LORD SCOT

**Lords of the Masquerade
Book Four**

Jade Lee

ARE YOU SIGNED UP FOR DRAGONBLADE'S BLOG?

You'll get the latest news and information on exclusive giveaways, exclusive excerpts, coming releases, sales, free books, cover reveals and more.

Check out our complete list of authors, too!

No spam, no junk. That's a promise!

Sign Up Here

www.dragonbladepublishing.com

Dearest Reader;

Thank you for your support of a small press. At Dragonblade Publishing, we strive to bring you the highest quality Historical Romance from some of the best authors in the business. Without your support, there is no 'us', so we sincerely hope you adore these stories and find some new favorite authors along the way.

Happy Reading!

CEO, Dragonblade Publishing

Additional Dragonblade books by Author Jade Lee

Lords of the Masquerade Series
Lord Lucifer (Book 1)
Lord Satyr (Book 2)
Lord Ares (Book 3)
Lord Scot (Book 4)
Lady Scot (Book 5)
Almost a Scot (Book 6)

The Lyon's Den Series
Into the Lyon's Den
Lyon Hearted

CHAPTER ONE

6 months ago

HORSES THUNDERED PAST Lord Loughton as he wandered along Rotten Row. His quarry, Lady Clara, was further ahead on a bench in Hyde Park. Her bonnet tilted askew as she gestured with a hard slash of her hand to a severely dressed gentleman sitting with her. Rather than adjust her bonnet, she ignored the sunlight on her face, and her freckles appeared like dots of burnt sugar on her cheeks. Fortunately, he was a fan of freckles, so they didn't diminish her allure but made him smile as she continued to press her point, whatever it was, to the gentleman beside her.

Lady Clara was a lovely woman with a passionate nature, at least in conversation, and Liam cared not a whit. It was her dowry and her brother's position in government that had caught his attention. Still, she appealed to him, so he approached her the only way a Scotsman could approach a titled English lady—by apparent accident.

"It's not possible," she was saying to the man. "Think of the height of those castle towers. You'd have to get water all the way up there. You'd have to carry it up. Imagine the amount of work!"

The gentleman shook his head. "Begin with a cistern to catch rainwater. And then, with the right application of pulleys, a single maid could bring water up from a well."

"A well, yes, but not all the way up to the top of a castle." The lady gestured with her hands to a place high above her head.

"Yes, she could," the gentleman countered. "Think of a line of buckets on a pulley that dunked buckets in the nearest stream."

"But that could be miles away!"

She took a deep breath in preparation of continuing her argument, but Liam grabbed the opportunity to intrude. "Excuse me," he said, doing his best to hide his accent. "I couldn't help but overhear. By any chance, have either of you ever lived in a castle?"

Lady Clara blinked. "I've toured them, of course—"

"Myself, as well," the gentleman said.

"But they're drafty, awful places compared to a modern home," she finished.

They could be, he thought, but his expression was one of challenge. "I live in a castle, and I can tell you that it's not always that way." He smiled. "Were you talking about plumbing? I would very much like to hear your ideas."

The gentleman frowned. Liam could tell he wasn't interested in sharing the lady's attention. Fortunately, Lady Clara lived up to her reputation of being willing to talk to anyone about anything. "You live in a castle? Is it in Scotland?"

So much for hiding his accent. Either he'd been very bad at it, or she had a good ear. He bowed again. "Lord Loughton, at your service."

"See here," the gentleman said as he pushed up from his park bench. "You can't go up to strangers and introduce yourself. That's not the way it's done in London."

What he meant was that as a Scotsman, Liam couldn't approach strangers. Fortunately, Lady Clara was more open-minded.

"Don't be a prig, Julian. I'm pleased to meet you, Lord Loughton." She held out her hand and he made a show of being excruciatingly proper as he kissed it. And if he squeezed her extra tight, she seemed pleased by his strength. She smiled as he eyed her over her gloved hand, and her companion huffed at the insult.

"This isn't proper," he said.

"It wasn't proper for me to meet you, Julian, and yet here I am without a maid in the middle of the afternoon." She turned back to Liam. "Lord Loughton, pray allow me to introduce you to my fussy friend, Mr. Julian Russell. He's got a passion for architecture that has lately turned to plumbing. I think we would both benefit from your knowledge of castles."

"I would be happy to answer whatever questions you might have. Indeed, I could even arrange a tour if you were so inclined."

"All the way in Scotland?" Mr. Russell exclaimed. He might as well have called it Hell, for that was the tone of his statement. "I assure you, we have plenty of castles in England if we need further education."

"As you wish," he said. "But I doubt your castles have the same kind of ghostly tales that we Scots enjoy."

He watched Lady Clara closely as he spoke. His information on her was sketchy at best, but everyone had heard of her love of the occult. It was said she went to séances with regularity.

"A ghost story? I do love those. Is it a murdered bride?"

"I'm afraid not," he said. "An old lonely cleric who wanders the halls and terrifies boys who don't do their lessons."

Lady Clara laughed, her nose wrinkling such that her freckles pressed together. "Sounds like a tale to keep young boys in line."

"It would be," he acknowledged, "if I hadn't seen the terrifying sight myself."

"And did you then complete your lessons?"

"Every single one."

"Then I would say that is a ghost who should remain exactly where it is." She tilted her head. "Is that the only ghostly tale in your castle?"

"Goodness no. In fact, there *is* a murdered bride, but..." His voice trailed away.

"But you don't think them appropriate for my delicate, female ears?" Her voice was tart.

No, he wanted to intrigue her so that he could spend more time with her. "I meant no offense," he said quickly. "We have just met, and some ladies do not enjoy bloody tales of ghostly apparitions."

"Then you weren't listening closely, were you? I told you I love ghost stories." She didn't appear angry so much as challenging him. Apparently, the lady enjoyed battling wits.

"Unfair! There are several types of ghost stories, my lady. I only began with the most proper."

"And there you have it wrong again. I also said I was a most improper lady."

Yes, he thought, he was counting on it. "True point, my lady." He held out his hand. "May I buy you an ice at Gunter's as my forfeit?"

That was too much for Mr. Russell, who stood up forcefully enough to knock Liam's hand aside. "Lady Clara is otherwise engaged." Then he turned to the lady with his own warm smile. "I believe we were going to promenade this afternoon."

Lady Clara looked at her friend and then back at Liam. Clearly, she was at a loss here, unused to having two gentlemen vie for her attention. She shook her head. "You're both being very vexing," she said firmly.

Then she straightened off the bench. And kept straightening. Good lord, the woman was tall. She nearly looked him in the eye. And that dusting of burnt sugar on her face now stretched out on a *long* face. He hadn't noticed it before, but now that she stood, he saw how very angular she was. Long limbs, a full slash of a nose, and a wide mouth pressed tight.

And she did not like Mr. Russell demanding her sole attention.

Best to give way, lest she tar him with the same brush. Except he couldn't make himself small beside this arrogant Englishman, so he attempted a compromise.

"Can we three not walk together? There is plenty of time

before the fashionable hour."

"Don't listen to him," the man said, his tone a dark warning. "He's *charming,* and you don't like that."

"Neither do I like peevish," the lady countered. Then she twitched her skirts into place and headed off in the other direction. She didn't say *good day,* or any other polite formality. She rounded on her heel and walked away, her long legs covering distance with ease.

"Lady Clara!" cried Mr. Russell, his hands lifted in disgust. "Now she'll be skittish for weeks." He turned to glare at Liam.

"So run after her. Blame it all on me." Clearly, the man was smitten with her, and if an attachment was in the offing, Liam would like to know now.

"She hates being chased. Almost as much as I despise impertinent Scotsmen."

Liam allowed his accent to roll through his word. "Och, we know. That's why we do it." And no truer statement had ever been spoken.

"Well, it won't work with her. Or me." And with that, the man gathered up his papers and stomped away.

Liam watched him go while his thoughts spun toward the seduction of Lady Clara. Clearly Mr. Russell favored the mealy-mouthed approach of letting the lady set the pace of their interactions. Probably a wise choice for an Englishman with little bottom. But Liam was cut from different cloth, and his ancestors favored boldness when acquiring their women. Abduction was not the plan, even though his father had suggested it. His thoughts were more "charming nuisance." No woman had ever resisted him beyond five interactions.

This was his first, and quite successful given that he'd removed a rival.

His second came at the opera where he visited her booth. Her brother was in London for one night and was known to use his booth as way to advance his political ambitions. Easy enough to slip in behind several Members of Parliament. He found her reading a book at the side edge of their box. He greeted her and was rewarded with a grunt. He teased her, and she grudgingly looked up.

He could tell she remembered him. Her eyes widened then narrowed. "Castle plumbing, yes?"

He smiled. "Yes."

"I've moved on to botany now," she said as she flashed him the cover of her book. Something about plants, he assumed. The light was weak enough that he couldn't make out the title. He wondered how she managed to see the words on the page.

"What about ghostly tales? Have you lost interest in those?"

That did catch her interest, but her gaze landed beyond his shoulder to her brother. "Aaron will never allow it, and since it's his birthday, I shall oblige him this once." This time she dismissed him in the polite way. "You may wish him happy birthday over there. Good evening."

Not an auspicious conversation for Interaction Number Two. Fortunately, he was able to wish her brother a happy day. Since the man was no fool, Lord Chambers correctly guessed Liam's interest was in Lady Clara. Discreet inquiries into Liam's character followed within the week. Indeed, if the man had stayed in London, Liam might very well have resolved the matter immediately. Unfortunately, Lord Chambers left for his father's sickbed too soon for a meeting of suitor to older brother.

Interaction Number Three had him dancing attendance on her at a ball. Except she never arrived. Same with attempted interactions four, five, and six. But by this time, his tracking skills adapted to the urban environment. Certainly, he did not follow her footprints in the dirt, but he was able to learn of her movements from any one of several dismissed servants. Thus he located her at a meeting of the Astronomical Society and again at an Alchemical Investigation lecture.

He charmed her to the best of his ability, but he was sadly uninformed when it came to the composition of comets or the formulae of various compounds. It was unpleasant to be viewed as an idiot. Worse still to be called a Scottish one, as if that made him even more stupid. And though the lady cried foul at such disparagement, she nevertheless lost interest in him when distracted by scientific discussion.

But far from losing faith in his charm, Liam switched to a different plan: cocky declaration.

Rather than bribe another of her ever-changing servants, he waited at her door until she chose to come out. He didn't ring the bell, but sat upon her front stoop reading the morning paper. If she had better servants, he would be shooed away within a quarter hour. She did not. It wasn't until nearly noon that she stepped out and discovered him there with a gasp of surprise.

"Lord Loughton?" she cried. "Whatever are you doing here?"

He looked up at her with a smile, taking his time to fold up the newspaper. "I've come to tell you that we're to be married."

"What!" she cried.

"We are. Your family approves." He winked boldly at her. "Shall we rush to the bedding or get to know one another first?"

She gaped at him. Indeed, it was perhaps the first time he had seen her rendered speechless.

He straightened up to his full height. Given that he was on a lower step than she was, they ended up nose to nose. He fully intended to take advantage of this position. More than being nose to nose, they were nearly mouth to mouth, and he planned to give her a full kiss. No woman had ever resisted that, and since this was their fifth actual encounter, it was well past time for her to tumble into his arms.

She did, but not in the way he expected. She was leaning close to him, no doubt to complete the kiss, when her heel caught. Her foot twisted, her knee buckled, and she tumbled straight into his arms. She landed with a heavy *umph*. The lady was not as light as she appeared. But he was strong enough to twist her in his arms such that her headfirst tumble ended up as a backwards collapse against his chest. Then he completed the move by settling her more firmly in his arms such that he could kiss her as passionately as he wanted.

Perfect.

But when he leaned down to claim her lips as his reward, she batted at his face.

"No," she said. "No, no, no!"

He pulled back. It was that or get a broken nose.

"Och, girl. What's the matter?" She appeared genuinely alarmed, and all he was doing was cradling her as gently as a babe in arms.

"Stop it!"

Stop what? Stop keeping her from bashing her head on the stone walk?

"Rest easy, lass. I promise you'll never forget your first Scottish kiss—" He might have said more, but she planted the palm of her hand over his mouth. If he hadn't flinched at the last moment, he would have lost an eye.

"Let me up," she grumbled, but he was hardly in a position to help. She'd fallen down the stairs and her feet were well above her head. Besides, he was still trying to get her accustomed to him.

"Calm yourself, lass," he muttered, because her palm was still over his mouth. Then to tease her, he stroked his tongue across her skin.

"Ugh!" She pulled it back with a grimace.

Damn it, the woman had no ability to flirt whatsoever. Bowing to the inevitable, he helped her adjust her feet. Soon, he set her down on the steps right where he'd been waiting for her. Then he rocked back on his heels as he pondered her indifference to him.

"Is it because I'm Scottish?" Damnation, she'd seemed so open-minded about everything, not at all like the prissy English girls of equal fortune. She discussed castle plumbing in Hyde Park. She attended lectures on chemistry. She was a woman of logic and yet she appeared shocked by the idea that he'd intended to kiss her.

"Yes, of course, it's because you're Scottish," she drawled, the sarcasm thick. "That would be the only reason I would catch my heel and fall."

"You know what I mean. I've had the devil of a time getting your attention. I'm not ugly, and your family approves of me." That was a stretch. Her brother had not waved him off.

Lady Clara's eyes widened, and her jaw hardened. "My family approves?" she said, her voice slow.

"Yes, of course they do." What else was he to say? At least they didn't disapprove, as far as he was aware.

She straightened her spine so hard he was surprised her spine didn't crack. "That's it. That's why." Again, her tone implied sarcasm, but he wasn't completely sure. The woman never acted as he expected.

"Why what?"

She grabbed hold of the railing and hauled herself upright. "Why I will not marry you."

"Because your family approves?" He hovered beside her, ready to catch her if she fell again. She didn't. Indeed, her feet seemed to be firmly planted on the ground. "Lady Clara, pray try to make sense."

"I don't care what arrangement you've made with my mother, I will not marry you."

"Your mother? What does she—"

"She's the only one who approves in my family. Which means I do not."

He blinked. Damn it, he'd erred here, but there was still time to recover. "My apologies, Lady Clara. I have never spoken to your mother. I know nothing about her."

The lady frowned at him, then sniffed hard. "My mother and I do not get along."

Obviously. He raised his brows and attempted a *Scottish* wink. "Leave it to me. I'll charm her too."

Wrong tact. Her expression tightened. "You said we were going to marry."

He smiled, scrambling to find a way to make her smile. "I was flirting. With you."

"But you also meant it."

True hit. He did intend to marry her.

"No," she said.

"Lady Clara—" he tried, but she cut him off.

"It's not because you're Scottish. It's because you *live* in Scotland! And in a castle no less!" Then she threw up her hands in disgust. "I told you that on the very first day we met."

"Whatever are you talking about?"

"Castles are drafty, miserable places. My home is not." She pointed to the house behind her. "Scotland is far away. London is not." She pointed again at his chest. "I don't care that you're Scottish. I care that you're *charming*." She spit out the word like bad meat. "And I'm not marrying anyone, no matter what my family has said to you or anyone else!"

He thought she would go inside then. Indeed, the butler was standing in the doorway with his jaw slack as he watched the entire encounter. But instead of running inside, she looked hard past Liam's shoulder. "Good day, Lord Loughton. There is a lecture on beekeeping that I am most anxious to attend."

"Lady Clara!" the butler called in a nasally tone. "Shouldn't I call a maid for you?"

The woman rolled her eyes. "No. It's embarrassing when she falls asleep."

She stomped down the remaining steps, her head lifted high enough that the hard slash of her nose seemed to cut the air around her. Such magnificence. She'd make a fine bride.

Unfortunately, that was encounter number five, and he'd exhausted the breadth of his charm. He didn't want to think of his father's plan, but he really had to consider it now.

Abduction.

CHAPTER TWO

CLARA'S INSIDES WERE knotted tight as she stomped away from the Scotsman. Her hands were clenched tight and though she headed to the lecture on beekeeping, she knew she would not be able to focus on it. No, when she got this distraught, there was only one thing for it.

She walked.

She loved London and knew its many corners. Thankfully, her brother Aaron had taught her the rudiments of fisticuffs and fencing. He'd also gifted her with a walking stick nearly identical to his own, one with a sword inside. She'd never had use of the blade so far, but the stick had come in handy when thieving children from the rookeries had accosted her. She knew to keep away from those areas, but there was still plenty of St. James' to wander, not to mention Piccadilly and Mayfair. She'd be pickpocketed for sure, but she barely cared for the few coins in her purse. She had a more substantial sum tucked in a secret pocket stitched onto her stays.

All that information flashed through her thoughts along with a steady stream of beekeeping information that she already possessed. She was unlikely to miss anything by avoiding the lecture. She tried to calm her frenzied thoughts by listing all the facts she already knew, but even that would not settle her. She would have to face her fury in the only way that worked.

She stomped on their faces.

Not literally, of course, but it absolutely gave her satisfaction as she stormed down Bond Street to imagine every foot stomp was on her mother's face. The woman knew she had no intention of marrying. Clara had declared as much from her earliest days. She'd thought her mother understood. Indeed, Mama had given her a bookshelf for Christmas last year and had declared that—since Clara was well and truly on the shelf—she might as well have a nice place to sit.

It was one of the few times she'd ever won an argument with her mother. But now she saw that the woman had merely cast her net farther afield—to Scotland!—to find a man who would lower himself to marry her. She didn't blame Lord Loughton. She knew that a man wasn't considered mature until he had a wife on his arm and children to carry on his name. But that said nothing about what a woman wanted.

Clara had no quarrels with any woman who chose to marry into a lifetime of drudgery as she served her husband's needs, but that was not Clara's choice. And thank God, she had the money to stick with her choice despite her mother throwing men at her at every turn.

She'd liked Lord Loughton! That was the worst of it. He didn't steer the conversation to his favorite topics. He didn't try to tell her how to dress or behave. He let her do and say as she willed and either enjoyed her conversation or made himself scarce. They had yet to discuss the plumbing at his castle, but she supposed that was due to Mr. Russell's churlishness.

And now she wouldn't ever get to talk about his life in a Scottish castle because—damn it—she had to dissuade him from pursuing her hand in marriage.

Stupid, stupid Mama! Why wouldn't she accept that her daughter was unmarriageable?

Stupid, stupid men! Why couldn't they ever be friends rather than suitors?

By the time she'd harumphed down Bond Street, she'd made her plans. First was to write a letter to Mama to tell her that her schemes with Lord Loughton had come to naught. Clara did not for one moment believe the man had pursued her this fervently without encouragement from someone. Since it wasn't her father or brother—they had long since given up on her marriage prospects—it had to be Mama.

Next was to give the Scotsman the cut direct. It was a harsh thing to do, but he needed to understand that she was serious. And she'd learned to her cost that most men—when absolutely determined upon a course—would not be dissuaded without firm, consistent denial.

She went home and wrote her letter.

Then she gave Lord Loughton the cut direct at the musicale evening she attended two nights later. She didn't know how he knew she'd attend. She rarely went to society functions, but he was there as if he too enjoyed the mezzo-soprano Fiona Verany. He sat close to the center of the room and listened with rapt attention while Clara twisted and fidgeted. She kept questioning the wisdom of giving him the cut direct. She didn't want him to think that she was opposed to Scotsmen, and that would certainly be the appearance. But she absolutely could not let him believe that she was open to his suit.

It ruined the evening for her, especially since when she finally did cut him, his response was a full and open laugh. And she heard—as did several others—as he remarked that her backside was as appealing as her front and was no displeasure to him.

Most unsettling! She spent the next few days in research on beekeeping as penance for her inability to remove him from her thoughts.

And then he was there again at the next meeting of the Naturalist Society. He said not a word to her at the beginning, but winked whenever she looked at him. He had some understanding of the material because he asked intelligent questions regarding the anatomy of an African civet as compared to a hyena. She wondered if he was showing off his knowledge for her benefit, but she could not be sure. What Englishman even knew of the hyena, much less could intelligently compare it to a civet? But he could and she would have discussed that very fact with him, were he not trying to marry her.

Unless, of course, he really did have a passion for comparative anatomies. She resolved to find out.

She allowed him to meander to her side after the lecture. And as he bowed over her hand, she blurted out the one question she had resolved to discover through subtlety.

"Are you here to pursue me or to discover African mammals?"

"I love all sorts of warm-blooded creatures—"

Excellent. She understood shared academic interest.

"But it's your warm blood that appeals the most."

She winced. He was here because of her. "My blood is not for you," she said tartly. Then she felt her cheeks flush as she realized her wording had been unfortunate.

"Then perhaps I'll just admire the packaging of it."

She frowned at him, thoroughly flustered. "I believe I have explained that we will never marry. You should direct your attention to ladies who wish to become servants to the men who would master them."

His brows arched. "I begin to understand your objection is to marriage and not my person." He smiled. "That is excellent progress."

"That is not progress at all! And your ridiculous pursuit of me will only end in disappointment."

His smile widened into a grin. "I assure you, Lady Clara, no lady has claimed disappointment with me."

"Then you have surrounded yourself with witless women."

He nodded. "True enough. It's why you appeal so greatly."

She opened her mouth to argue with him further, but he held up his hand in a gesture of surrender.

"My lady, I assure you that Scottish brides are not servants. Our land can be harsh, and I would work alongside my bride."

"So says every *charming* man, but it is a lie. The Scotsmen control the purse, the home, and the product of their wives' work. Just as it is in England, France, and every other country you are likely to name. It is the way of the world."

"Why do you despise it so if it is the natural way?"

She snorted. "You have just attended a naturalist lecture. Do you know of any animal who subjugates the female as thoroughly as man? I submit that it is a perversion of the natural order of things created for man's convenience, and not a woman's."

"You are making a false comparison, my lady. Do you see animals building castles?"

"Nests. Dens. Burrows."

"Do they farm crops or husband cattle?"

"Both sexes forage."

"Unless the female is busy caring for the young. In which case, the male—"

"I do not care about that, as I have no intention of having young."

He arched a brow. "A sad life that might be."

"There are plenty of children available if I have the urge to mother."

"I wasn't referring to the children," he quipped, his eyebrows waggling.

How like a man to think of sex first. "This is a waste of time and that is something I abhor." She nodded to him in dismissal and was about to say, *Good day*. But he spoke faster than she and—worse—he piqued her curiosity with his words.

"On the contrary, this has been the best use of my time since arriving in London."

"Because you are considering the plight of a female for the first time in your life?"

He chuckled. "Because I have now learned your conditions for marriage."

"Hardly that."

"You care not about children nor the entertainments in bed. Your time must be valued, and your labors set into your hands for your control." He spread his arms such that his entire body was on display. "I can offer you that *and* the pleasures of the bedroom as well!"

She would not be alive if she didn't notice the muscles that shaped his torso and strengthened his legs. He had muscles that built out his large frame. Though he was lanky, like her, there was no denying that he had callouses on his hands, muscles that no doubt crisscrossed his body like a Greek statue's, and legs that supported him well as they covered vast distances.

He was a man built for the wilds of Scotland, she supposed. He would look magnificent in a kilt. He looked quite spectacular in English attire. If it weren't for his roguish smile and that arrogant twinkle in his eyes, she might find him attractive. Instead, she thought him much too impressed with himself for her to be interested.

"Good day, Lord Loughton. I hope you find a woman to meet your needs."

"I have found her," he said to her back. "We're just negotiating the terms of surrender."

She stopped walking. She knew he was teasing her. That he was being *charming*, and damned if it didn't work on her a little. She was smiling, after all. And her heart was pumping in an excited state. But it wouldn't work. Boyish charm meant that the lady would end up marrying a boy. And she could barely tolerate a man.

She turned back to him. "I will not marry. Look elsewhere."

"I am too bewitched to look away."

She shrugged. "I'm not."

She left. She walked straight out of the room and into her beloved London where she looked into shop windows before wandering through Hyde Park. What need did she have for a handsome Scotsman when she had all of this?

She did not.

And yet, she couldn't stop thinking of him.

Which meant she would have to go to more extensive efforts

to cut him from her life. Fortunately, she had a plan.

She decided to spy on him and find out whatever appalling thing she could discover. Every man had something to be ashamed of, didn't they?

He did not. Or she was such a lousy spy she discovered nothing more than that his friends liked him, and his landlord thought him a fine man for a lady such as herself.

She decided to frighten him off with a fake séance. She knew that to the uninitiated they could be quite terrifying. She paid a fake psychic to put on a show of channeling his dead grandmother and warning him away from her. She even paid a man to throw knives at him "from the great beyond."

Lord Loughton was laughing so hard, he had to hold his sides. He declared the evening the best time he'd had since arriving in London. And in case he missed the part about his dead grandmother warning him off, he said that she'd never been right about anything while she was alive, so he didn't think he should listen to her once she was dead.

It was thoroughly disappointing, especially since her brother returned from the country and declared Lord Loughton to be a perfectly acceptable suitor. He encouraged her to go walking with him in Hyde Park at the fashionable hour.

And her mother wrote to say she had never met the man, and who would want to marry a Scotsman anyway?

In the end, Clara agreed to walk with Lord Loughton in Hyde Park because she had another plan. No man wanted to be thought a fool for the woman he courted. She dressed in her most outlandish outfit. It was clothing of her own design, specifically created for those days when she never wanted to see anyone. No stays. No tight fabric. Her attire resembled something she had seen in the Arabic countries for men: white linen that flowed about her body with ease. It covered her from neck to toe and yet felt extraordinarily freeing.

She loved wearing it…in the privacy of her own home.

But today she was going to be bold. While the servants gaped at her, she swung the front door open and dared his lordship to say one word.

"Good afternoon, Lady Clara. You are looking especially fine this afternoon. What innovative attire. I love it." And if she doubted him, his eyes lingered on her chest where her breasts bounced completely unrestrained beneath the shift.

He was completely unfazed. And even worse, he outdid her in outrageous attire. The man had come in his kilt. Nothing else except for his boots. He wore a full tartan over his bare chest and equally naked legs. Presumably there was open air beneath the kilt, but she blushed whenever she thought of it, so she set her mind on other things. Or rather she tried to.

She was so shocked that when he offered her his arm, she took it without objection. And she promenaded beside him—in Hyde Park, no less—as if it were the most normal thing in the world. She walked without a shift. He walked without any underclothes at all! She spent the entire promenade in high color in part because of his nakedness. And in part because she realized she'd been entirely wrong in her supposition about Lord Loughton.

She'd assumed she would embarrass him because she was odd. It was important for him to understand that their marriage would subject him to constant pity from his compatriots. What she discovered was that he loved being the object of attention whether he was thought a fool or not.

And damn it, she was not used to being completely ignored when she had specifically set out to be outrageous. The women didn't bother with her at all! They were so intent on speaking with Lord Loughton. And the gentlemen thought nothing of a Scotsman appearing in London in his clan attire.

"They don't even notice what I'm wearing," she murmured, completely shocked.

"On the contrary, they think it a new Scottish custom and are probably envious of how sweetly you move in it." He flashed her a lascivious grin. "I am certainly thinking about it."

He paused then in the shadow of a tree. He pulled her hand to his lips, grinning because her outfit did not include gloves, and pressed his lips to the back of her hand. His lips were rough where he pressed it to her flesh, a twin to his calloused finger that stroked her palm. The sensation when he touched her wasn't unpleasant, and his gaze as he looked at her was winning.

Not winning. *Charming.* And damnation, she hated charming!

She steeled her heart against him.

"You cannot win me like this," she rasped.

"Of course not," he said. "We have merely been playing the games of society. I haven't yet proved to you that you can be my equal at home."

She scoffed, but he cut her off as he straightened to his full height before her.

"Let us be done with this nonsense. Let us meet as people and let me tell you what it would be like as my wife."

"I already know—"

"Och, do ye now?" He let his accent roll thick and heavy off his tongue. "You have mis-guessed my reaction at every turn. Not one thing you have assumed aboot me has proven true. So what do ye know fer sure, lassie?"

Nothing. Only that he was charming, and her opinion about that was not his fault.

Chastised, she nodded. "What would you have me do?"

"Come riding with me in the morning. A good Scottish wife needs to manage a horse." He cocked an eyebrow. "You can ride, yes?"

"Yes."

"To which question, lass?"

"I can ride, and I will meet you tomorrow morning to prove it."

"I'll bring the horses."

Her brows arched. "I didn't realize that you kept horses in London."

"I don't, but I have friends who do. Do you want a spirited

horse or a sweet one?"

She grinned. "Bring me the most spirited horse you can find."

He did.

And she loved the rollicking wild ride.

Over luncheon, he told her about his life in a castle, making it sound like jolly good fun.

They went to a musical evening next, and the opera after that.

Her heart softened to him. He made her laugh, his eyes sparkled when he looked at her. And she began to think that *charming* wasn't so bad.

And then he disappeared from London.

CHAPTER THREE

L IAM HATED TRAVEL. He enjoyed a long ride on horseback as much as the next man, but rapid travel from London to Edinburgh required either a coach and many, many horses—which he did not possess—or a seat on the mail coach. Thankfully, the weather was good and the cheapest seats—on top of the vehicle—were actually the finest. He could set his face to the wind and not smell the onion vinegar stench rolling off the person next to him. He could lean against the luggage set at his back and dream of what he would do with all of Lady Clara's money. And—on the return trip to London—he could plot the best and most dramatic way to save Clara's best friend Lilah from a potentially unwanted marriage.

Still, the entire trip had been exhausting and he barely managed the time to clean up before rushing to the big ball that marked Aaron's ascension to his title as the Earl of Kittrel. Liam was dressed in his best English finery, but he still had trouble making it inside the ball. In his haste, he'd left his invitation in his rooms and the new staff appeared to be very good at their jobs.

When had Clara figured out how to manage her servants? She was notoriously bad at it.

In the end, he had to slip in through the back where the entertainers were departing and then duck through the guests just in time to disrupt Aaron's very public proposal to Miss Rees.

Oh hell.

But before he could explain himself, one lady—the most important one—cried out.

"Liam! You're back?" cried Lady Clara.

He flashed a smile at her and would have winked, but he was momentarily struck by her beauty. She was not a lady who cared about her appearance unless she was deliberately going against trends and wearing something outlandish, as she had on their walk in Hyde Park. But this time she had dressed as hostess to her brother in a gown that reflected her family's colors.

She wore burgundy in a shimmery dress that emphasized her height and plumped her breasts enough to show an enticing shadow of cleavage. Her hair—normally trapped in a tight bun—now flowed in soft brown curls that caught the light enough to give her highlights of gold. Even her eyes picked up the golden hue, turning her normally green eyes into a mesmerizing cat's eye as she unconsciously stepped toward him.

He'd caught her, he realized. She was coming to him now, happy to see him, and anxious to be by his side. All he need do was close the trap. But first they had to wait until Aaron finished his proposal.

It was a surprise to see the normally unflappable man drop to his knee before Miss Rees. The lady was a lovely woman, but a known bastard. Liam never would have guessed that an earl would propose to a by-blow, even one as sweet as Miss Rees. But he was learning that when it came to Lady Clara and her brother, nothing was exactly as it seemed.

Except, of course, for now when it seemed that the two were desperately in love. Hopefully, the romantic scene softened Lady Clara's heart as well. With that thought in mind, he took Clara's hand, intending to take advantage of the moment.

"Let's step outside," he began, but she cut him off.

"Why didn't you tell me you were going to Scotland?"

Because he'd run out of ways to capture her wandering attention. That meant it was time for a sudden, mysterious absence. He'd hoped to spark a longing in her for him, and from the way she was beaming at him now, he'd succeeded.

"There wasn't time," he said.

"Is Lilah really a Scottish heiress?" she asked. "I cannot believe it."

Neither had he, at first, but the clues were there. All he'd had to do was follow them. "She has to go to Edinburgh to claim it, of course. But now she need not marry your brother for fear of poverty. She has her own money."

"But she loves Aaron!"

He nodded. "I can see that, and now so can he." He'd managed to get them walking, heading away from people who tried to get her attention. She was in a talkative mood, and he was loath to share the moment with anyone else.

"Lilah wasn't impoverished. She runs a registry office."

He nodded. But he knew much better than Clara how very little profit came from that endeavor. "In my experience," he said sadly, "money or the lack thereof taints every human endeavor."

The lady frowned at him. "That is a very cynical statement."

Only a wealthy woman would think that. "Perhaps you can persuade me differently as we dance?"

The musicians were starting again, and he had already noted that she did not wear a dancing card upon her wrist. That wasn't so unusual. She was the hostess of the event, and would have other tasks beyond dancing the night away. But it also allowed him to claim her hand whenever she was free. Which was now.

"Oh, my lord," she said with a rueful smile. "I would much prefer to take a walk. Perhaps we could stroll to the refreshment table."

The idea appealed. He hadn't eaten since early this morning and was very hungry. But something in her expression told him she was lying. He hadn't quite determined what exactly was her "dishonesty tell" but he knew it, nonetheless.

"Are you perhaps embarrassed to be seen dancing with a Scot?"

Her eyes widened and she drew back with an angry glare. "Of

course not! Whyever would you say that?"

"Because I cannot think of another reason why you would be so averse to partner with me."

She snorted. "Are all Scotsmen so arrogant? Did it never occur to you that it might have nothing to do with you?"

He arched his brows. "Are you hurt in some way? Do your legs pain you? Is your breath short?" He leaned forward, only half-teasing. "Shall I call a doctor?"

"No, you should not! Honestly, if you wish to dance, there are scores of ladies who would love your attention."

"But I am not interested in them."

"Then you will respect my wishes and ask me no more about dancing."

A polite Englishman would accede to her request. A polite Scotsman would too, so he offered her his arm and they began to promenade about the room. But he would not leave off the topic. "You must tell me if you are injured in some way. Truly, I am concerned for your health."

She shot him a wry glance. "I am not injured."

"And you are not embarrassed to be seen with me," he said, "because we are promenading in full view of everyone." Indeed, every few steps they were stopped as someone greeted them. He fobbed them off and returned immediately to the topic at hand. "If you were offended by my heritage, you would have turned tail the moment I appeared in Hyde Park in my kilt."

She snorted. "My consequence with the *ton* increased after that afternoon. Being in your handsome presence made me interesting by association."

He snapped his fingers. "That is how much I care about the *ton*'s attention."

"You are a flirt, my lord. And all flirts care about attention whether it be from the *ton* or from the lowest scullery maid."

He slanted her a glance. There was a note of bitterness there which he would need to explore, but he would not be distracted. "I flirt with you, Lady Clara." Then at her sideways glance, he shrugged. "I endeavor to be amenable with everyone. That is no crime." Despite the way her tone suggested otherwise.

"I find nothing objectionable in you," she finally admitted.

"Damned by faint praise." He gazed hard at her. "So why won't you dance with me?"

"Nothing objectionable except for your dogged interest in my dancing."

She scowled at him. He arched his brows back.

"I'm not going to tell you," she said, her tone dark.

"I'm not going to stop asking."

"Then I will find you tiresome and leave you to your own amusements."

Impasse while they were stopped by yet another group of people. It took ten minutes before he could extricate them.

"I find you fascinating," he said as he finally drew her outside, where the night air cooled his skin. Behind them, the musicians had begun the set and the tromp of feet could be heard louder than the notes. "I want to know every tiny detail about you. That includes your—"

"I'm very bad at it!" she snapped out as she rounded upon him. "There. Are you content now? I'm a horrible dancer. I'm tall, you know, and uncoordinated. My partners shoot me horrible looks when I accidentally bump heads with them. It's worse when the gentleman is very short. I'm supposed to dance with my knees crooked so as to not tower over him. Have you ever tried to dance for an entire set with your knees bent? It's awful."

He nodded slowly. "That sounds awkward and painful. My knees ache just thinking about it." Especially since most dances were an intricate interchange of partners and steps. She was of a height with most men, but would indeed have to stoop with the short ones.

"I hate it." She blew out a breath. "Plus, I never remember the steps. I'm stupid like that."

Laughter burst out of him in a sharp bark. And then he abruptly had to rein it in at her offended expression. My God, she was serious. "Lady Clara, you are the most intelligent woman I've ever met."

"Everyone is stupid about something," she shot back. "With you, I suspect it's an inability to stop when told explicitly to do so."

He acknowledged that with a nod.

"With me," she continued. "I'm stupid about dancing."

"Everyone would appear stupid if they had to do it with bent knees."

She walked away from him until she stepped on the small green that backed the property. "That has nothing to do with forgetting the steps. Which I do all the time."

This was a woman who could recite the tiniest details about African mammals and then switch seamlessly to obscure historical facts. Memorizing the steps of a dance would be child's play for her. "You don't forget the steps. You get bored with the steps and think of something else. And when your partner is boring as well—"

"I wander off," she said dully.

"What?"

She turned back to him. "I have done it, my lord. I have thought of something else interesting in the middle of a dance and—"

"Wandered off?"

Her cheeks turned crimson. "My attention is caught by a myriad of things. All the time. It is not unusual for me to stop everything in the pursuit of a random fancy." Her gaze turned upward to the three-quarter moon. "I would not insult you like that. Since I cannot promise to remain attentive, I merely remove myself from the dance all together."

He nodded. "Prudent."

She blew out a breath, her shoulders sinking to their natural place as she visibly relaxed. "Thank you for understanding."

"But that wouldn't happen with me. You should definitely

dance with me."

Her lips quirked. "I ask you again, are all Scotsmen so arrogant?"

"Possibly." He grabbed her hand and drew her back. "First of all, I am taller than you, so no need to stoop."

"But the dances require me to change partners—"

"Not the waltz."

She pressed her lips together. The waltz was considered scandalous by many because it was so very intimate when compared to the other dances. And with him, it would be very intimate indeed for he would draw her close enough to feel the heat of his body on hers, the movement of his hips, and the press of his hands. It was not lovemaking, but he knew how to make an innocent girl blush fiery red from the dance done with him.

He did not yet know how innocent Lady Clara was. And that was why he wanted so badly to draw her into his arms. That was she was brilliant was obvious. But would they dance well in bed? He could not have that conversation, so he would dance the waltz with her instead.

Or maybe he would not, because she was shaking her head.

"I do not dance, my lord."

"Do you kiss?"

She jolted. "What?"

As if God himself had ordained the timing, the first strains of a waltz began in the ballroom behind them. While she was still gaping at him, he gathered her into his arms as if they were to dance. Her arms were stiff, her face pulled back, but he didn't force her to move. Indeed, he did nothing more than step close and set one hand on her waist while the other intertwined their fingers.

She could step back from him, but she didn't. Neither did she melt into his arms. And when he began to sway with the music, she resisted as if she were made of a thick mud. She moved, but only from his effort. And so he stopped pressing her in favor of standing nose to nose.

"Tell me you have thought of it," he said. "For I have dreamed of kissing you from the first moment we met."

Her lashes fluttered and she looked away. "Such a thing would be improper."

"And when did you become proper, Lady Clara? You don't even use a maid when you go about London. I wager you have discussed the mating habits of several animals as well as the anatomy involved." He leaned forward. "Did you think of my anatomy? I have thought of yours."

Her gaze shot back to his. And to his delight, she wet her lips.

"If I kiss you now, lass," he said, the burr of his accent slipping into his words. "It will be a declaration to everyone here. We will wed then or you lose your reputation."

"I don't have a reputation to lose."

"Yes," he said, as he lowered his mouth to hers. "You do." She was known as a bluestocking, which was a great deal more elevated than a courtesan. One public kiss would not make her into a demi-rep, but it would begin her fall.

So he held back. He let their lips touch, but only by the barest degree. He felt their breath mingle and knew that her pulse was beating fast. It had to be, because his was thundering in his ears. It would be so easy to finish the kiss. So wonderful to thrust himself inside her and plunder as he willed. His hand that should be on her waist was creeping upwards. So easy to curl slightly around to cup her sweet breast.

He began to move her then. The slightest sway to the music, enough to get her angled such that his back protected her from view. Anyone could be watching, but there was no one near them where they stood on the grass.

She whimpered, a slight mew of need. And he rewarded that sound with a sweep of his hand across her breast. Her nipple was tight! Of course, it was, and yet the feel of that nub against his palm had him wanting to crow aloud in victory. Especially when she trembled at the caress.

"Allow me a kiss," he whispered, knowing that he would

likely take it whether she agreed or not.

"One kiss," she returned. "If you never press me to dance again."

He grinned. "You drive a hard bargain."

He took her then. Not the full way he wanted to, but it was enough for his plans. He pulled her tight against him until she arched her back and lifted her face to his. He felt her hips full against his erection, a womanly cradle to his darker desires. And in the most glorious of moments, she pressed against him there. She surrounded him, held him, and offered herself.

He took her mouth. He thrust himself inside while she opened her teeth and parried with her tongue. A dance of sorts, filled with twisting and thrusting. And when he thumbed her nipple again, she whimpered even as she pulsed against him.

They would do well in bed, he decided. That was what the throb in his cock told him, as well as the scent of her musk that befuddled his thoughts.

"Travel with Miss Rees," he rasped against her ear. "Come to Scotland with her while she claims her inheritance."

Clara pulled back and he gloried at the way her eyes blinked in dazed confusion. "What?"

"Come to Scotland with me," he repeated.

"What? No. I live in London."

"You can visit Scotland, can you no'?" His accent was thick again, as was his cock and the surging need to throw her over his shoulder and carry her himself straight to his home.

"A visit?" She bit her lip, and his blood surged again. Then she shook her head. "No. No, I cannot. That's too far away. I don't know anything about it."

"I'll teach you."

"What if there are highwaymen?"

"I'll protect you."

"What about all my friends here?"

She was throwing up excuses. Bad ones at that. Her mind was foggy, her normally quick wits scrambling. His were too, but even he could see that she was fighting him for no rational reason.

"What do you fear?"

She looked him in the eyes, and he watched as the truth tumbled from her lips. "That I'll never come back."

She probably wouldn't, if he had his way.

"A psychic told me that once. That if I ever travel to Scotland, I'll be lost to the land forever."

He quirked his lips. "It's a beautiful land, Clara. Why not get lost in it for a time? I swear I'll take you back myself if it comes to it." A lie. Once there, he would have her for sure.

"I don't believe you." The woman was clever. No one could argue that.

She stepped back from him, and he released her. Her nipples were still tight, and the pulse beat a rapid tempo in her neck, but she stood tall and faced him squarely.

"I will never go to Scotland. Not even to visit."

He sighed. "You force me to abduct you. I'd rather not flee the city with your brother on my heels."

Her eyes widened. "What are you talking about?"

"It's for your own good."

"What?"

He shrugged and turned her around. There, just bursting through a crowd of onlookers, was her brother. His hands were clenched in fists and his expression was murderous. A half-step behind him was Miss Rees who was flushed bright red. Liam labeled her expression as chagrined and more than a little intrigued as her gaze hopped between them. Given the size of the audience, there was no question of what was to happen next.

He swept into a deep bow before angry brother and chagrined fiancée. "Miss Rees, please allow me to escort you to Edinburgh where I shall assist you in the legalities regarding your Scottish inheritance."

Miss Rees was able to keep her composure enough to dip into a curtsey. "Your help would be most welcome."

"And perhaps, you would appreciate a companion, wouldn't you? Lady Clara, for example, might enjoy getting out of London for a time."

To his side, Clara sputtered an objection. "I don't want to leave London. That's the whole point—"

"I think that's an excellent idea," Lord Kittrel interrupted. "And naturally, I will accompany my fiancée."

"Of course!"

"And you and I will have ample time for a thorough conversation." Dire threat sounded in the words.

"My thoughts exactly," Liam said amiably.

Then her brother took a step forward, the movement menacing. "And rest assured that if I do not like your companionship, I will relinquish every penny of my wife's money rather than have more association with you." He paused a moment. "I'm also a good hand with a sword and a pistol should I feel the need."

As threats went, this was a serious one. He was saying that he was fully ready to duel Liam should he find the man lacking. Clara knew it too as she squeaked in alarm.

"Aaron! You're overreacting!"

"I see no reason for violence, my lord," Liam said quickly. Aside from the fact that one of them would end up hurt or dead—he was not at all sure which one of them—such a thing would go counter to all of his plans. "I am offering assistance to your intended bride."

"It's not Lilah I'm worried about."

"Aaron," Clara cried. "This is quite unnecessary."

"On the contrary," interrupted the most unlikely of people. It was Miss Rees who stepped between the two men. She also gripped Clara's hand and tugged the woman to her side. "I think it a capital idea that we travel to Scotland together. Very soon, in fact."

That would be the most prudent way to quiet any gossip. Liam nodded and tried not to be gleeful. "Most wise."

Clara sniffed. "Does anyone care what I want?"

Her brother shot her a hard glare. "No."

Two days later, the four of them left for Scotland.

They travelled light. The ladies acted as chaperones for each other, which kept things proper. Another carriage followed with a maid and a valet to serve them all.

No abduction was required, thank God. Though from Clara's mulish expression, he knew it would take all his wits to keep her there forever.

CHAPTER FOUR

"D O YOU LOVE him?"

Clara glared at Lilah in the confines of the coach. They'd left this morning for Scotland and her friend had wasted no time in peppering her with questions. The two men—Aaron and Lord Loughton—were riding postillion, each trotting along opposite sides of the carriage as if they couldn't bring themselves to even look at the other.

"Your brother is still furious," Lilah said. "To kiss you like that where everyone could see."

"We were in the garden in the dark. No one would have noticed if he hadn't brought attention to us."

Lilah pursed her lips. "You know that's not true. He pushed his way through several gawkers."

"It was a mistake," Clara muttered. "Obviously."

"But was it really? You're no green girl, Clara. You knew the risks and yet did it anyway. That tells me you have tender feelings for the man."

"Well, of course I like him. I kissed him." Clara grimaced. "That is to say I *used* to like him. Now he thoroughly disgusts me."

"That's just pique."

"Of course, it's pique! I do not want to leave London. Ever. And yet here I am." She gestured disdainfully at the carriage. "On my way to the one place in the world I never wanted to go to."

"Yes, about that," Lilah said as she folded her hands in her lap. "Why exactly do you despise Scotland?"

Clara leaned back against the squabs and glared dolefully out the window. It gave her a view of her brother's unamused expression. That would usually cause her to look the other way, but the opposite window showed her Lord Loughton's gleeful expression. The man was enjoying himself a great deal more than any man ought to at the beginning of a five-day trip.

"Clara!" her friend huffed. "This is going to be a very long ride if you refuse to talk to me."

"It's going to be very long in any event." Then when Lilah opened her mouth, Clara slashed her hand through the air. "I'm on the shelf, Lilah. I'm too old for anyone to care who I kiss at a party." That was a ridiculous statement. She was the daughter of an earl. That made her a person of interest. And even if she weren't, people always gossiped about who kissed whom.

Lilah, of course, wasted no time in pointing that out. "You're neither naïve nor stupid. So out with it. Why were you kissing him?"

"Because I wanted to!" she huffed. "Because I liked him. Past tense. *Liked.*"

"And you don't like him now because…?"

"Because he's happy about it." She turned and pointedly glared out the window where he was now whistling as he rode. Blasted man. "He couldn't be more delighted to be whisking me off to the one place I despise!"

"So you've said," Lilah huffed. "But *why?*"

Clara measured her answer before she spoke. She knew that the words of a psychic would not have any weight with Lilah, even if the fortune teller had been adamant that Clara would die in Scotland. Lilah indulged Clara's fascination with the occult. She did not share it. So Clara turned and looked behind them at where the last London buildings were long gone.

"I love London, Lilah. I have built a life I adore there. I go to museum exhibitions. I have friends I see every week and lectures

I attend. Aaron even stopped pestering me about bringing a maid with me everywhere. Everything about my life is perfection, especially with all the new servants you've trained for me." They'd gone several weeks now without a single servant quitting or disappearing. "In London, my life is perfection. There is nothing I lack, no entertainment I cannot find. Why would I ever want to leave it?"

"For a change of scenery, perhaps?"

"It is illogical to change to a lesser thing."

"It is illogical to think that a place you have never been cannot offer something new, something intriguing, something unique to itself."

"I do not want anything new," Clara huffed.

"You *live* for everything new!" Lilah shot back. And Clara was shocked enough at her friend's raised voice that she straightened in her seat and frowned at her friend.

"You are overwrought," she finally said. "That's what happens when one travels."

"That's what happens when one's most sensible and logical friend suddenly turns irrational."

That was a damning statement. Clara's best asset was her intelligence, and to call that into question was guaranteed to provoke a fight. She was just rising to the bait, when Lilah's eyes suddenly widened, and her mouth dropped open on a gasp.

"You're illogical!" she cried. Then she clapped her hands together. "That means you're falling in love! Clara, that's wonderful!"

"I am not in love," Clara snapped. She had fallen desperately in love once in her adolescence with a man who turned out to be a fortune hunter. It was a horrible memory, and she'd decided then to never be subject to such wild feelings again. Such was her force of will that she had succeeded. She'd never been troubled by love again, except for a love of science.

Lilah, however, completely disdained such discipline. "Of course it doesn't feel like love to you. You are a creature of deep intellect. Only something momentous could break that. And since you've suffered no blow to the brain, the answer is obvious."

"I am not in love!" Clara repeated.

"Are you sure?" Lilah pressed. "Really, really sure? Because, honestly, how would you know? Have you ever been this irrational before?"

"Yes!" she responded. "Back when I was sixteen."

Lilah's brows rose in surprise. "You fell in love." It wasn't a question.

"Yes." He was clever, he laughed at her jokes. "He was *charming.*"

"And?"

"And he was a fortune hunter through and through. Every word he said was a bold-faced lie." She sniffed. "I came close to running away with him when my mother brought me the evidence."

"Oh, dear."

"It was awful." She tried to block the memory of her mother getting the man to admit that he was courting her for her dowry and that he had no interest in her whatsoever. It didn't work. She relived every excruciating moment. And when it was done, she looked at her best friend. "So, yes, I know what it is like to be in love." It felt thoroughly wretched. "And I feel no such thing for Lord Loughton."

"But you cannot—"

"As for being irrational," she interrupted, her voice high. "You are the one who is jumping to illogical conclusions."

Then rather than discuss things further, she grabbed one of the books she'd brought, slammed the pages open, and pretended to read. It was what she always did when she preferred not to be disturbed. She had pretended to read a myriad of tomes through-out her childhood, which had worked until her mother started quizzing her on the contents. Then she began to actually read the books, but at this moment, she'd obviously reverted to pre-pubescence.

Meanwhile, Lilah released a low chuckle. "I'm so happy for you, Clara. I know it's upsetting now, but really, being in love with a good man is the best thing in the world."

"You would say that as my brother is a paragon of masculine virtue. He's titled, generous, and a genuinely good person." She glanced out at Lord Loughton who had given up whistling in favor of eavesdropping. He was riding practically on top of the door and looking in as if he were trying to read her lips. And when she gaped at his blatantly ill-bred behavior, he winked at her. So she raised her voice and nearly bellowed her next words.

"Lord Loughton, on the other hand, is a… a…" Damnation, even in the height of her fury, she couldn't lie about him. He wasn't a lecherous cheat. He was outrageous, but that was her mother's favorite insult, and she was hardly going to be so prosaic as to use that. "A scoundrel!"

"Really," Lilah gasped, all too aware that the man was listening in. "How so? What *exactly* has he done?"

Kissed her. Just once, but it was a really, really good kiss. He'd also made her laugh, dressed outrageously when they went to Hyde Park, and had a body that would tempt any student of anatomy. But none of that warranted the name "scoundrel." She resorted to the kind of vague, ignorant response she usually detested.

"I do not require specifics. I know it nonetheless."

"Well," her brother shouted from the other side of the carriage. "I require specifics!" Apparently, he'd been listening in.

She had no response, except the general complaint that she was now in a carriage headed north and she did not want to be. So rather than argue, she stared like a grumpy toad down at her book while her mind chewed like an old dog on her feelings. She got nowhere, of course. Feelings were not something that one could dissect into component parts. Feelings had to be experienced and survived. Which is exactly what she planned to do— with no discussion with anyone else—until that blessed moment when she returned to London.

Too bad no one else wanted to fall in with her plans, most especially Lilah.

"You know," she began, "you could take this time to see if it's love. Say yes to anything he wants to do—"

Clara's head shot up in shock at that.

"No, no! Not *everything*," Lilah hastily amended. Then she dropped her voice as she leaned forward. "Agree to anything that is not scandalous. Avoid anything that could get you pregnant. And at the end of the trip, you'll know if you like his amusements."

"I don't want to like his amusements. I have plenty of my own." She was being petulant. She could hear it in her voice, but she seemed powerless to stop it.

Lilah shot her a look that said, very clearly, exactly everything Clara was thinking. That only a child whined like this, and Clara was no little girl. So Clara lifted her chin and resolved to consider the task.

"He does not like the normal amusements. Or at least not in the normal way."

"Neither do you."

True enough.

"Will you at least try?" Lilah pressed. "If nothing else, it will make this a much more pleasant journey for everyone else. No one enjoys being around a sulk."

Again, truth. And one that cut Clara deeply. She had prided herself on never sulking once she had escaped her mother's overbearing interference. She had spent her younger years steeped in tantrums, which always bled into long weeks of sulking. That was the pattern she'd had with her mother, and it was Aaron's one condition when she had escaped her parents' home to live with him: no sulking. Ever.

She hadn't until now. She'd stomped out of the house when she'd gotten angry. She'd fired a drunken servant – once. She'd even gotten drunk and fallen asleep downstairs. But she'd never, ever sulked until now.

"I beg your pardon," she said, thoroughly ashamed.

"Just say you'll give him a chance."

"Even though I told him that I didn't want to go to Scotland and here I am."

"Yes. Even though."

She glared down at her open book. She thrust out her lower lip until it could go no further. She screwed up her face into a comedy of childish, *I don't wanna!*

And when Lilah released a musical cascade of laughter, Clara gave in.

"Very well. I promise to say yes to all his non-carnal amusements. But if I end up dead in a peat bog from some stupid Scottish custom, then it shall be all your fault."

"I shall confess my guilt at your funeral."

"You'd best cry too."

"Buckets of tears. I swear."

And so it was that her fate in Scotland was sealed. Not by any nefarious machinations by Lord Loughton, but because she'd promised her best friend to give someone else's amusements a chance.

CHAPTER FIVE

L IAM WAS TIRED of being entertaining.

Knowing that Lady Clara was less than thrilled about this trip, he had worked extra hard to be delightful. He teased her with winks and smiles, he filled their meals with delightful anecdotes, and when the weather forced all four of them inside the carriage, he became as fascinating a conversationalist as he knew how to be. Which was to say, he asked about everyone in the carriage, doing his best to get them talking about whatever struck their fancy.

After five days and nights of entertainment, he was feeling the strain. Plus Aaron snored, and they'd had to share a room at the last posting inn. Liam was ready to be done with this charade. They were in Scotland now, arriving in Edinburgh this afternoon.

It was time to close the trap. He had to find a way to get Clara to his home in Kipcoille. And yet, perversely, the closer her came to capturing Lady Clara and her large dowry, the more distempered he became.

"Look at all those buildings!" the lady exclaimed as she pressed her face against the carriage window. "And there are people everywhere!"

"Did you think Scotland was just cowpies and hovels?"

She looked back at him. "No, of course not. No more than England is. But this is quite beyond what I'd expected."

"It's called the modern Athens. The topography and the

architecture in New Town are reminiscent of Athens."

She frowned, obviously trying to create a mental picture of both cities. "But Athens was a center of intellect and—"

"As are we, my lady," he chided gently. Or maybe not so gently because he was tired of this argument. "Have you heard of the *Encyclopaedia Britannica?* It is published here. I shall take you to see it if you like. Sixteen thousand pages in twenty volumes, all written and printed here. Every page filled with the categorization and explanation of knowledge."

Her mouth opened in a shocked O. "I have heard of the publication, of course, but I did not know that it—"

"It's Scottish, Lady Clara."

She bit her lip. "I didn't know."

Of course, she didn't and damned if that didn't rub him raw. Meanwhile, Miss Rees turned to him. "Is that something you enjoy doing, my lord? Visiting publishing houses? Categorizing bits of knowledge such that others can learn from you?"

Not in the least. "I am thinking of entertainments for Lady Clara."

"Yes, I can see that, and it is very kind. But perhaps you could share what you enjoy most."

He'd been telling tales of Scotland since the first day of travel. Anything he could think of that might intrigue his three very English companions. But he supposed he never stated his favorite amusements. Probably because they weren't appropriate for polite company.

"I used to love the Highland Games," he offered. "I was never the top competitor, you understand. I can toss a caber—that's a very big log—with the best of them, but I never developed the full brawn to beat my neighbors. They said it was because I spent too much time studying. I think it was because I didn't stuff my face with haggis." He shook his head in memory. "My mother used to complain that they ate their weight in meat, then came back for more."

"You throw logs?" asked Miss Rees.

"And hammers and iron balls. There's a lot of heaving and hurling of big, heavy things, and a tug-o-war that is great fun."

Aaron stretched his legs a little in the tight confines of the carriage. "I ran the footraces when I was young," Aaron said. "Clara was the fastest at those, but I could beat her."

"That's because you're older." she shot back. Then she looked back at Liam. "We didn't throw a lot of things at our fairs. People competed to see who had the biggest pig or the prettiest flower. Things like that."

"Would you like to see some Highland Games?" Liam asked, striving to be casual about the offer. It was his best hope of getting her to Kipcoille.

"Oh, I don't think so. I shouldn't like to wait around—"

"Are they fun, Lord Loughton?" interrupted Miss Rees. "Do you enjoy seeing them?" There was a pointed note to her question as she shot a look at Lady Clara. No doubt because she'd challenged the lady to try new amusements. His amusements, to be specific, and that was the best way to get her to his home.

"They're great fun even if I haven't thrown a weight over the bar in years. I'm usually in England during the festival."

"So this is a favorite pastime of yours?" Miss Rees pressed.

Not his top choice, but it counted as an entertaining event. "It can be great fun."

"Then wouldn't it be fun to experience something Lord Loughton enjoys? Clara was just saying she wanted to learn more about what makes Scotland special."

He sincerely doubted that, but Lilah was determined while Clara flushed dark red. Then she turned a brittle smile at him.

"Of course, my lord. I should love to experience a Scottish fair day. Unfortunately, we'll likely be returning home—"

"Actually…" he began. He'd spent some time last night sorting through the logistics. He would have to send a letter to his father as soon as they settled in the inn. Then he calculated the number of days it would take to bring the whole county together for a fair. "I believe there will be games at home this coming week. I'm sure we could attend if Miss Rees' business does not take very long." He flashed Clara his most brilliant smile. "How lucky is that?"

She looked at him, her expression steady. He gave her credit for not using a polite phrase that she didn't mean. Instead, she spoke with blunt honesty, which he appreciated. "I do not want to find Scotland charming."

"You have something terrible against charm, my lady. I assure you—"

She held up her hand. "Don't. I have sworn to Lilah that I will give you and Scotland a chance. I know you think I'm being ridiculous." She swept a hand at everyone in the carriage. "You all do. But London is the only place that I have ever felt comfortable, and it was a long, hard battle to find my place there." She turned back to Liam. "You are going to show me the best of Scotland, ply me with treats and show me fair days. Aaron and Lilah will remind me that by kissing you publicly, I have lost my reputation. Worse, they are to be married soon and no newlywed wants a spinster sister hanging about."

"Clara," inserted Aaron, "you will always have a place in my home."

Miss Rees was quick to agree. But Liam could see that Clara's intellect had already written out her future and she already hated it.

"I have some fondness for Lord Loughton," she said, her tone one of dread. And at Lilah's happy gasp, she rolled her eyes. "I did kiss him, after all."

Aaron interrupted. "Then what is all this fuss about?"

She glared at her brother. "Any man, no matter how char—" She abruptly cut off the word "charming" to substitute another. "No matter how delightful, cannot replace the happiness I have found as a spinster in London." She looked at Liam. "I will not change my mind."

"So you have said," he drawled. "Many times."

"I have to repeat it because no one believes it! And all of you will be terribly upset with me when I want to go home."

He could see her genuine distress. For all her independence, she disliked being at odds with people, especially with her brother and his fiancé. But most of all, he could see in her the constant pain of being discounted or ignored. She knew her own mind. And he knew how hard it was to stay true to oneself against the constant pressure of others.

"Clara," he said. "You've a strong mind and a good heart."

"I am immune to flattery," she said dryly.

He chuckled. "You're immune to genuine compliments, too, because you think them all lies." He leaned forward. "I intend to get to the bottom of why that is."

She didn't respond. Indeed, she looked as excited as he probably did at the beginning of one of those interminable lectures she loved.

"Lady Clara, I have bet my future upon changing your mind." Not an understatement. "Can you not take up the bet as well?"

"You want me to bet against you?"

"That is the nature of the game, is it not? But you must fully engage yourself with me and the entertainments in Edinburgh and at my home. For a full week, each location."

She shook her head. "That's much too long. A week in the city will be enough."

"You must see my home to fully play this game."

He wondered if she would play fairly and was pleased when she nodded. "Very well. One day at…" She frowned. "Where do you live?"

"A day's travel north in Kipcoille. You must spend several nights—"

"One night—"

"Five nights. My home is large and has many amusements. And you did say you wanted to live in a castle."

"I said I'd *toured* many a castle," she corrected. "But that does hold some small appeal if only to argue plumbing with Mr. Russell when I return. Very well, I shall allow for two nights—"

"Five."

"Three."

"Five."

"Three, my lord, and not a second more."

"Oh, for the love of God," Aaron burst out in exasperation. "Four, it is. And to compensate, we shall cut one night in Edinburgh. Is that acceptable to you both?"

Liam nodded. He doubted he would need that long. Lady Clara had told him a great deal in this last exchange. She'd shown that she'd been hurt badly in the past and had fought for her independence in London. No doubt it had been a terrible time for her, but despite all that pain, she was sorely tempted by a game.

That made her fun as he was a man who also enjoyed contests. Not the silly ones about who could throw a tree farther, but the ones that involved money and status. He played the deep games that gambled with the survival of his entire clan. And it pleased him that she brightened when things were framed as a game between the two of them.

"I will agree to that," she said.

"As do I," he echoed.

Aaron rolled his eyes. "You two make my head hurt."

"I think I have never been so entertained in my life," quipped Miss Rees.

CHAPTER SIX

A S A CITY, Edinburgh had its appeal. Clara could admit that now that the rules of this trip had been firmly established. Lord Loughton took her not just to the publishing offices of *The Encyclopaedia Britannica*, but also to the offices of *The Edinburgh Review*. Indeed, he appeared to have a childhood acquaintance with Francis Jeffrey, the editor, who encouraged them to visit a certain pub that evening.

Clara had no idea what that meant, but after Lilah and Aaron went off to a musical entertainment, Clara and Lord Loughton listened to a woman spin tale after bloody tale of ghosts and mayhem. The Scots had a special way with storytelling, and Clara was entranced. Enough that when the evening's tales were finished, she rushed forward to introduce herself. And that led to the most interesting discussion of all. The lady knew of all sorts of phony and real practitioners of the arcane arts. She gave Clara a short list of people and places to explore inside the city. And that was nothing compared to what could be found in Scotland as a whole. And damnation, it was maddening that she couldn't explore them all on this trip. A dozen trips would not suffice, though all four of them managed a nighttime visit to Greyfriars Krikyard where Lord Loughton embellished the tale of Bloody MacKenzie.

She loved listening to his voice. He spoke of the most bloody things with in a matter-of-fact tone that sent shivers down her spine. And then, he tugged her behind a very tall gravestone, pressed her against the cold stone, and whispered into her ear.

"Bloody Mackenzie, come out if you dare. Draw the sneck and lift the bar."

After five days inside a carriage together, all four of them had become familiar with one another. She knew his scent and the feel of his legs against hers. She knew how he breathed when he slept and that his hands were very large, especially compared to her own. And now he pressed himself against her more intimately than ever before. A week ago, she would have screamed at such liberty. But instead of being afraid, her breath caught in excitement while her skin tingled.

"I don't think this is the right door for that," she responded, her words coming out on a whispery laugh.

"My mistake," he said as his face lowered to hers.

A proper woman would push him away. But she had seen Aaron pull Lilah aside for just such a dalliance a moment earlier. If her brother and best friend could kiss between the crypts, then why couldn't she?

She didn't have time to argue as his mouth caught hers. He stole her breath, plundered her mouth, and pulled her hips against his such that she felt the hot thrust of his cock. Never had she felt something so erotically as he pulsed against her. She gripped his shoulders to hold herself upright. And she allowed her body to feel every movement of his while her tongue twined with his.

And then he pulled back, dropping his forehead to hers.

"I am mad with wanting you," he gasped. "Marry me, Clara."

How easily she could be swept away by his charm, by his kisses, by his whole body as it burned against hers. She wanted to explore these sensations. She wanted to feel everything he offered. But marriage was a business arrangement, and this was not the time to speak of business.

She let her head fall back against the stone wall and she looked into his eyes. She could see when disappointment darkened them and when his jaw firmed with frustration.

"Why won't you see reason?" he growled.

"You kiss me like that and expect reason?" She shook her head. "You expect me to be swept away with lust." She was. Oh, how desire pulsed through her body. "But marriage is a contract, and with you, that contract rests in Scotland."

"We could come to an arrangement."

She shook her head. "Lust is not enough for me to give up my life in London." Then she ducked under his arm and wandered back to the main path. She wasn't surprised when Aaron and Lilah came out soon afterwards. Lilah's hair was mussed, and her lips swollen. Clara no doubt looked the same, but when Lord Loughton joined them, he was decidedly more sober. It was left to the others to carry the conversation until they returned to their rooms in the inn.

Lilah's inheritance took several days to secure. There were visits to a law office and a bank, plus one to the Edinburgh residence of her nearest cousin. The man was disgruntled, disagreeable, and disgusted that a by-blow could claim any money from his family. But it was the law and he could not stop it. Still, he made it clear that Miss Rees would not be welcome at the family seat.

Lilah retorted that he would not be welcome in London and that she now saw why her mother chose life as an actress rather than be associated with them. And with that, she bid him good day, then treated the four of them to a night at the theater. Far from being upset, she was pleased to relegate her mother's troubles to the past as she started a bright new future with Aaron. Indeed, she seemed brighter and happier than Clara had ever seen, and she kept saying how she "owed it all to Lord Loughton's assistance." Indeed, she praised him so much that Aaron began to grumble that it hadn't all been the Scotsman. He'd asked Lord Loughton to ferret out the truth, so he deserved some credit for Lilah's wealthy status.

Naturally, Lilah made it up to her fiancé. She was deeply in love with Aaron. It mattered not a jot where the praise went, her heart was with Aaron. But her gratitude to Lord Loughton was real, and Clara was treated to a detailed description of how the Scotsman had cut through all manner of lawyer and banking reluctance to pass her inheritance on to her. Enough that Clara was impressed by his ability to bend bureaucrats to his will.

They left for Kipcoille the very next day.

Clara thought Lord Loughton would ride postillion again because it was a fine day. Clara certainly wanted to do so rather than sit inside a stuffy carriage. But he didn't. While Aaron lifted his face to the sun outside the carriage, Liam sat beside Clara and pointed out landmarks and interesting tidbits. She thought he might grow happier the closer he got to his home. Instead, his body tightened with increasing tension. His gestures shortened and became more abrupt. And his gaze would not steady but hopped from window to window while alighting on her and Lilah along the way.

"Arc you feeling well?" she finally asked after he had shifted his position on the seat for the umpteenth time. "Your mood seems to sour the closer we get to your home."

"Don't be silly," he countered in a tone that was firmer than any he'd used so far. "Whyever would you think that?"

"Well," she drawled, half-teasing in hopes of making him smile. "Could it be that you know your castle cannot possibly compete with the lures of Edinburgh? And if you have not seduced me to Scotland with the city, then you will no doubt fail with your home, no matter how charming it is."

"Clara!" Lilah said, her tone admonishing. "Don't be mean. Lord Loughton has been nothing but kind this entire trip."

Clara frowned at her friend. She hadn't intended to be mean. Indeed, she'd been trying to tease him about their bet. But a part of her believed that he was coming to realize that he had no hopes of luring her away from London. If the delights of Edinburgh could not tempt her, then what could a castle in the middle of nowhere do to bring her around?

Rather than speak her mind, she chose to be extra polite. "I beg your pardon, Lord Loughton. You have indeed been wonderful this entire holiday. What can I do to make up for my thoughtless words?"

He opened his mouth to speak, but then shut it again. His gaze finally settled on her face with the air of a man about to throw a pair of dice. Then before she could understand more, he found his words.

"You can make amends by remembering that Scotland has some rough areas, Lady Clara. A harsh land produces gruff people and sometimes very angry people. But my clan also has a fierce spirit, a generous heart, and a wily way about it that canna be denied." He smiled as his accent thickened, and she found she liked the sound and look of that.

"You think I will not like them."

"I think you will judge them too quickly. They are good people, but they are undoubtably *not* English."

What was she to say to that? "As I am often referred to as an odd duck—and those are the kindest terms I have heard—how could I possibly judge people who are different as well?"

He snorted. "Because there is English different and Scottish different."

"And now I am intrigued." She arched her brow at him. "Which I gather was your whole point."

He grinned and settled back against the squabs. "Also, I hope you will indulge me a little as well. Our activities in Edinburgh have been for your entertainment. Finally, you shall get a look at my favorite pastimes."

Lilah leaned forward. "Will you be throwing things then, Lord Loughton?"

"I am sure Connall—my neighbor to the west—will challenge me so that he and his clan will show well in comparison. But that will not be my main source of delight."

"Then what will it be?" Clara pressed.

"We have a glass works factory, my lady, at which I am moderately skilled. And whisky to fill the bottles." He glanced out the window as Aaron. "I hope to interest your brother in touring the distillery."

"Touring and tasting, no doubt," Clara said. "Indeed, I should love to see it as well."

He arched a brow at her. "Do you enjoy whisky, then?" There was no condemnation in his tone, and so she answered honestly.

"I have enjoyed hard spirits now and then." She winked at Lilah. "And we should definitely expand Miss Rees' palate in that regard."

"I am not an innocent in all things," Lilah returned. "But in this, you've caught me out. I've never tried whisky. Would it be improper if we sampled a little?"

"Not improper at all," he said. "At least not in Scotland."

So it was decided that in the morning, they would tour the distillery and the glass works. But first they had to arrive at his home in the highlands. It was a long journey with the three of them in the carriage, but after lunch, Aaron joined them inside as well. The conversation was desultory. The weather hot enough to make all of them testy. In the end, Clara retreated into her books while the others dozed.

That usually worked for her. Reading always settled her mind—except today. She thought instead about Lord Loughton's words. She was not normally a judgmental person. She believed in common courtesy, and she extended it to others as a matter of habit no matter what horrible things they said about her. That he would worry that she would be rude toward his family was upsetting. She was never rude on purpose, only by accident. She resolved to be on her best, most cordial behavior throughout her stay in his home.

It was dusk by the time they passed the remains of a curtain wall. Even in the fading light, Clara could see that it was falling to ruin, if it had ever been strong. It appeared more like reinforced hillside than wall. She wanted to ask Lord Loughton about it, but he was sitting with the coachman as he directed their path. She resolved to look at it more closely in daylight as she tried to separate shadows into forms she recognized.

They travelled up the road to the raised flat of land on which the castle was built. She should have expected the size of it. It was a castle after all, one large enough to have a curtain wall. But she had not expected this.

An entire English village could fit inside the main keep, and indeed, there seemed to be stalls and carts everywhere, but none occupied. No doubt, she'd have a lively time seeing them in the morning. She heard Lord Loughton call out, and soon there were lanterns lighting the gloom, guiding their way into the main keep. Anxious to get out of the carriage, she thrust open the door before they fully stopped moving. She waited a moment more, then she jumped out into a slightly muddy bailey. Two young boys ran forward while Loughton, too, jumped down though from a higher perch.

"Art, Mungan! How you've grown!"

The boys were there to see to the horses, though one child was barely tall enough to reach the harness. The front door opened, spilling more light onto the ground. Large dogs came running out, barking with canine glee. They clearly knew Lord Loughton, but were unsure about her. She was suddenly surrounded by four large dogs with big teeth and deep barks which made her shrink back against the carriage beside Lilah. And it effectively pinned Aaron inside the carriage. She was accustomed to dogs, of course, but few people kept animals this size in London. They easily came up to her chest and were a hundred pounds of muscle and teeth. Or so she felt.

She squeaked in alarm as they sniffed her, and Lord Loughton snapped a sharp command.

"Come! Lukos, Ogre. Come!"

Two of the nearest creatures lifted their heads, but they didn't leave her. Probably because Lord Loughton wasn't their master. And while Aaron calmly encouraged Lilah to step back into the carriage – she was closest to the door – Lord Loughton cursed and roughly pulled the dogs back. They didn't bite him, but they didn't give way easily either, even as he cuffed the nearest one to her on his long snout.

"Back! Back, you stupid—"

A long whistle cut through the air, sharp and clear. The dogs immediately retreated, running back to stand next to a man now silhouetted in the light streaming out of the open castle door. He was a large man, outfitted in a fur mantle as if he were a king roused from his mead. Servants flowed out around him holding lanterns aloft so that light filled the courtyard.

"Who comes this evening?" asked one of the servants.

"Who disturbs the MacCleal?" asked another servant from the opposite side.

Lilah whispered to Clara. "Isn't he a viscount?"

"Yes," Clara said, equally quiet.

Fortunately, the exchange was buried under Lord Loughton's muttered grumble of, "Pompous ass." But then he spoke loudly. "It is me, your son, Liam, come with friends to show them the glory of your halls."

"What friends?" asked the first servant.

"Do they appreciate the depth of the honor you request upon their behalf?" asked the second.

Clara was also close enough to hear Liam grind his teeth together. "It is your son who requests entrance. And as such, I vouch for my companions."

Clara noted that he said nothing about appreciating the honor and all the rest. Like her, it appeared that Lord Loughton disliked the formality of whatever this was. However, her brother—who was just now exiting the carriage—was well used to pomp and circumstance.

"I am the Earl of Kittrel. This is my fiancé Miss Rees, and my sister, Lady Clara. We greet you with utmost respect and humbly request your tolerance as we visit your beautiful home." He said nothing more, but he bowed as deeply as he would when greeting the Prince Regent. Beside him, Lilah curtseyed such that her knees cracked after the long time spent in the carriage. Clara didn't see if Lord Loughton's father eyed her, but she felt his eyes upon her as a heat upon her cheeks.

Normally, she would have given the barest sketch of a curtsey. She had no love for people who demanded nonsensical bowing and scraping and usually avoided them at all costs. But she had vowed to be extra polite, and so she curtseyed as well, keeping her head lowered even after she regained her full height.

There was a long ponderous wait that irritated Lord Loughton more than them, if the grinding of his teeth were anything to go by. She worried he'd break a tooth, but he said nothing. He simply stood beside her in the dimming light and stared at his father who presumably stared back. It was hard to tell with her eyes lowered, though she did sneak a peek.

Finally, the MacCleal spoke, his voice less full than she had anticipated from all the fanfare. "If my son vouches for you, then you shall be welcomed. Mairi will see to you." And with that, he turned and stomped away.

It took a moment for him to disappear back into the depths of the castle, trailed as he was by the first and second servants, but eventually he was gone, and a woman stood in his stead. She was younger than Clara expected, though she wore the keys and the clothing of a chatelaine. Weren't they normally older since they functioned as a housekeeper? Either way, the woman walked closer and dropped into a curtsey in front of Lord Loughton.

"Welcome back, my lord."

"Mairi," he said, his tone soft and warm. "You've grown into a beauty." Then he pulled her into a rough hug which she returned.

"You always say that."

"Because it's always true."

Mairi shrugged out of his grasp and glared hard at him. "I've been a woman grown for ten years now, and I'm past waiting for you to notice."

He frowned at her. "I always noticed, Mairi, and I acted accordingly."

There was a weariness in his tone that Clara heard but couldn't explain. She could guess, of course, but she wasn't good at that, so she kept her tongue. Instead, she smiled when Lord Loughton introduced her, then busied herself with studying her surroundings when the conversation became too thick with Scottish accents for her to follow.

She did catch that Mairi was actually Miss MacAdaidh, and she served as housekeeper—or chatelaine—to Viscount MacCleal. If there was a butler, Clara did not see him as she and Lilah were led up a tower to a third floor room that had a thin rug on the floor and a freshly made large bed. Presumably she and Lilah were to share. And though this was a very common practice among most everyone, Clara hadn't ever shared a bed. Not even with her nanny.

She glanced at Lilah, who was thanking the servants bringing up their trunks on thick shoulders. Meanwhile Miss MacAdaidh was not one to dip her chin again. She directed the settling of the trunks then turned to face the ladies.

"I've set your maid in the south tower, but she's feeling poorly. I doubt she'll be much help tonight. I've found a maid to help you tomorrow morning, but there were none to spare tonight. Everyone's getting ready for the games." Her tone turned especially hard with that last sentence, but Clara had no idea why. "I'll send a tray up for your dinner, but there'll be no baths tonight. I canna set out a decent place for a ladies' pleasure no matter what Liam says in his letter." She lifted her chin. "You'll find that the viscount is laird, but I am the one who directs the comings and goings throughout the castle. You'll have everything you need, but I haven't the time to waste on nonsense."

That was a frank speech, and though Lilah appeared to be shocked enough that her jaw hung open, Clara found she appreciated being able to be blunt back.

"I'm not one for nonsense either. We're perfectly capable of maiding each other, and I see water in the basin. Send up a simple tray, we shall be very well set indeed."

"Good. But don't use the chamber pot. Won't be a soul to clean it out tomorrow. The garderobe is down through here, and you'll not be running in there undressed. It's the one that works best, so you're not the only one to use it."

Nothing to say to that except that the castle was cool enough that she wouldn't want to go anywhere in a simple nightrail anyway. "Thank you—"

"The men will have their revels tonight. Nothing like tomorrow, but it will get rowdy enough. Don't think to join them. I run a fine home here, and you'll not be turning us common."

"Common?" Clara echoed, her annoyance at the insult growing by the second. "And what—exactly—constitutes common behavior?"

The woman sniffed. "If you don't know that, then you're not the lady his lordship claims you are." Then she gave the briefest of nods and walked out, all but slamming the door behind her.

Clara and Lilah traded arch looks.

"Well," Lilah finally said on an exhale. "Lord Loughton did warn us they were a proud people."

"He said gruff and angry," she corrected, "which seems to match Miss MacAdaidh exactly." He'd also said his people had a fierce spirit, a generous heart, and a wily way about them. She'd have to wait and see on that.

"We're fine in here," Lilah repeated as she bounced lightly on the bed. It appeared to be in relatively decent shape. "And tomorrow we will get a good look around." She smiled. "I consider it a grand adventure."

As adventures went, this didn't compare to the lurid tales Clara had read in novels. Having to share a bed was hardly the equivalent of an abduction at gunpoint or being lost at sea. Even so, this was the most unusual place she'd ever stayed, and she had promised to reserve judgement as long as possible.

So she smiled at Lilah and declared it her experiment in castle living. And she wondered what Lord Loughton would be doing tonight in his manly "revels."

CHAPTER SEVEN

L IAM WAS HALFWAY up the east tower stairs when Mairi blocked the way. It wasn't just her body filling the narrow stair, but her attitude radiated from her folded arms and dark scowl. She and her father were the last of the MacAdaidh clan. Though they'd been absorbed into his clan in order to survive, the woman radiated all the pride of a laird's daughter. If Culloden had turned out differently, she would be sought by every Scotsman who might catch her eye. But her people were gone, along with her land—taken by the English fifty years ago. And yet, she still acted like a queen of all she surveyed. And she was none too pleased with the look of him.

He didn't bother with pleasantries. He knew she wouldn't appreciate them. So he waited, knowing she could not tolerate silence for long.

"It's her, then?" she demanded. "Is she stupid or desperate because she's old?"

"She's barely two years older than you."

"Stupid, then. Have you had her yet? Have you claimed her in public?"

Liam glared down at his childhood friend. She was the first to ask him this, but she wouldn't be the last. Best to make it clear from the start. "No, and no. I'm playing a different game with her."

Mairi snorted. "Whatever game, you'd best do it tonight.

Your father won't wait beyond tomorrow." She glanced behind them. "I put the women together to hold him off tonight."

Liam jerked upright. "He's gotten as bad as that?"

"He's a mean drunk to be sure. You have to stop him from drinking the stock."

"What stock? The whisky?" Liam cursed under his breath. "Damnation, we need that! We can't sell what he drinks, and I can't put a royal mark on his belly."

"Och, the king will no' give you his warrant any more than he can dress hisself. He's mad and—"

"But Prinny will. What have I been working for these last years except to secure our future with our whisky?"

She arched her brows and leaned forward. "*Our future*, is it? And just who are you including in that?"

He blew out his breath. "The clan, Mairi. A royal warrant will let me charge ten times over for our whisky. That money'll pay for food and clothing. We can repair the grounds and hire teachers for our bairns."

She straightened away from him, her expression wary. "So you'll not be marrying that Long Meg for her dowry?"

"Not for her dowry, no."

"But for something else then. Her smiles? Her bonny—"

He cut her off before she became crude. "The whisky, Mairi. Tell me how much he's drunk. Is there any left?"

She didn't look like she would answer at first. She was too interested in Clara to want to be deterred, but in this, he held firm. In the end, she relented.

"Half of what was made—"

He cursed.

"But he thinks it's all. I had Brian hide the rest. It's out behind the old bathhouse because for sure, your father won't be going there."

"Good thinking," Liam said, as his gaze jumped over her head to the bedroom above. He heard a thump and then laughter. Clearly the two women were settling in, but the urge to see that for himself had him stepping higher on the stairs. Mairi still blocked him, but now he stood taller than she.

"You made me a promise," Mairi said. "We were going to change things here. Fix what's broken—"

"I still plan to do that."

"But with her? Or just her money?"

He looked back at the girl who had—years ago—been his closest friend along with their neighbor Connall. They had indeed plotted a grand future for the MacCleal clan, but hard facts often trumped youthful dreams. "You remember, don't you, how we said the lying was the worst thing. The way my father cheats friend and family alike."

"So you mean to remain true to our promise, one to another."

"We were children, Mairi."

"And here I've been thinking I was a woman now and you a grown man. With the both of us making plans to turn this life into a future." She spread her hands wide, giving him a view of more than her full breasts and strong body. He also saw the callouses on her hands and the chatelaine keys bound about her waist. "I've been here minding it all while you found the money."

"I'm working on it," he said.

"With her."

"Yes."

"And with me?"

What could he say to that? She was the logical choice, and indeed if she'd had any money of her own, they'd have married years ago. But she hadn't, so he'd left to gain English money. He'd also gained perspective and wisdom. She was not the woman for him, and he had to make that clear now.

"I'll always favor you."

"But not love?" Trust her to see the truth behind his words.

"Aye," he answered. "You're beautiful and intelligent, Mairi. You'll make someone a fine wife—"

"Och, be done," she snapped as she shoved her way past him.

"You were useless to me these last five years, and you're useless now."

He wanted to call her back. Indeed, he turned to say something, but no words formed. She was the reason he'd survived his childhood in this place, and now she wouldn't even look at him. She did pause long enough to throw words over her shoulder at him.

"Leave the Sassenach alone. They need their beauty rest, and you need to see to your father before he's too drunk to be handled."

He would have ignored her. He had spent most of the day sitting up top with the coachman and had missed conversation with Clara. But then Mairi opened the lower door. It brought sounds from the main hall beginning with his father's bellow and followed by raucous cheers. It sounded like a full battalion of men in their cups.

"How many are down there?"

Predictably, Mairi didn't answer. If he wanted an answer—and the ability to manage his father to his liking—then he would have to see for himself. He could already tell that the crowd was growing rowdy. He had fifteen minutes at most before some became mean. He needed to find out where his father landed on that scale and make sure any extra emotions were not directed at the English. Or at himself, for that matter. He was here to lead the clan now, and he couldn't do that if his father turned them all against him before he'd even begun.

After one last look at Clara's bedroom door, he went back down the tower stairs, though his thoughts remained with her. What did Clara think of her first stay in a castle? Did she see the strong bones of the place? Or did she feel the damp, even in early summer? Did she fancy herself a princess as she gazed out the turret window? Or was she already nose deep in one of the books she'd brought along, having dismissed the entire place as dreary?

He was thinking of ways to change her mind when his father's favorite crony called out to him.

"Liam, my boy! A drink for the man who brings us the Sassenach money."

Oh hell. The last thing he needed was for everyone to applaud that before anything was settled. Especially with Aaron somewhere in the castle. He held up his hand in greeting and forced himself to smile. Then he allowed his father's friends to surround him and club him on the back as if beating him was an appropriate greeting. It was a game, he knew, said to make a boy manly. And though he had the size and stamina to withstand the blows, that hadn't been the case when he was ten.

Nevertheless, he wended his way through the crowd—a dozen men—and made it to the high table where his father sat like a chieftain of old. The man shoved a tankard of whisky into Liam's hand and grinned from ear to ear.

"What do we spend the bitch's money on first?" he asked. "I say we double the distillery! We've got fine wheat growing and copper pipes from the Aberbeag. Next year we'll be swimming in it!"

There was a great cheer from everyone as Liam held up his goblet and drained it. Fire burned down his throat and he knew he'd need food soon or he'd be as mutton-headed as his clansmen. But after he slammed down the tankard, he held up his hand.

"Easy, friends," he said. "I've not caught the lady yet. That's why we're showing her the best of the Highland tomorrow."

"Bah!" his father said once he'd drained his own tankard. "Go bed 'er now and be done with it."

Liam felt his smile strain, but he knew better than to show his temper to his father, especially when the man was in front of his men. "She's a fine lady," he said. "She'll take some courting yet."

"Says a man with a small stump," his father scoffed. Then he wiped his mouth with his sleeve. "I'd do it," he cried, "but I like a woman wi' some fire to wet her box." Then he grabbed a woman who'd just brought a plate of bread and cheese for Liam.

The woman—whom Liam did not recognize—squealed with

laughter before slamming her mouth down on his father's face. She got a slap on the rump for her troubles, while the entire room grunted or bellowed encouragement.

Must be his father's new mistress. At least she was large enough not to break under his coarse attention. Meanwhile, Liam laughed in a good-natured way though the sound came through a tight chest. "I'll be bedding the woman in my own time, thank you verra much."

There was a great deal of ribald comments from that, thankfully the situation wasn't out of control. His father had a saucy woman in his lap and free flowing whisky. That meant the man wouldn't move from the table until he was carried out. Assuming, of course, that Liam stayed close to make sure no one got a wild idea. Meanwhile, he had time to take the measure of men he hadn't seen in a year.

He remembered most of them. Farmers, herders, and the like, all good men but with a bad example leading them. He noted that Brian—the man who ran the distillery—wasn't here. He was probably protecting the stock from drunken revelers. And none of their neighbors—the Aberbeag clan—filled the hall. They would come tomorrow.

"More whisky!" his father bellowed. Apparently, he'd grown tired of fondling his woman.

"Och!" Liam bellowed back, doing his best to drown out the cries of agreement. "You'll empty our coffer before the games tomorrow. What kind of host would we be without drink after the games?"

His father peered at him with an angry scowl. Hell. That meant he'd entered the mean phase of the night. "The Sassenach will fill them again."

"Aye," he said because there was no use disagreeing about that now. "But there'll be no more drink until we flatten the Aberbeag tomorrow! Show the Sassenach what kind of men we are!"

There was a full round of cheers from that but also a great

many grumbles as women started filing in and grabbing their men. He looked to the side where Mairi stood with her hands on her hips. No doubt she'd been listening closely to the revels and had prompted the women to get their men. And as he watched, she waded in to the sourest of his father's clan.

"No one fights well with a sore head," she chided as she helped bully the herder to his feet. "Get thee gone and show us your mettle tomorrow!"

The man grumbled at her—along with several others—but did as she bid. Liam helped where he was needed, but mostly she managed them well. Before long even the worst drunks were out the door. And when she at last shut the doors, she turned and pinned him with a hard stare and a raised brow. He didn't need words to know what she was asking.

Can your Sassenach do the same? What will you do without me?

He didn't know. He had big plans for his people, and he had no idea if Clara was up to the task. But he wouldn't be stopped by Mairi. He turned around—it was time to get his father to bed— only to pull up short.

Aaron sat near his father. His hand was wrapped around a tankard, but from the look on his face, it hadn't pleased him in the least. How long had he been there? What had his father said? Damn it, if Aaron chose to be prickly, he'd pack up the women and leave at first light.

Liam approached with a wary smile. "Aaron, how do you like the whisky?"

"Better than the company," he said flatly as he pushed his drink away. His eyes were hard. "There's been some crude talk here about my sister."

He couldn't deny it. "We can be a crude people, but no one will hurt her. I swear it."

Aaron looked hard at the mess around the great hall, the dogs—Scottish Deerhounds—who were settling down for the night, and the MacCleal who was being cajoled out of his seat by his half-naked mistress. Disgust curled his lip, and he shook his head.

"I believed your clothing and your speech. You've spoken intelligently about matters of state, and I've heard you argue science with my sister at a level I can't follow. Your education is good, your appearance is good, and no one has a dark word to say against you."

"You thought me a fine husband prospect before. That hasn't changed."

Aaron's fist slammed down hard on the table. "Not changed? Do you think I will let my sister step into this? That I would leave her to—"

"English men have revels such as this with dogs and whores. Do not deny it, because I know it's true. I'd wager you've even attended a few."

"Not with my sister!"

"And she was not here." Liam used a cloth to wipe down the seat that his father had used. Thankfully, the man had been led away by his woman. Then Liam sat in the laird's seat and faced his future brother-in-law. "You saw tonight the old way of doing things. Drunken revels and coarse talk. Did you see the faces of the loudest men here? They are aging, as is my father." He composed himself in the chair as a refined man of elegance, such as would be suitable in a royal court. "I am the future here. My plans for the clan are modernization, commerce, and education. Things that you and your sister support."

"Then come back to her when you have cleaned up this place." And by "place," he clearly meant his "people."

"That is not how it works, and you know it. The new generation must show the old how to do better. And so I am."

"How?" he asked with a sneer. "By all accounts you've barely been back here in years."

Liam pushed Aaron's tankard back toward him. "That's how."

"What?"

"Scottish whisky. It's the finest in the world."

Aaron arched a brow, then at Liam's encouragement he picked up his drink. He sniffed it, then took a slow drink, before setting it back down. "It's good, I'll give you that."

"It's better than good. It's fine enough to be served at the king's table." He grinned. "I hear Prinny has a taste for it." In truth, Prinny had a taste for all kinds of alcohol and could likely be convinced to enjoy Scotch whisky. But only by a man with access to the prince. A man like Aaron, or his second cousin who worked at Carlton House supplying the regent with all his food and drink.

"You want a Royal Warrant for your whisky."

"I do. A mark will make it easy to sell everywhere. Not just London, but on the Continent too."

Aaron frowned down at his drink. "It's not that good."

"Yes, it is." He was staking his clan's future on it.

The man pursed his lips and nodded slowly. "Very well, it might be that good." Then he looked around. "All of this was not to get Clara's dowry?" Doubt laced his tone.

"I brought you here to taste the whisky, to see how we make and bottle it. And to get you to bring it to your cousin and put it in Prinny's hand."

"You could have brought me a bottle in London. I would have been more amenable to it then." Aaron's eyes narrowed. "But then you wouldn't have Clara here."

Liam let his admiration and his desire show through his expression. "Clara is a fine woman who can make up her own mind."

Aaron snorted. "She's a sheltered woman, and I'll not have her exposed to that." He gestured with his chin to the mess that was the great room. A kitchen maid was cleaning in the far corner, but the debris of a hearty celebration were everywhere. And lest Liam thought he meant only the hearty enjoyment of the clan, Aaron's gaze moved from the dirty tables to the stairway where Liam's father had disappeared. "He's the viscount and laird," Aaron said, his voice thick with scorn. "You're powerless against him."

Liam smiled. It was a slow shift in face accompanied by a steady rise to his feet. Soon, he towered over Aaron. "You promised four days—"

"Not anymore—"

"I'll take one—tomorrow—and I'll show you who has the power in this land."

Aaron stared at him, his expression as unforgiving as any protective brother could be. But in the end, he nodded.

"One day."

And one night. That was the important part. They wouldn't leave until the morning after tomorrow.

"Done."

CHAPTER EIGHT

CLARA WOKE WITH a sore head thanks to the very excellent mead she and Lilah had enjoyed last night. They'd had a right jolly time of it, as they always did together, and neither had missed joining in the manly revels from the night before. Or at least Lilah hadn't, and she had managed to keep Clara distracted well enough that she had not gone exploring.

But now it was morning, and she would not stay cooped up like an errant child. She was quick with her ablutions and dressed in a gown that she could button up on her own, which was to say it was a good dress for a tradeswoman. If Lilah were awake, she would have stopped Clara from wearing it—it was important to dress to one's class when in a foreign land—but to Clara, it was a matter of expedience. So she put it on and slipped outside as the sun began to light the day in earnest.

The inner bailey was filling with people selling their wares. It was too early for most of them to be ready, but every one managed to greet her good morning and offer her a quick early look for her eyes alone. She refused them, promising to return later, but a few managed to suck her in. She was impressed by the quality of their woolen hosiery. She purchased a stunningly tatted fan. And then she marveled at an array of glass bottles and other pieces. She'd never seen such beautifully rendered glassworks, but before she could ask who had fashioned them, she was distracted by a jewelry vendor who sported beautiful copper pieces for "a lady's head and hair."

They were quite lovely, and she nearly bought a bracelet as a wedding gift for Lilah when Mairi caught her elbow.

"You cannot be buying Aberbeag goods without matching your purchase among the MacCleal," she said. "You've done got a fan from them. If you don't balance it quick from the MacCleal side, you'll be declaring yourself on their side, and you won't be welcome on this one." She gave Clara a pointed look. "Is that what you want?"

Clara grimaced. This was why she hated anything outside the city. Her own home county had a rivalry with the neighboring one. She never remembered whose pig was to be praised and whose was to be ignored. And if she said she liked one flower over another, it became the talk of the parish.

"In London, I can buy a beautiful fan, and no one thinks twice about it."

"Then you should'a stayed there. But you're here now, and you need to think. The copper mine is on the Aberbeag side. The glass and whisky is from here."

"And who made the mead?" she said. "I've never had better."

"That's from Father Andrew and his ladies. It's right fine mead, but he serves both the clans equally, so it's no help to you."

"And the wool?"

"Everybody does wool. Depends on who you mean." Then before Clara could answer, Mairi cursed under her breath. "And now the fighters are here, and I've got to see that they don't kill each other early. Quick make up for your gaff or the whispers will follow you all day."

"How?"

"Buy something from us!" the woman said with a huff. She shoved Clara toward a stall of heavy wool scarves that would probably itch, then rushed off to a group of twenty large men clattering in through the gate.

The seller perked up, but Clara reasoned it would do no good to buy something and discard it immediately because it was itchy.

Instead, she turned back to the glassworks. That was undoubtably MacCleal work, and she was fascinated by the different shapes and colors. One perfume bottle was shaped in a lion's face with his mane streaked in copper. She had no intention of buying, but she was impressed by the craftsmanship. It looked like the creature was in mid-roar.

"This is exquisite," she breathed. "I can't even imagine how it's done."

"Tis skillful, indeed, Miss. But maybe you'd appreciate something more like this."

He passed her another perfume bottle with the stopper in the shape of a wolf's head. The skill was evident in every line, especially as the wolf was stretched up to the sky as if howling. But for some reason, the bottle was blue, and she could not reconcile a wolf done in blue.

"It is lovely," she said, her eyes going back to the lion. At least this was done with clear glass and copper highlights. That made sense to her mind, though she kept comparing the intricacies of both animal heads. The work was extraordinary.

"Don't like the blue, do you?" a voice said from behind her.

She spun around, grateful that she had a good grip on the two bottles otherwise she might have dropped them. As it was, the merchant held out his hands as if to catch them should they drop. "Lord Loughton," she cried as she looked up at his rugged face. "You're awake." Awake and dressed in his barest highland kilt. He had fabric wrapped around his waist and thrown over his shoulder, but much of his torso remained bare.

"A poor man I would be to sleep on the day of the Highland Games," he responded, while she did her best to not look at his partially naked chest.

"I believe the Aberbeag competitors have arrived," she managed, realizing belatedly that they too had been dressed, or undressed, in a similar fashion. And how embarrassing it was that she had not noticed their attire at all, but that Lord Loughton's flesh suddenly had her blushing.

"Aye, they did," he was saying. "But don't think about them. Tell me your thoughts on the two pieces of glass."

"They're both beautiful. I've never seen work this skilled. How are they made?"

"In heat and sweat, my lady. Like the fires of hell." He pointed to the back side of the castle. "The furnace is back there, and all MacCleal men have the burns to prove it."

Her eyes widened. "Really? Even you?" She couldn't imagine him like a blacksmith hunched over an anvil.

"Even me," he said with grin. "Will I have to prove it to you?"

"Yes. Definitely!"

He laughed as he turned her attention back to the two perfume bottles. "You seemed to prefer the lion's head."

"I don't like the blue," she said. "Not for a wolf."

The merchant inhaled sharply at her words, but Lord Loughton kept her attention on the pieces. "I think the color pretty."

"Well, it is. Quite pretty, but this is a wolf with a long snout and great teeth. It should be brown or black." She ran her finger along the tiny sharp points fashioned in glass. Then she saw something else, a flask set toward the back of a pile. "Now this is a good use for that blue." She picked it up and turned it toward the light. It was a short, small rectangle, suitable for several drams of whisky. On one side etched in copper was a tree branching to the sky. And on the other side was a wolf, also done in copper, but with outlines that were uneven, as if drawn by an unsteady hand. Obviously not the master's works. Probably one of his apprentices, but she appreciated it nonetheless.

He lifted it from her hands and frowned at it. "The copper work is bad. The wolf is blotchy."

"Not true!" she said, outraged that he could be that critical of a piece that was probably the best some young apprentice could do. "It's not perfect, but I value the endeavor." She lifted it from his hands. "My mother wouldn't buy anything that had a blemish on it. Everything had to be perfect to suit her tastes." She lifted her chin. "But in so doing, she missed the beauty in evolving things. She misunderstood that life is never perfect." Then she held up the flask to where a man was walking with one of the wolfhounds. "See?" she said. "The real animal is never tidy. His fur lifts in places and drops in another. Why should the drawn wolf be any different?"

Lord Loughton stared at her, his mouth slightly ajar. It was the first time she'd ever managed to silence him. Flushed from finally besting him in something, she turned to the merchant. "I should like to buy this," she said. "How much?"

"No—" began Lord Loughton, but she cut him off with a hard look.

"I shall buy it and once I find out who made it, I shall make a point of complimenting him." She pictured a young boy laboring over the glass as he learned his trade.

"Will you now?"

His accent was coming back. She was getting to him, so she pushed her win with an arch look. "I may even give him a kiss for his troubles." She almost left it at that, but propriety insisted she make herself clear. "On the cheek, of course, to show that effort is of value no matter what the result."

Then she handed over a shilling without dickering over the price. The merchant grinned at her and said nothing, but he was all ears as Lord Loughton's expression turned wicked.

"Oh, I think it will be somewhere other than his cheek, Lady Clara. On that you can be sure."

"What?"

He didn't respond to her question, but instead cupped her arm. "Should you like to see how glass is blown now? It must be done before the games begin." He shot her a glance. "Maybe the creator of your flask is in there now."

"Well, yes. I really would like to see this is done."

He was in an odd mood today. He seemed both excited and tense as he steered her through the growing crowd. There was a roughness to him that was new. Usually he was relaxed as he asked her grand questions. How did she feel about educating children? Could they get enough at home or should there be proper schools like there were for the aristocrats? What did she think about modernization in a kitchen? Would she spend money on buying a modern convenience or rather employ more people to do the work as it had been done for years? They had spent many hours on the trip here exploring the choices facing the leaders in a community.

But suddenly he had a fierceness to him. She was honest enough to admit that if he'd first appeared to her this way, she would have refused him the acquaintance. Fierce gentlemen were uncomfortable at best, in her experience, and not prone to cerebral discussions. But Lord Loughton had already shown his ability to match her intellectually. Now he seemed intent to prove something else to her.

But what? She was surprised to realize how very intrigued she was. Just what could the always entertaining Lord Loughton have in store for her today?

They crossed the bailey while everyone greeted him. They showed him great respect as was due the son of a laird, and Clara had to admit an inner thrill at being on his arm. He was a great man to these people, and she was given deference merely because she was beside him. Even the Aberbeag gave her grand smiles and courtly bows. Especially the very tall, very handsome Connall of Aberbeag and his father, the duke.

They were helping to set up the field of play, but they came close to greet her with courtly bows and a wicked grin for Liam.

"Tis a fine morning, my lady," Connall said after the introductions were made. "Why would you want to spend it on this coarse fellow's arm?"

Good lord, it seemed all the Scots here were broad shouldered and half-naked. She'd never seen so much tanned skin in all her life. But of all of them, Connall's golden hair and bushy whiskers shone the brightest as he retained hold of her hand after kissing it.

She tugged it free. "Because he has promised to show me how the Scots make such beautiful glass." She held up her bottle for all to see.

Connall grinned as he released her hand, his gaze fixing on Liam's. "I see he has made his claim, but…" He leaned down suggestively. "If you wish to handle something less…delicate, then I offer myself for entertainment."

"I assure you," Liam returned with good cheer, "MacCleal glass is as strong and smooth as any Aberbeag."

"That remains to be seen," said the duke. Then he bowed politely over her hand, as courtly as any gentleman could be given that he was obviously frail. She feared the man would not survive long, and she was relieved to see that someone was setting up a chair for him to use while watching the games.

They conversed some more as Lilah and Aaron joined them. She found she liked the duke and his son quite well, but her interest remained with Liam and the glassworks factory. She had never seen one before and was intrigued by the idea. Also, she did not like the way everyone—Aberbeag and MacCleal—seemed to be staring at her and judging her in ways she couldn't imagine. For the first time ever, she wished she'd worn something for show rather than convenience. She should have realized how everyone would want to look at her.

Going to the glass factory would be the fastest way out of the public eye, but she didn't know how to end the conversation to get there.

"My apologies," Liam interrupted, "but I have made a promise to Lady Clara, and I mean to keep it. My lord, Miss Rees, would you care to join me?"

Smooth as silk, they took their leave and headed through the bailey to the back side to the castle, Lilah and Aaron trailing behind her like a shield.

"Thank you," she whispered to Lord Loughton. "I began to feel like a spectacle."

"But that never bothers you," he returned as he looked down

at her. "Why now?"

He didn't understand. "It doesn't bother me in London where I am one of thousands of people all rushing to their own life. The country is different where everyone knows everyone else, and the smallest detail is examined and criticized."

"You feel that way because you do not know them. If you did—"

"I will still have to watch my words, my attire, and my purchases to see that I offend no one." She sighed. "It's exhausting."

"Because they don't know you and you don't know them. In time—"

"It will remain the same. As it does in all villages where the souls number less than 300."

"And here I thought you bold enough to make your own way no matter what the biddies say."

She winced. He was right. She had long since declared herself free of other people's thoughts. She made her own way and be damned to them. But in this, she found she wanted Liam's people to like her.

She was still chewing on this revelation when they made it to the glass factory. It was an open air building and on the far side, she saw a blacksmith doing a brisk trade. Of all the Scots, this man was huge with a meaty fist that wielded his hammer like a Norse god. The clang rang in her ears and Clara was grateful that they were led to the opposite side of building. Though on this side, she was blasted by the heat coming from a blazing hole in a furnace.

A man stood nearby with gnarled hands and skin puckered with burn marks up and down his arms. He was short, but his face remained serene as he drew a glowing blob of glass out of the furnace. The glass was attached to a long pole, and a teen boy immediately began to blow through the pole while the short man used pads then tongs to shape the glass into a rectangular bottle. It was fascinating to watch despite the heat, and Clara's hands itched to try even though she knew she hadn't the strength to do what even the boy did. The heat alone would defeat her.

Lord Loughton stood beside her describing the process of blowing glass as the master worked. It took ten minutes for the bottle to be completed and another fifteen to shape a stopper as a wolf's head. Then the bottle was set inside a cabinet to cool. And beyond that was a large bench of shaped glass bottles, most exquisitely made.

When the bottle was finished and set in the cooling cabinet, Lord Loughton made introductions. The short man with thick-set muscles was Master MacAdaidh. He glanced at them, dipped his chin once with a curt grunt, then returned to his work. The teen boy was Tas Dubh, and he stood tall and strong beside Lord Loughton, though his gaze remained lowered in respect.

"Mr. Dubh," Clara said as she held up the blue bottle she'd purchased. "Are you the creator of this fine piece of glass?"

The boy looked up and flushed a fiery red. His gaze hopped to Lord Loughton and then to Master MacAdaidh who snorted loudly.

"No' that piece of trash," the master said. "Tas made those." He pointed to a shelf of bottles behind them that she hadn't seen. Large round bowls like basins only with wings on the back to hold towels and the like.

"They're beautiful," she breathed, and Lilah echoed the statement. But she still wanted to know about the one she held. "Who made this piece?"

No one answered her. Instead, Lord Loughton unhooked the clasp at his shoulder and wrapped his kilt firmly around his waist. As the others in the building were equally undressed, it should not have surprised her. And yet, it did. Clara was used to seeing laborers without a shirt, but this was Lord Loughton. He was an aristocrat who debated politics with Aaron and discussed nutrition with Lilah. He was well-educated, and yet he now stood before her with his entire upper body outlined by the light from the furnace.

And what a sight he was. His body stood taller than the master and more mature than the teen. Though he didn't have the bulky power of the master, his muscles were longer, more fluid, and more beautiful by Clara's reckoning. She stood transfixed with awe as he began working a blob of molten glass. She watched the sweat bead on his face and wet his torso. She stood transfixed as he set his mouth to the blow tube and the glass expanded. His chest swelled to a stunning degree and then his belly tightened, seeming to draw up into his ribs which in turn pulled together through his taut neck all to be expelled into glass turned molten gold.

As she watched, she remembered the way his lips had moved across her own mouth and her neck. And now she saw what he could do with molten glass.

He replaced the glowing blob into the bright furnace several times, and each time he pulled it out to expand it further. Before long, he handed the pole to the teen who supported it while he took pads and blocks to force it into a rectangular shape. And then, he dropped copper onto it, crafting it as finely as any great painter would with a brush.

And when he tapped the piece off the rod, the master looked it over with a dismissive grunt.

Lord Loughton sighed. "I'm out of practice."

"Aye," was all the man said.

He didn't look out of practice. He looked like a Scots warrior of old. She had no love of warriors rushing into bloody battle. The sight of weapons gripped in sweaty fists did little to spark her interest. But here was a man as powerful as any fighter putting his strength to the creation of something beautiful.

It awed her.

"Try the stopper," said Master MacAdaidh. "See if you remember how to sculpt."

Lord Loughton nodded and began the work again. Lilah and Aaron had backed away from the heat, but Clara wanted to go closer. She didn't care that her face was flushed, and her dress wet with sweat. She watched again as he heated the glass then sat on a bench as he used tongs to stretch and pull it into shape. She kept watching his hands—strong fingers to grip the tongs—and the muscles of his forearms as they bunched and twisted the glass to his will. Several times she thought the glass would break. Indeed, the teen had started his own work and the boy cursed loudly when his creation shattered on the floor.

She looked at Lord Loughton's face. His concentration was fierce, his brows knitted as he worked. Even his back rippled with the strain of forcing molten glass to his will. Then under his hands, a wolf's head appeared. The glass dimpled into eyes, the jaw extended into a howl. Drips of glass became teeth, and pinches became ears. He even carved fur into the glass until he sat back with a pleased grunt.

As if on cue, the master came over to survey the work. "Still a deft hand," he said as he caught the stopper when Lord Loughton tapped it off the pole. "You could be a fine man at this if you stuck around."

Loughton wiped his face off with a nearby rag. "A laird has more tasks than the furnace and the tongs."

"Aye," the master said as he set the stopper into the cup-board. "But you've got the wit and patience to learn quickly." He glanced at Clara. "If'n you stay around."

She couldn't tell if the words were directed at her or Lord Loughton. Either way, the master stomped away to help Tas while Loughton gave her a wide grin.

"What did you think?"

"You made this bottle, didn't you?" She held up the one she'd purchased.

"I did, last Michaelmas." He leaned forward. "And I believe you owe me a kiss for it."

She could smell his scent and feel the heat of his body. She lost seconds in wondering why it pulled her in rather than repulsed her. They were indecently close, everyone was watching them, and he was still half-naked. And yet her body tingled with his nearness. She was aroused—obviously—and the realization was so shocking to her that she immediately rejected it. She hadn't been afflicted by those feelings since she was a teenager. She knew how unreliable the sensation was. And yet it had been so long that a part of her relished the experience.

That was the part that had her leaning in until they were nose to nose. "You want a kiss?" she challenged. "For something you made in a half hour? My kisses don't go so cheap." In truth, she was incredibly impressed by what he had created in so short a time. But she had to say something to set him back on his heels.

It didn't work. Lord Loughton laughed then stole a kiss from her lips. It was quick, fierce, then done as he straightened up to his full height. "Perhaps I shall find another way to earn it. And maybe a bit more."

His eyes sparkled as they looked down at her. She realized suddenly that she was leaning over the bench that separated them, and his height now gave him an excellent view of her breasts, including the tight points of her nipples as they were outlined by the fabric of her wet dress. And damned if his appreciation didn't set her entire body to flaming.

She straightened up and turned around, unable to look at the cocky man any longer. But as she spun, she ended up face to face with Aaron and Lilah who had been watching the exchange. Typically, Lilah was smiling, her knowing look saying she understood Clara's flustered behavior. Aaron, on the other hand, was scowling fiercely. And when his gaze met Lord Loughton's, the Scotsman arched a brow.

"A man under a deadline must act fast," he said. Then he gestured out to the fairgrounds. "The games will be beginning soon. You should hurry to your seats." Then he winked at Clara. "There's a great deal more to come this day."

He held out his hand to escort them, but at that very moment Mairi ran up to him. "Och! What are you doing in here playing with Da?" She cast a hard glance at the master. "And don't you be looking like that. You were supposed to help set up the field." She jerked her head at them both. "Now get. Tas, you can mind the furnace here, yes?"

The teen gave her a brisk nod. "I'll see that it's kept safe from the children."

"Many thanks," she said with a warm smile. Then she turned on the men. "Go! Everybody's waiting on ye."

Then she shooed the men out. Loughton went slowly, his long legs taking him away even as his gaze lingered on Clara with a cheeky grin. Her gaze followed him as he strode out of sight. And then, when he was lost behind a tight crowd of people, she turned reluctantly to Mairi who stood glaring at the bailey with her hands on her hips.

"You and your father are MacAdaidh," Clara said as she put the pieces together. "What relationship is that to the MacCleal?"

"They took us in after Culloden. My grandma and a few others were all that were left, and she heavy with my father. We've not fared badly here, but I'm the last of us." Her eyes grew cold as she looked at Clara. "You'll not fare well here, Sassenach. You're too soft, too lost, and too weak to do what needs to be done. He's mad to think any London lady can match what I do on my easiest days, but the MacCleals have a reputation for climbing into English beds." She looked to the three of them. "Go home. Now. Afore the games begin. You've no future here but pain and that's the truth."

"I promised—" Aaron began, but the woman cut him off.

"I know what you promised and why, but I tell you true." Her gaze cut hard to Clara. "If you value your sister, you'll go now and leave the MacCleal and the MacAdaidh to find our own way."

Aaron looked like he was considering it. His mouth was pursed, and his brows lowered. But Clara had her own promises, and she didn't like being dictated to by a woman who clearly wanted to be mistress here.

"What an ignorant thing to say!" she cried. "Of course I can't run a castle like you do. I've never tried. But then, I can navigate a boat using the stars and a sextant. Have you mastered that? I doubt it because you've never tried. Do not guess what a person is capable of, especially when you've never done a thing beyond this narrow, little world."

She hadn't meant to sound so contemptuous of Lord Loughton's home. By all appearances he had good people behind him. But the idea that she was somehow less because she'd never attempted the things the Scots had conquered made her furious.

"You're a Sassenach idiot," the woman spat.

"And you've seen nothing beyond a square mile of your home. You know nothing of the world." So saying she swept past the shrewish woman and headed to the fairgrounds. She would see these Highland Games and she would marvel at Lord Loughton's people and his own prowess. But if even one child chose to suggest she was not up to their mettle, then she was determined to grab hold of some big tree trunk and hurl it straight at them.

CHAPTER NINE

L IAM HAD NEVER strutted for a woman. Not even when he was a randy teenager and had preened through his first Highland Games. Then he'd been drunk on his own swagger as he laughed with the other boys his age. This time, he was aware of her eyes upon him, the direction of her body as she met the people of his life, and the sound of her words so rarely heard but every moment imagined.

As the host, his father opened the games. As the only son of the laird, he competed in the grand events. It had been years since he hefted a tree, but he grunted and strained as he threw the caber a respectable distance. That was won by Connall, the golden Aberbeag heir, who'd been Liam's rival since the day they were born. Clearly, Connall had spent his last years in Scotland while Liam was in London learning the ways of the English. The man was cheered loudly by his clan and even drew a pleased clap from Clara. That was fair-minded of her, since even he admitted that his rival had done a great toss, but he was jealous of her applause nonetheless. Which is why he put all his concentration on the open stone put. That event was more about technique than brute force, and indeed, his youthful training stood him in good stead.

He won the contest and turned immediately to her when declared the winner.

"Does that earn me a kiss, lass?"

Connall lifted his silver cup, the prize given to the caber toss winner. "Aye, lass. Come give up a kiss to the greatest Scot on this field."

Clara looked around, obviously flustered by the attention as several Aberbeag cheered at Connall's claim. Fortunately, her attention came back to him.

"Am I to kiss all the winners then?" she asked. He noted the flush to her cheeks and that her lips were wet with mead. The drink had softened her usually prickly exterior such that her body didn't seem as guarded as usual. Her eyes sparkled beneath the bright sun, and her lips flashed red with her smile.

Damn, he'd never seen her so beautiful.

"Kiss me and not another," he said firmly. "Not unless you want to start a clan war."

She laughed at his comment as if he weren't serious. He could tell that she had no understanding of how many people were invested in her presence here. Everyone knew her to be the English heiress brought here to be wedded and bedded by him. None of them knew her, but they all wanted her money, including every Aberbeag here. And if she showed the slightest inclination to any man but him, the lure of her money could bring on a fight which would add in old grievances until it became a war. He would like to think his people were cleverer than that, but with whisky and women came stupidity. He kept his expression serious as he looked in her eyes.

"Me alone, Clara. Do not tease about that."

She frowned as she focused on his face, then she tilted her chin. "You have not won me yet, Lord Scot."

She spoke loud enough for others to hear, and he winced as they chuckled at her audacity. One even said, "The Sassenach has some fire."

That alone convinced him to claim her, though truthfully, he would have done it anyway. Until now, he'd always been restrained with her. She flinched too often when he came quick at her. She claimed to like refinement and education. But they were in Scotland now, and her gaze had feasted upon him all day since the moment he'd unclasped his tartan in the glass factory. It had fired his blood and stiffened his rod.

He caught her around her waist with one hand and he planted his mouth on hers before she could cry out. She was a tall woman, but he had a few inches more, which meant she fit well against him. He knew the curve of her hips, the swell of her breasts, and the shape of her mouth because he had kissed her before by slow degrees and with patient caresses. This time he flattened her body against his, heedless of the sweat on his body or the shock in hers. He tasted the alcohol she'd drunk and inhaled the musk of her arousal.

He invaded her mouth, taking it as a Scot storming a castle. He breeched her lips, bypassed her teeth, and then stroked his way through every part of her. She scrambled to react—faster than he expected—and suddenly they were dueling tongue to tongue. That would have been enough. It was the statement he'd meant to give every man on the field. But as he eased back, she pursued him. She thrust her tongue at him, trying to breach his walls, and the shock of that had him bending her backwards as he re-possessed her.

She tangled one hand in his hair and another on his back. Then to his surprise, she gripped his hair in a fist and yanked him back. She had more strength than he expected, and he couldn't stop the wince of pain. But for all that she'd made his eyes water, he lifted barely an inch away from her face.

"Is that all ye've got?" he asked.

The men watching hooted in delight, and Liam had a moment of gratitude that her brother and Miss Rees had wandered off to see the display of herding dogs, else he might now be challenged to a duel. But what he saw most was the way Clara's eyes narrowed and her brow knitted. Their gazes were locked together, but he could see her confusion grow even as her body seemed to mold against him.

She had fire for sure, but he was pushing her to feel the surge of lust, and in a very public way. That was not the best way to handle a sheltered English flower. And while he was thinking that—and scrambling to find a way to ease her fears—she accomplished the feat herself.

While still bent nearly halfway back, she managed to lift her leg straight into his balls. He'd had to straddle her one leg to get her into that position, and so he was exposed. Thank the God above that she was pressed tight to him or his stones would be lodged behind his eyes. As it was, her knee clapped him in the arse and her thigh merely flattened his balls to an eye-watering degree.

His breath caught in a tight wheeze, and it took all his strength not to drop her. He stumbled backwards though, or more accurately, he hopped back. She followed, showing surprising dexterity in keeping her balance. Now they stood eye to eye because he was still crumpled over his balls. And while the hooting around then grew even louder, all could hear her response.

"I'll give my kiss when I'm ready to, Loughton, and not a moment before."

It was a contradictory statement given that she had been the one to haul him back to her mouth, but that didn't matter to the women who cheered at her audacity. Meanwhile, Connall pressed the silver cup into Liam's hand, then splashed whisky into it. "Here. You need this more than I."

He used it to toast Clara with before drinking it back. The pain was receding enough for him to straighten to his full height. And when he was done, he rasped his question.

"Who taught you that?"

She snorted. "I have a big brother, you know."

He grinned. "My admiration grows."

"But not your staff!" bellowed one of the Aberbeag men.

He took the ribbing with good cheer, and so passed the afternoon. He finished the games, performing respectably in the other events. Then he ducked away to wash off the sweat before showing Aaron the distillery.

Aaron's eyes were dark as they headed to the building. The man had heard about the kiss, of course. He would have been deaf to not hear the ribbing that followed Liam wherever he went that afternoon. The man did not mince words as they crossed the bailey. "She's fond of you. You've gotten farther with her than anyone else ever has, but I don't think she's changed her mind."

"I hope you're wrong, because the day is almost played out." And by nightfall, there would be other games about. He would have to see that she was safe from the worst of them.

"I'm not," said Aaron. But at least he agreed to tour the distillery with him. He'd already sampled the whisky, but there would be a great deal more shared tonight.

With the games finished, the dancing began. Traditional displays judged by elders and audience alike. If Clara appreciated them, he was not around to see it, being too intent on convincing Aaron to sponsor their whisky. He expected she would wander to the corner where tales were told by old men and women who knew how to keep the children enthralled. It wasn't until after he and Aaron were well filled with cheer that they made it back to the bailey and the remains of the feast.

Mairi had outdone herself here. Food was plentiful and well-liked. He and Aaron had to rush to grab the last of it before the way was cleared for the full revel. The end of the festival came in a raucous dance where lord and pauper danced together. It wasn't until his muddled head noted the masks and costumes surrounding them that he realized he'd been tricked.

He'd been so intent on showing Aaron every inch of the distillery that he'd forgotten his father's machinations. For surely it had been that man's idea to make the night's revels into a masquerade. And when he finally saw Clara, he knew that her time had run out.

She was caught, and it would be up to him to make it work.

CHAPTER TEN

CLARA HAD NEVER enjoyed herself more than she did that afternoon. After putting her knee to Lord Loughton, men and women alike praised her for her fire. Never in her life had so many people grinned at her while raising their glass or lifted their knee and laughed with good cheer. Women praised her, men saluted her, and everyone tried to press a drink into her hand.

So she drank. It would be impolite not to. And when her head began to get dizzy, she pretended to swallow, then made a big show of licking the liquid from her lips. That always drew gales of laughter and several winks from the men. Sweet heaven, these Scots were a raucous bunch. The English enjoyed their drink, too, but as a gently bred woman, she was kept apart from those people. Here, she was not only allowed to participate, but she was the center of the spectacle, celebrated for kissing a man in public and then nearly crippling him.

It was a heady sensation. She'd never been popular, much less celebrated. And everyone here seemed to love her.

"Mistress!" A girl rushed to her side. "Mistress!"

Clara turned, careful not to wobble as she did so. "Yes?"

"Mistress, this way." A girl of about fourteen years tugged on her sleeve and tried to lead her out of the crowd.

Clara dug in her heels. She was not a woman to go anywhere with anyone without an explanation. It had nothing to do with the fact that she really needed to stand still at that moment. She did not want to get sick in front of everyone. Fortunately, before she could frame her question, an older woman with a low-cut red gown sauntered forward. She had a warm smile and an easy manner that Clara appreciated, and she spoke slowly enough that Clara could easily understand her despite her thick accent.

"Lady Clara, I'm so pleased to see you. We haven't been properly introduced, but I'm the MacCleal's lady. You may call me Lady Beitidh."

Clara dipped into a curtsey. It sank a little lower than was appropriate, but that's what came of drinking too much in the afternoon heat. Fortunately, the young woman was beside her to help her recover her feet. "Lovely to meet you, Lady Beitidh," she said.

"If you would come with us. I understand you have no costume for the masquerade tonight. I have a gown that will serve you."

"A masquerade?"

"Yes. A gown that is favored throughout Scotland." She leaned forward as to confide a secret. "You are to be dressed as the Bride of the MacDhubhthaich."

"The what?"

"Aye, it's a sad tale of a lass who wanders this very castle in search of her laird."

"This castle?"

"Aye. Come wi' me—"

"I cannot change into a fine gown as I am." Thanks to the heat and spillage from several drinks, she was a mess. "Where is your bath house?"

The lady shook her head. "In a sad state, for sure. But we can help with a bath, isn't that right, Deirdre?"

The young woman's eyes widened. "But—"

"Your cottage is near the stream, yes? We can use your ma's dress and have a right fun presentation. Fetch you a lamp, and you'll be the bride come in from the storm to find her laird and all her people dead."

"Tell me more about this ghost lady," Clara said. She already guessed that it was one of a thousand ghost stories about a tragic female figure, but it was always interesting to learn the details. And if it were tied specifically to this castle, then she would enjoy discovering if there were any truth to the tale.

"I will," Lady Beitidh promised, "but you have to come now. If we're to wash and dress you in time."

Clara agreed, thinking it would be best to get her away from all the people pressing drinks on her. And if she could manage some bread to settle her stomach, all the better. With Beitidh and Deirdre leading the way, they moved quickly through the crowd. Lady Beitidh shooed her onto a donkey cart, commandeered from one of the vendors, and off they rushed as fast as the beast could take them.

Clara perched as steadily as she could manage on the bench while her entire body shook from the sad state of the road. It made her grit her teeth against the nausea. Fortunately, she was able to distract herself by watching her surroundings. She noted the increasingly sad state of the homes around the castle. Many were little more than hovels. Most of the men were at the castle, but she saw women and their young children working or playing as was their wont. They wore threadbare clothing on their thin bodies. And they watched Clara go by with empty expressions.

Clara had seen poverty before. London had desperate people, too. But this was a need that startled her. With all the food and drink at the castle, she had not expected the kind of poverty she saw now. Certainly not this close to the castle.

"Is this how most people live?" If she were less drunk, she would have phrased the question more clearly. As it was, Beitidh laughed in a way that sounded cruel.

"Och, no! Are you thinking that we all sit in our own shite? The village is the other way, and they all be fat and happy there. Big sheep, thick woolens. But this side here is the other part. It's a hard life for some, and they do what they can with little help out here, right, Deidre?"

Deirdre immediately responded with, "Yes, mum."

And then a whole slew of ridiculousness followed. Beitidh began telling tales of the goats that gave gallons upon gallons of milk every day. On how the ladies at the castle often bathed in it. And that the trees nearby gave off the most amazing fruits—as big as your head—and then popped out nuts in the evening. But none of that happened on this side, of course. This was the poor side, and a shame it was. She was not to judge Scotland by this side of the castle. And that soon enough, she would visit the streets lined in silver and gold at the village on the other side.

At first Clara thought the lady drunk as she poured out one ridiculous tale after another. Then she believed perhaps she was the one drunk, because she must not be hearing the words correctly given how silly the tales were. In the end, she ignored all of the woman's talk in favor of looking about herself. And as she stared, she became sober, both in drink and in affect. There was need here, and she was saddened to see it.

Eventually they made it to Deirdre's home. A single dwelling with little more than a dirt floor and a pile of rags in the corner that served as a bed. There were sheep nearby. Five heads, according to Deirdre, that her father tended while she worked at the castle. The main benefit of the property was the stream that ran through the back. It was shallow and muddy, except for a stretch about three feet long where the water ran deep enough for her to wash with the aid of a cloth.

"But I cannot bathe outside—" she began, but Beitidh snapped at her.

"We've got no time to fill a fine bath for you," she said. Then she grabbed hold of Clara's gown and yanked the front apart. Buttons scattered as she stripped it off her. The woman was a great deal stronger than she looked. Clara ceased fighting. In truth it made her dizzy to struggle. So she closed her eyes and stepped into the bracing water if only to get away from Beitidh.

"Oh my!" She gasped at the temperature, but it helped to clear her head.

Meanwhile, Deirdre collected her gown and what buttons she could find. "I'll wash it for you as soon as you're done."

"You'll wash it? Where?" She saw no large kettle to hold the water, no way to boil it when it came to that, and no lines to dry what had been cleaned.

"In the stream," she said, and then she pointed to the far side where a boy's shirt and pants were draped to dry.

"Whose clothing is that?" Clara asked.

"My brother and sister share it. They're watching the sheep now." Deirdre looked around. "No sense dirtying the clothes when they're out in the fields."

Clara said nothing. What was she to say when she had several spare dresses, plus underthings, a coat, and well-shod shoes?

"Where's your mother?" Clara asked.

"Died of sickness several winters back." Deidre's voice broke on that. "She were never as strong after the twins were born."

Pregnancies were hard on a woman, even more so if she carried twins. Likely she hadn't enough food or rest to recover her strength.

"Right sad it was," interrupted Lady Beitidh. "I brought Deirdre to help me at the castle given that she's my cousin. She gets good coin for her service, and I get my family help for their pains."

Not as much help as she might, given the richness of Beitidh's dress and the thinness of Deirdre's entire body. The stark contrast between the two souls was all too obvious.

"Go on, girl," Lady Beitidh said as she pushed Deirdre back into the house. "Get the costume for Lady Clara."

Deirdre looked none too pleased with this order, but she complied nonetheless. Meanwhile, Clara climbed out of the stream and dried off as best she could with no towel. Then pulled on her shift and stays. By then, Deirdre had returned with a gown so diaphanous as to have no color at all. In truth, it was the perfect gown for arriving at a masquerade pretending to be a ghost, but it still looked too cherished to wear.

"Where did you get this?" Clara asked.

"It was my mum's," Deirdre answered. "She married my father in it, as did her mother with grandpa."

A wedding gown passed down from mother to daughter, likely worn for every nice occasion in the intervening years. This family didn't have enough to save gowns.

"I cannot wear something so precious."

"It's just for the night," Lady Beitidh said.

Deirdre nodded, though her eyes were sad. "It won't last until my day. And it's too big anyway."

That was true. Deirdre was not built along the sturdy lines that Clara sported. "I can't—"

Beitidh didn't let her continue as she abruptly cast the gown over Clara's head. She had no choice but to allow it, because any fight would rip the dress into pieces. And when it settled around her, she felt as if she wore nothing but her shift and stays, and yet it fell in pretty waves around her ankles.

"Now remember," Beitidh continued, "you're a poor girl come to wed at the castle. A storm kept you late, and you arrive to find them all dead. You expire on the spot from grief, but then your spirit wanders the halls looking, always looking for your laird husband."

"But—"

"Deidre, fetch some leaves and the like to make a crown on her head."

"Stop—"

"It's a sad tale, you know, but we all love it, especially since we change the ending at our festival."

Clara took a deep breath and kept her tone stern. "Lady Beitidh, I cannot wear this dress. It's immodest." Besides, it was too precious to Deirdre.

"It's a masquerade, Lady Clara, and this is what the favored lady always wears." She arched a brow at her. "You wouldn't want to embarrass the MacCleal, would you? It's expected. I was to do it this year, but Liam would have none of it. You're the ranking guest, he said. It was to be your honor and him to be the groom."

Clara frowned. "Liam—Lord Loughton wants me to do this?"

"Of course, he does!" the lady snapped, clearly impatient. "You wouldn't think I'd give this up easily, would you? It's usually my part!" The outrage in her face was clear, but then she abruptly softened. "It's tradition, you see. The ghost lady comes in, she spies her groom dead on the floor and collapses from her grief."

"It's a play, then? I thought it was a masquerade."

"Och, it's both, don't you see? He'll come rescue you, tell you it was all a mistake and then take you to bed. Bride and groom, happy as it should'a been. And we all celebrate as if it were a wedding feast!"

Clara wasn't so sure she wanted this. "If it was to be your part—"

"Stop it! I won't be disobeying my laird, and neither should you."

She had run out of objections, especially as Deirdre began to weave leaves and branches into her hair, her fingers deft. Clara tried to stop her, but the girl whispered into her ear.

"It's all right," she said. "It's supposed to be this way."

Clara turned. "But this is your dress."

Deirdre shook her head. "If it gets damaged, I'm sure the laird will repay me."

"You can be sure of it!" Lady Beitidh declared.

That was enough to convince Clara, especially since she meant to give the girl some coins herself.

Before long, it was time to go back. By that time, Deirdre's little brother and sister had joined them. The two children stood naked from behind a tree to watch the commotion. They said nothing, and Clara wanted to give them something. A toy, maybe. Food and clothes at a minimum. But she had none of that with her now and pointing them out might embarrass Deirdre. So she said nothing while Lady Beitidh hustled them back to the donkey cart. It would be dark by the time they returned to the castle, but Lady Beitidh assured her that was the plan.

She was to make a grand entrance at the masquerade. Everyone was waiting for it. She couldn't disappoint them now, could she?

And since the lady kept talking with barely a breath between sentences, Clara agreed to the plan. She sat on the cart bench and studied everything that went past. She'd known that Lord Loughton's clan was poor, but here indeed was proof that his people were hurting. One bad harvest would be devastating. No wonder he wanted his whisky to become the drink of kings. It would go a long way to filling his coffers, though not quickly enough by the look of things.

By the time they made it back to the castle, the games were all done. She guessed from the noise that the food had been consumed and the dancing was well underway. People were sprawled everywhere on the grounds with a center area filled with merrymakers. Clara didn't know the folk dance they performed, but there was a great deal of jumping and clapping. She smiled at the sight of some young men trying, with mixed results, to perform an acrobatic leap-kick maneuver.

"But no one else is in costume," she said as she realized most were still in whatever they'd worn throughout the day.

"You don't think the regular folks would put money into fancy dress, now did you? But look ahead there. That's the laird, and he's wearing his clan tartan, isn't he?"

Of course, he was, but that wasn't the same as dressing up as a ghost and wandering through the party. Meanwhile, Lady Beitidh pulled the cart to the side and grabbed a lantern from where it was hanging off a nearby stall and shoved it into her hand.

"Now wave this about and cry, 'Where's me husband? Where's me husband?'"

"But no one else is dressed—"

Deirdre caught her arm and pulled her close enough to whisper. "It's for the best, mum. You'll see. Everybody will like it."

She wanted to argue. She felt extremely uncomfortable, especially since the drink from the afternoon had worn off, but she wasn't given the chance to object. The moment she descended from the cart, Lady Beitidh started bellowing.

"Look! Look! It's the MacDhubhthaich bride, come to find her husband." Then she pushed Clara forward.

"Och, it's the bride!" bellowed one of the nearby men.

"The MacDhubhthaich bride!" cried another.

"Drink, lass. We'll find him for ye."

A flagon was pushed into her hand as everyone around urged her to drink.

"It's what turns the tale," said Lady Beitidh. "She drinks, we cheer, and then she finds her man." She pushed the drink toward Clara's lips. "Don't ruin it fer them! This is the reason for the festival, and it was given to you!"

This is why she liked to research things ahead of time. She didn't know anything about the customs in this part of the world, and she didn't like having a role when she had no idea what she was to do. Damnation, her home parish still talked about the time she tripped while dancing around the maypole when she was eight.

But there was no help for it now, especially with everyone cheering her on so joyously. So when the next flagon was pushed into her hand, she took a healthy drink. And the next. And the next. It steadied her nerves—if not her feet—and allowed her to cry out as if she truly were a lost bride.

"Where is my husband?" she asked. "I am the bride of... of..." She couldn't begin to say the word. Fortunately, everyone else could.

"The MacDhubhthaich bride!"

"Over here! Over here!"

When they'd climbed off the cart, it hadn't seemed too far to the center of the merrymaking. But now that she was walking through the people—many of whom kept trying to get her to drink—she was turned around and pulled in different directions. The pathway seemed five times as long, and when she arrived in the center clearing, the chanting had become a battering of sound.

"The groom! The groom!"

She looked around, trying to get her bearings. Deirdre was nowhere to be seen, but Lady Beitidh had moved to the MacCleal laird's side. Liam's father was a big man with a booming voice and—right now—a full grin.

"Welcome, MacDhubhthaich bride!" he bellowed. "Your groom awaits."

"He does?" Clara asked. "I thought he was dead."

"Not dead. Your kiss revives him."

Two men had hold of her. She supposed they were helping her along—she'd been passed from one to another all the way up here—but she found her footing and steadied herself in the center of the clearing. She shook the men off, elbowing one of them when he would not step away.

Damnation. The gown she wore was in tatters. She would definitely have to buy Deirdre another. Meanwhile, she held up her lantern and slowly turned a full circle. Flushed and happy faces surrounded her. Men toasted her with their drink and women smiled slyly at her. So many people all seeking to applaud her role in tonight's festivities.

She took a breath. Might as well do it for all she was worth.

"Aieeee!" she cried in her best attempt at a ghostly wail. "I have arrived too late at my beloved's castle. They are all killed."

A roar of denial followed her statement. Then Lady Beitidh cried, "There he is! Your groom is here!"

She looked where the lady pointed and saw Lord Loughton pushed forward. His expression was dark, and his gaze landed hard on the laird.

"Father!" he snapped. "This is not the way to win a woman."

"It's our way!" the man bellowed, to which a chorus of men roared their approval.

"Clara!" someone bellowed, and it sounded like Aaron, but try as she might, Clara could not find him. Too many people crowded around.

"Clara," Lord Loughton said as he stepped closer. "Don't...word..."

She peered at him where he was struggling through the crowd. Lord, her head was starting to swim. Whatever he'd just said was lost amidst the sound of his clan cheering.

"I'm the...the MacDub...something bride."

Lady Beitidh nodded happily as she coaxed Clara on. "Say, you're here to wed the MacCleal."

"Right," Clara said. "I'm here to wed." Then she shook her head. "But I'm a ghost, right? I die because I find you dead."

"But he's here, now," the lady said. "Kiss him and declare yourself wed."

Clara looked at the crowd. Of course. That's what they all wanted to see. A kiss between bride and groom was the end of the tale. She could see that Liam was none too pleased to be in the center of this, but it was only harmless fun. *She* would not be the reason this festival was bad. She would play her part.

So when Liam finally closed the space between them, Clara went willingly. Thankfully, he caught her around the waist and kept her upright. Good heavens, just how much had she drunk? Her legs were like wet paper.

"Careful, Clara," he said against her ear. "I've got you."

She set her head against his shoulder to steady herself. All she needed to do was say the words, and it would be done. She could go inside and rest. Maybe even get some bread to settle her stomach. She just had to finish it.

She reached up and touched his face, investing all her strength in saying the words Beitidh had told her.

"My groom," she cried.

He caught her hand and pulled it back from his face. His other arm pressed her tight to his body, steadying her against him. "Clara, don't say anything—" he began, but she wouldn't be stopped now. It's what the crowd wanted. And she never minded kissing him anyway.

She used her free hand to grab his broad shoulder and jerked herself high enough to press her mouth to his. It was a perfunctory kiss. He had not helped her do it, being more occupied in keeping her from falling, but she managed the feat. Finally. Their lips had touched enough that it probably worked for the play, though she thought Liam could have made a better show of it.

Then she allowed herself to fall backwards some and cry, "My lord lives!"

The crowd cheered, but the MacCleal's voice boomed over it. "You are wed then? To my son?"

Loughton's arm tightened around her. His face was a hard mask of fury at his father. "Don't answer—"

"Yes!" she cried. "We are wed."

She felt Liam's sigh as if it went through his whole body. She frowned, not understanding his reaction. Had she done a bad job?

Meanwhile, the laird clapped his hands. "It is done!"

"Clara!" That was definitely Aaron, but she could not see over Loughton's shoulder enough to find her brother.

"Let me—" she began, but her words were cut off as Loughton swung her into his arms. She cried out in shock, but then she relaxed as his arms gripped her tight. Ah! It was so lovely to be held like this. No need to support herself on wobbly legs, and all the time in the world to nestle against his broad chest. She let her head drop into the space between his head and shoulder, and she inhaled his scent.

"Hold tight," he said to her. "I'll get us clear."

She didn't understand what he was saying until a few moments later. It seemed as if everyone was guiding them into the castle. Dozens of hands were pushing them forward, others were clearing the way ahead.

Oh yes. Bride and groom would have to go into the castle at the end of the performance. That made sense. She even managed a wave to the crowd as he carried her inside. She'd thought that they would be free once they made it through the castle door, but they were followed. The men pushed them on, climbing through the tower stairs and into a bedchamber.

It wasn't her bedchamber. She saw that immediately. She also saw it when Mairi stood inside the room glaring at her as if she were vermin dragged into the castle. Clara felt her ire rise at that. She hadn't wanted to play the role of some ghost bride, but she'd done her best to make everyone happy.

Fortunately, before she could say anything, Mairi turned her tart tongue on the men following them.

"Out! Out you go! Get out!" She shooed them back and back, closing the doors until all the revelers were on the outside, leaving the three of them on the inside.

Lord Loughton set Clara down on the bed. His bed, she now realized, as she looked about the room. They were in his bedroom. Those were his items of clothing hanging in the wardrobe.

"It's done then?" Mairi asked.

"Aye," Loughton answered, though he sounded none too pleased about it. Then he squatted down in front of Clara. "How much have you had to drink, Clara? How are you feeling?"

She blinked at him. "Lady Beitidh said it was part of the play. That I was supposed to drink it."

"*Lady* Beitidh?" Mairi snapped. "She's no lady at all."

"What?" Clara asked. "But she said—"

"Never mind that now," Loughton interrupted. He looked back at Mairi. "Get her some food and water. I'll explain it to her when she's sober."

Mairi's brows shot up nearly into her hair. "You'll *explain* it? Like it's a way to cook a pheasant. You'll *explain* this to the Sassenach?"

"Enough!" Loughton said, the word loud enough that Clara pressed a hand to her head to steady it. The word echoed inside her skull.

She must have made a sound of distress because he immediately moderated his tone. "Sorry, Clara. Mairi, go. Get us some food."

"It's right over there, you idiot. Do you think I'd be in here for any other reason?"

Clara looked over to where a tray of bread and cheese sat, as well as a full pitcher of water. Oh good. She reached out, but Liam was there before her. He handed her half the loaf of bread.

"Start on that," he said. She did. And while he was filling a cup with water, he looked over at Mairi. "Keep the bastards out," he said as he glared at the door where the sound of a drinking song came through loud and clear.

"Aye," Mairi said. "I know my duties." Then she snorted as she headed to the door. "*Explain* it," she mocked. "What I wouldn't pay to see that. Best you keep your sword handy, Liam. I hear she's already knocked you one this day."

And on that, she maneuvered her way out the door while the men still clustered outside roared in enthusiastic approval.

CHAPTER ELEVEN

LIAM TRIED TO block out the drunken singing outside his bedroom door and focus on the woman he'd just ruined. They were married now for sure, but she didn't know that yet. Which meant he had a short moment in time to convince her to throw her lot in with him.

He began by tending to her physically. That meant water and bread. Whatever she was wearing was torn to shreds leaving her in a dirtied shift and stays that smelled of drink. He would need to get her out of all that, but not until her head and stomach were settled.

"Here," he said as he handed her a cup of water. "This will help."

She'd already managed most of the bread, and she took the cup with a loose-limbed ease. "I have to buy Deirdre a new dress," she murmured before she drank the water. Then she looked down at her stained clothing. "Do I smell like the distillery?"

"Only a little," he lied. "Who is Deirdre and why must you buy her a dress?"

She touched a trailing thread. "Everyone was tugging on me. They tore the gown to pieces." She finished the water and then seemed to lose strength. He was sitting beside her, so it was an easy thing to encourage her to sink against him and close her eyes. He thought she might have gone to sleep, but a moment later she spoke in a small voice. "Did I do a good job?"

"What?"

"As Laird Dub… itch… whomever's ghost bride?"

"You were wonderful," he said as he pressed a kiss to her forehead. "Who told you the tale?"

"Lady Beitidh. She said it was the most important part of the festival day and that I'd replaced her."

Of course, she did. His father's mistress—who was no lady in any sense of the word—would have gotten the idea from his father and together they manufactured this disaster.

"She's not a lady," he said gently. "And she tricked you."

Clara lifted her head off Liam's shoulder. "What? But she said—"

"It doesn't matter, Clara. It's over." He refilled the cup with water and pressed it on her. "Drink up. We've got some talking to do."

She did as he bid, but when she was done, her expression was cloudy. "I don't think I want to talk. I don't think I'll like what you're going to say."

He was sure of it. "Why not lie down a bit? Until you feel better?"

She proved she wasn't completely lost as she peered around the room. "But this isn't my bedroom."

"You can't leave now. Not with everyone outside the door."

She sighed. "They are rather loud."

Yes, they were. He stretched back on the bed and pulled her with him. She lay down against him, settling sweetly into the curve of his shoulder.

"Does your head hurt?" he asked.

"Not really. I'm sure I'll have a sore head in the morning, but right now, it's just nice to lay down."

He let her rest there while he stroked his hand over the curve of her waist and up along her ribcage. She fit him so well, hip to hip, long leg curling around his legs. His cock was standing tall and a little twist would have him rubbing delightfully against her.

If ever he had imagined his wife, he would not have landed on a lanky bluestocking with moderately-sized breasts. But that's because all boys were idiots. As a man, he couldn't wait to unlace her stays and discover the glory beneath her clothes.

"Do you know when I first realized you are beautiful?" he asked.

She shifted against him, making his cock throb. "What? How much whisky have you had?"

Enough to make him mellow. "When we walked in Hyde Park, and you wore that shapeless thing without stays. It was like you'd put a bag on and everything underneath was free."

"I was perfectly covered," she said.

"I know. And yet when I touched your sides, this wasn't there." He tugged lightly at her stays. "I learned the shape of you then. That you weren't all hard angles and knobby knees."

"My knees are definitely knobby."

"But not the rest of you." He shifted her as he tried to untie her stays. "Let's take this off, hmmm?"

She sat up with his help and shed the remains of her gown. Then she untied her stays and, with a sigh of relief, dropped the thing on the floor before flopping back onto his bed with her arms spread out. He could see the movement of her breasts beneath her shift and the shadow of her nipples. But more than that, he could see that she breathed with full inhales, and he heard the sweet sound of her sigh.

"Clara?"

"Hmmm?'

"You'll have to say, stop, if you don't like it."

"What?"

Unable to resist touching her, he caressed her breast through the fabric of her shift. Her eyes popped open on a gasp, but a moment later, her mouth curved into a smile.

"I should stop you," she said.

But she wasn't going to. And while she pressed her breasts into his hand, he kissed her shoulder. Then she turned her head such that he had the full length of her neck available to his mouth, and before long, he was able to nibble her jaw before teasing up toward her lips.

"This is very wicked of us," she said.

At least she said, "us" and not "him."

"It's not wicked if we both want it," he said. Then he caught her mouth in his. He thrust his tongue between her lips and felt her stretch against him. Her mouth opened, her tongue dueled with his, and she sounded like she was humming low, like a purr while his body burned for her.

He stroked his hand down her belly then across her groin to her thigh. He wanted to pull off her shift, but she was trembling. A fine ripple that had him wondering what she was feeling. He broke off their kiss.

"Clara? What—"

"It's nothing," she whispered as she pulled him back to her mouth.

It definitely was something. Her whole body was shaking against him. Not violently, but with a subtle energy that surprised him.

"Are you afraid?" he asked.

"No." She smiled up at him. "It's like emotions build up inside me, and I tremble. That's all."

He set his hand on her belly, resting lightly so he could feel it without stopping them. "What emotion?" he asked, awed by the delicacy of her.

She bit her lip, her cheeks turning rose. "I'm feeling daring, my lord. Very daring."

"Call me Liam." He stroked his hand along her leg, as far down as he could reach, and then skimmed back up as he brought her shift with it. "And what do you dare?"

"I should like you to teach me something please."

"Yes?"

"I should like to experience a quickening. I've heard about them, you know, but I didn't... I haven't..." She shrugged. "You needn't if you don't want to."

He grinned at her. "I very much do."

"I'm told I can do them by myself, but—"

"They're not nearly as much fun that way."

She grinned. "I knew you would know about them."

"Of course, I do." He nibbled along her jaw. "They were invented by the Scottish."

"They were not!" she said, giggling in her outrage.

He chuckled, his hand now trailing over her hip and across her still shaking belly. "No, but we do enjoy them." He waggled his brows at her. "And every Scotsman worth the name has his own special way of bringing his lady to her peak."

Her brows rose. "Really? And how do they learn such a thing?"

"It's a secret handed down from father to son on the eve of his wedding."

"Then how do you know such a thing?"

He grinned. "I might have learned it early."

She snorted. "I bet you did."

His expression sobered at her tart tone. "In all honesty, Clara, I learned by talking to a woman who cared to teach me. But if you think I have been hopping from bed to bed in pursuit of this, then you have the wrong of me. I had better things to do with my time."

She touched his face. A single finger stroked along his jaw, fire trailing in her wake, while her gaze met his and held. "You are the most interesting man I have ever met."

High praise coming from her. "How can that be?"

"I do not know. Perhaps it is because I never know what you are going to say. And I cannot guess what you are going to do."

"Can't you?" he asked as he stroked beneath her shift to cup her breast. "Surely you know what comes next."

She smiled, a lazy happy smile that bewitched him. "Not exactly," she said. "But I like that you have pulled up my shift, I like the way your callouses feel against my skin, and I cannot stop thinking about your kisses. I have let no one but you touch me like this. I have never kissed anyone the way I kiss you."

She could not have said anything more erotic. In that moment, he wanted her as a drowning man wants air. He wanted to work by her side and sleep in the same bed. He wanted to spill his seed inside her and meet the child that would be as much her as him. He wanted her as his wife and so he set about showing her. But he could not do as he willed with her shift between them, so he tore it apart with his bare hands.

Then he kissed the hard peak of her breasts, laving her nipple with his tongue, and sucking it hard while she gasped in surprise. He spent a great deal of time on her breasts. He liked how she arched against him, and he loved how her legs twined with his.

It was no easy feat to pull off his own clothes. He feared she would change her mind if he left her body for even a second. Such was his need for her that any hope of common sense was lost. He tossed aside his boots and socks while she sat up and pulled off her shift. But as he unwrapped his kilt from his own body, she draped it across hers. She covered her groin first, hiding her wet curls from him. Then she teased it across her breasts.

She meant to throw it aside, but he caught the end and wrapped her tighter and tighter in its length until she appeared bound in his clan colors.

"Lie down, lass," he said as he tugged his tartan toward the bed.

She let him do it, laughing lightly as she landed. "It's like I'm surrounded by you," she said as she toyed with the ends.

He tried to laugh then. He wanted to match her ease, but hunger had claimed him. His hand slipped between her knees, coiling around her thigh as he squeezed her flesh. "Kiss me," he said as he leaned over her.

She did. She wrapped her arms around him and kissed him with all the passion he wanted. And while their tongues dueled, his hand rose between her thighs. His knee followed to hold her open. And when his fingers cupped her sex, she clutched his shoulders in surprise.

"Am I going to feel it now?"

"Yes."

He stroked her, his pace slow while his fingers remained thorough. He spread her open, he pressed his fingers inside, and he painted her with her own moisture. She liked it when he drew everything high to her clit. She arched when he plunged back into her. And she whimpered when he stopped for a moment, just to see her there, open to his touch and wrapped in his kilt.

"I would you never wore anything else."

She had no breath to answer as he increased his tempo. He watched her passion grow, and it was the most glorious sight. Wrapped in his kilt, she undulated, pressing up against his hand when he was at her clit and seeming to pull him inside when he plumbed her depths. She threw back her head, her eyes were wide as she stared at nothing, and he saw her naked belly between the wrap of his kilt as it fluttered and flexed.

He took her to a faster pace, a wilder place, and when she finally came it was as if her whole body exploded with wild abandon. He nearly came from watching her. And, because his fingers were deep inside her, he felt the waves she rode. Tight then release, tight then release, pulse after pulse while she smiled as if he hung the moon and the stars for her.

He'd certainly try.

And when she finally rested, she stretched like a satisfied cat and curled her body around his.

"Now I know," she said.

"Now you know," he echoed.

Then he took her face in his hands and kissed her hard and deep. He leaned over her and felt her nipples brush his chest and knew the welcome openness of her legs. His knee was already between hers. His thighs lowered and she opened beneath him. But he didn't thrust, though his organ wept from nearness to her.

"Marry me, Clara. Be my bride." He kissed her again, thrusting his tongue inside her as he wanted to do with his cock. "I'll see you never regret it. Not once, I swear."

She pulled back, her hands stroking the hair from his eyes. Her expression was tender, and she smelled of her glorious musk. "You cannot promise such a thing."

"I can try. I will spend my life trying. For you, Clara."

He nuzzled her neck and she trembled in his arms. An excess of emotion, she'd said.

"You want this," he said. "You want me."

"I do," she whispered, and his body tightened at the words. "But I will not marry." While his body went cold, she pressed kisses to his jaw and mouth. She even used her teeth for tiny nibbles that would have aroused him before. Now, he caught her by the shoulders and held her away.

"Clara, you must see—"

"Liam, I told you from the beginning that I would not marry you." She gestured to the room about them. "You live in a castle. There are men singing drinking songs outside your door. This has been a wonderful adventure for me. One that I will never forget. But you cannot think I will live here. It's not what I want."

"Edinburgh is as modern a city as London. More so!"

She nodded, and her smile faltered when she realized he was not smiling back. "Yes, it is, but you don't live there. You live here."

"And you despise my home?"

"Of course not!"

"Then it is my people—"

"Don't be ridiculous."

"Never say it is me," he said. "I am between your thighs right now, Clara." He sank hard against her, and she gasped at the weight of him.

She also scooted back from him, though she couldn't dislodge him. And damnation, he wanted—he needed—to be embedded inside her. But he didn't, though the blood pounded a needful rhythm throughout his body.

"Clara—" Her word came out as an angry growl.

"Liam! Nothing has changed!"

"Everything has changed!" he shot back. "Everything!"

He nearly took her right then and consequences be damned. His blood, his cock, his anger all willed him to possess her in the most primitive way possible. No one would damn him. Hell, they were already married, and the men outside were there to make damn sure she was not a virgin in the morning.

But he couldn't do it. He couldn't look into her eyes now or afterwards if he took something she had not given. So he wrenched himself away. He rolled off her and landed on the balls of his feet beside the bed. Then he stayed there, crouched over his own nakedness, while desire killed any softness inside him.

"Liam?" Her voice was small. She sat up slowly and curled herself into his kilt such that her breasts and groin were covered. As if that would make him want her less! The sight had him gripping the bed, his knuckles white.

"Clara, I am not a man who begs, but I am doing so now. Be my wife."

She was silent a long time, her gaze holding his, her breath measured to the same tempo as his. And then a single tear slipped from her left eye.

"I'm sorry, Liam. I'm so sorry."

Tears? Tears! Damnation, she didn't understand anything! "How can such a brilliant woman understand so little?"

It was a rhetorical question. It burst from him as he shoved away from the bed and stomped to the corner. He grabbed the nearest shirt from a pile there and hauled it on with rough movements. He was acutely aware of her gaze following him. Of the way she sat on his bed watching him as she might a wounded animal.

He spun back to her. "Do not look so tragic. I will not hurt you!"

She frowned at him—a small tuck between her brows—as she tried to understand what was going on. "I have done this all wrong, haven't I?"

Yes! "No," he ground out. She had only remained true to what she had said from the very beginning. She would not wed him. He was the one who had betrayed her. But he was in no mood to confess that. "Go to sleep, Clara. The morrow will have plenty of problems. Best get what sleep you can now."

Her eyes narrowed, and he could see that all vestiges of drink—and of passion—had been wiped from her eyes. She focused now on the door where the singing had died down to two voices praising a tavern wench.

"They assume you have ravished me."

"What do you care what a bunch of Scots think?"

She nodded as if that made sense. "I wouldn't, as a general rule," she admitted. Then her gaze returned to him. "But you are angry, and I don't understand why."

"Then you are being willfully stupid," he snapped. "I have been courting you, Lady Clara, from the beginning. And now you are in my bed. What did you think this was about?"

Her gaze dropped to the floor. "You are right, of course," she said, her voice small. "Though I've told you from the very beginning that I would not marry you. I thought you understood. I thought you could show me things and not think it meant more."

He took rapid steps forward until he towered over her. "I do not bed ladies I will not wed."

She arched a brow. "That's obviously not true. What about the woman who taught you…" She gestured weakly at her lower half. "You did not wed her."

"She wasn't a lady!" he all but shouted.

She sniffed. "Well, pretend I'm not one either."

He threw up his hands. This was ridiculous. He should tell her the truth now before she learned it from his father in the morning. But to do so now would be to ruin their remaining hours. Part of him still held hope that he could convince her, that some miracle would have her changing her mind before the sun rose.

Instead, she blew out a breath and lifted her chin. "I am a demi-rep now, not a lady at all."

"That's ridiculous, and you know it."

Except, apparently, she didn't. "No, no, it's easier this way. After all, I'm a spinster, long since on the shelf. I have odd friends, dress strangely at times, and go to séances when I can find them. I only tried to keep up appearances because of Aaron's political career. I was a bad hostess, but I tried. Lilah will do that for him now." She nodded, clearly accepting her changed circumstances as if it were the easiest thing in the world. "I shall find a private room for myself in London. I don't require much, and Lilah will help me set it up. That way I can entertain whomever I want and be like a courtesan of old."

He growled down at her. "You will entertain no one but me."

"Well as to that," she said as she scrambled out of his bed. "I should like you to visit me. Often." She stood there, her glorious hair tumbling down her back as she faced him fully. "We can be the best of friends." She bit her lip. "Lovers, even, if you should like, though I shall have to make sure there are no children."

He had no answer for that. What she was envisioning would never come to pass.

"You know how to do that, right?" At his incredulous look, she shook her head. "Never mind. I know about French letters, though…" Her gaze dropped to his still thick erection where it bobbed beneath his shirt. "Well, I know about them, so I can find some." She chuckled, the sound high and nervous. "You can find anything in London."

Those words broke him. They flashed red across his vision as he grabbed his tartan from her body. She squeaked in alarm as he pulled it off her. He wrapped it around himself in hard, jerking motions while she dropped to her knees in order to grab her shift. It was torn in half, but she pulled it on backwards such that her front was covered. Her watched as her glistening sex disappeared from view. He stood like a statue as her breasts bobbed from her motions. And he watched as she grabbed a blanket off the bed and wrapped it around her in much the same motions as he had his tartan.

"You're angry," she said again. "And I don't understand why."

"Yes, you do."

"Because I refuse to marry you."

"Yes."

"But I have refused you every day since we met. Nothing has changed."

"That's right," he lied, defeat washing through him. "Nothing has changed." And with that, he stomped to the door and hauled it open. "Don't leave this room," he ordered. Then he looked to the men grinning at him where they sprawled in the hallway. "She stays inside," he ordered. "And if any of you touch her, I'll gut you."

Then he stomped away while his father's men hooted drunkenly in his wake.

He shook with the need to punch every single one of them, but they weren't responsible for the current disaster. No, that crime lay at his father's feet. He stomped through the castle then walked in a steady pattern through the bailey and out around the castle grounds.

He found the MacCleal drunk beneath a willow tree. He lay half on his mistress while mumbling a song.

"You couldn't trust me," Liam growled as his father. "You couldn't leave it in my hands."

His father blinked owlishly at him. "What you yapping about?"

"Get up, you drunken bastard," Liam said. "The pride of the MacCleals," he taunted. "Tricking a naïve girl to steal her dowry. You disgust me."

Beitidh was awake now, though also drunk. "Aw, it got the job done," she grumbled. "What does it matter—"

"Say another word, and I will beat you. He may have ordered it, but you lied to her face, dressed her like a harlot, and set her to wander alone through the men." The idea of what might have happened to Clara made his blood boil. He reached down and hauled Beitidh to her feet, not caring when his father tumbled sideways into the dirt. "Go," he growled straight into the woman's face. "Get far away," he growled, as he shoved her toward the road.

"Och," his father cried as he righted himself. "Leave her be." The man managed to sit up, but he couldn't keep the position. He slumped back against the tree trunk and peered owlishly at Liam. "You were taking too much time."

"It was one day!"

"It's been years that you've been away. Years to bed one rich Sassenach." His father waved a limp hand at him. "We got tired of all your *thinking* and *planning* and wasting time."

"You're the one who taught me to think, but now it's all about your cock and your drink." He wanted to beat his father senseless. He wanted to choke him for poisoning Liam's future with Clara. But that would be like kicking a stupid dog. His father had had honor once and brains, but now he was awash in drink. It didn't matter if this started from grief at losing Liam's mother or was simply laziness plus the influence of Beitidh's loose morals. The end result was the same.

His father was not a fit leader for his clan.

Liam spit at the ground, repulsed by his own culpability in this disaster. He was the MacCleal heir, and yet he'd hadn't been here to stop his father's slide into debauchery. And he'd brought Clara into this disaster knowing full well that trickery was a possibility.

"You've poisoned everything," he said. "I still had ways to convince her."

Now his task with her was a million times harder. When Clara realized the truth, she would leave. And Aaron would move heaven and earth to block Liam from gaining her dowry.

His father wasn't listening. The laird's eyes were shut, and he mumbled incoherently as he slumped against the tree. Ten feet away, Beitidh was in a similar position curled up against a different tree trunk.

The sight made him nauseous. Even more so because he knew that in the morning, both would be awake and gleefully planning the spending of Clara's dowry. Such was their constitution that these two could be blind drunk now, and yet still able to cause mischief in the morning. They likely would not even remember that he'd been here.

Liam rubbed a hand over his face. He needed to figure out what to do. Was there any hope of salvaging the situation?

Maybe. If he could buy more time with Clara. Enough to convince her that his father's and Beitidh's perfidy was not Liam's choice. But the only way to do that was to claim that the situation was a fait accompli.

Liam and Clara were married. By Scottish law, the two of them were husband and wife.

The problem was that the English were famous for ignoring inconvenient facts. Aaron could deny everything that had happened here. At a minimum, with the right amount of bribery, he could annul the marriage, especially since Liam hadn't bedded her.

That meant Liam now had to bluff. He had to declare their wedding an undeniable fact. He had to be cold and uncompromising on that, showing not even the tiniest amount of sympathy to how Clara had been abused this night. He had to claim her dowry for his people, and then he had to keep her here while the finances were settled. Aaron would not hold back on the money as long as the cash supported Clara.

It was a cold way to begin his life with Clara. He wouldn't blame her if she never forgave him, but it was the only way forward for his clan. They needed her dowry, and if that meant that he had to spend the rest of his life with an angry, bitter wife, then he would do it. For his people.

But what a miserable, awful future that painted for himself and Clara.

CHAPTER TWELVE

L IAM WAS RIGHT.

Clara curled into herself on his bed as she thought through what had just happened.

She knew exactly why he was angry, though she'd pretended confusion. Most men became furious when she refused to conform to their wishes. Liam was no different than any other stubborn man in that matter. But of all the people she knew, he was the one she least wanted to upset, the one she most wanted to please. But not at the cost of her entire life.

He had touched her more intimately than any person she knew. Not just physically, but because he listened when she spoke, took her to activities that interested her, and never, ever laughed at her oddities. She valued him as a good friend and hoped they could become lovers now that she had become a demi-rep.

She would see about mending fences with him after she returned to London.

With that thought firmly in place, she wrapped herself in the spare blanket and lay down to sleep. It took her a while to quiet down, but eventually she relived the experience of climax in her memory. The feel of him between her thighs and the soaring explosion of sensation at the end had her relaxing into his bedding and enjoying the scent of him everywhere.

Eventually, she slept.

Sometime in the night, she heard him come in. She felt him settle on the bed beside her. When she stirred, he murmured to her, saying something to the effect of, "Hush. We'll rest a while together."

She didn't speak, but allowed her body to conform to his. He curled into her back, and she held his hand as he wrapped his arm around her waist. He surrounded her, and she smiled as she dropped off to sleep. He had forgiven her their fight. All was well.

They slept.

The door burst open with a bang that reverberated through her aching head. She jolted upright, but it was nothing compared to what Liam did. He leaped over her to stand unapologetically naked in front of her. And with a jolt of shock, she saw he held a wicked-looking dagger in his hand.

"Aw down with you, boy," his father boomed with an echoing laugh. "That little prick won't do naught to me."

"Get out," Liam said, his voice colder than she'd ever heard before.

She sat up, wrapping the kilt tightly around herself. Behind the laird stood his men rubbing their eyes as they peered in through the door. They'd likely been sleeping out there and were just now waking amid the commotion.

Meanwhile, the laird stomped forward. Liam paced him, keeping between his father and Clara. "Now isn't the time," Liam hissed.

"Oh, now is the best time," returned the laird as he peered past Clara to the bedding behind her. "Step aside, lass. We've got to have the proof."

Liam gripped his father's arm. "I didn't take her," he said in a harsh undertone. "She's still pure."

"What?" The word was equally quiet, though fury still throbbed in his words. The MacCleal looked at his son, then he spit on the bed. "You're worse than a Jesse dobber. To think that a son o' mine…" He shook his head. He abruptly straightened and gestured his men back. "Get back," he growled. "Let Beitidh in."

The men did as they were bid, and soon the woman maneuvered her way inside carrying a heavy robe.

"Go help my lady." The MacCleal sneered the last two words as his woman came bustling forward.

"Och, now, Lady Clara, there's no need to fear." She was speaking loudly while the laird kicked the door shut. Then she nudged Liam aside as she reached for Clara. "There now, lass, give the plaid back to your husband. I've a robe that will fit you nice this morning."

Damnation, her head really hurt. Every sound had her wincing, and she knew it would be ten times worse if she spoke. She remained silent as the MacCleal stripped the blanket off the bed to scowl down at the white sheet beneath.

"Och," said Beitidh as she shook her head. "You've got yourself a whore daughter-in-law then."

Liam reacted with violence as he grabbed Beitidh's arm. She'd just pulled a vial out of her bodice, but now her face paled as she flinched from Liam. It didn't stop his father, though, as the laird grabbed the vial, unstoppered it, and splashed red blood on the sheet.

"What are you doing?" Clara asked, her mind and body rebelling at the sound of her own voice. She watched in confusion as the man purposely smeared the dark stain with his hand, before lifting the sheet up.

"Open the door," he said.

"Not yet," Liam snapped, as he yanked the robe out of Beitidh's arm and passed it to Clara. She was quick to pull on the robe, dropping the plaid in the process. Meanwhile, the MacCleal stomped to the door carrying the now-bloodied sheet.

"Wait—" Clara began, but she hadn't the voice to stop what was happening.

Once the MacCleal swung the door open, the men crowded forward.

"It's done!" he bellowed as he held up the sheet, bloody side in full view.

The crowd roared in approval and several bawdy comments were shouted into the room. And while Liam shoved Beitidh away from Clara, the MacCleal carried the sheet to the window, pushed aside the shutters and unfurled it to the wind. Another cheer rose up from the courtyard below, and Clara finally figured out what was happening.

It was "proof" of her virginity—or loss thereof—set out for all to see. It was a custom from hundreds of years ago, clearly still used here, and Clara could do nothing but gape around her at the scene. The laird waved at the people below the window, his men crowded into the doorway, all while Liam stood naked with a dagger in his hand. And she stood in a robe that smelled as if it hadn't been washed in years.

"This cannot be happening," she murmured. When had she landed in a gothic novel?

At her words, Liam turned toward her. His gaze flicked a hard glare at Beitidh and jerked his head toward the door. "Out," he growled.

Beitidh stayed long enough to whisper into Clara's ear, "I've saved your reputation this day. Keep me happy and no one else will know the truth."

"That I'm still a virgin?" Clara asked, her mouth speaking before her brain fully caught up.

Beitidh sniffed. "I shall buy gowns of gold and velvet on your dowry." Then she grinned at the MacCleal as she held up her hand. The man took it and together, they sauntered out of the room. They were barely past the door, though, when another commotion filled the hallway.

"Clara! Clara! Where are you?"

It was Aaron, bellowing as he tried to force his way through the throng of men. He was being held back. Aaron was a large man, but even he couldn't get through a narrow passage blocked by five strapping Scotsmen and the laird.

She shot a terrified look at Liam. The last thing she wanted was for her brother to burst in on this, and she didn't even know what *this* was! But there was no help for it.

Liam sighed and stalked to the door. "Let him through. Let him through, damn it!" Then to make sure it happened, he grabbed one man by the shoulder and shoved him aside. A moment later, Aaron burst through the group. Liam stepped backward into the room to let him in. Aaron stopped, his mouth hanging open in shock as she saw Clara wrapped in the robe and Liam standing still naked nearby.

Then, with a hard, ugly growl, he slugged Liam.

It was a shocking sight. She'd never seen her brother in such a fury, never seen him lash out in the kind of hatred he showed now. And worse still, Liam didn't duck, didn't sidestep, did nothing but wait for the blow. Clara even had time to scream, "No!"

But it made no difference.

Aaron landed a solid punch on Liam's jaw. Liam's head snapped back, and he stumbled slightly from the force of the blow, but he didn't fight back. And when Aaron lifted his arm again, Clara lunged forward and grabbed his arm.

"Stop it, Aaron! What are you thinking?" she cried.

Aaron turned his head slowly to look at her. His eyes were wide in his mottled face, but his words were clear enough. "Get dressed!" he snapped. "We're leaving."

Well, she certainly agreed with that statement. She'd decided last night that everything would be better after they returned to London. But something was going on here, and she couldn't leave until she understood it. None of them could.

"Calm down, Aaron. You're making matters worse."

"I'm not sure how that can be," came a voice from the doorway. It was Lilah speaking calmly with her gaze averted. Damn it, Liam was still naked.

Clara quickly picked up Liam's tartan and passed it over to him. He took it with a quick jerk of his fingers. His gaze didn't quite meet hers, but he murmured his thanks as he wrapped it about his body. His chest remained bare, and if it weren't for the people in the room, Clara might have enjoyed looking at it in the sunlight. As it was, she could only wrap the robe around her tighter and gesture to the chairs in the room.

"Sit down, Aaron, before you punch someone else."

"That bastard—"

"Stop it, Aaron," Clara said, and Lilah seconded her words.

"Let's hear the full explanation, please."

They all looked to Liam, who stood with his body tight and his face clenched hard against any words. He looked as if he might explode, but he didn't say a word. Indeed, he simply stood there looking at her.

No one sat down.

"Very well," Clara said. "I'll start. Aaron, I'm a demi-rep now. I'll move out as soon—"

"You're my wife!" Liam boomed out.

Well, it seemed like he *had* found a way to explode. And yes, she'd already considered that given the sheet still billowing in the wind, but the central question remained unanswered.

"How?" There'd been no ceremony, no priest that she remembered. Certainly, she'd been drunk last night, but she would have remembered that.

Liam's expression faltered, but he spoke the words without flinching. "In Scotland, a couple is wed when the bride and groom claim before all that they are wed."

Aaron spoke up, his voice a heavy rasp. "Did you do that, Clara? Did you say you were wed?"

She thought back. "Only as the ghost bride. It was play acting."

"It was a trick," Liam said.

Aaron raised his fists. "And you went along with it!"

"It was already done. She'd said it."

Clara frowned. She didn't remember everything clearly, but she hadn't been insensate. She thought she recalled the moment. "You agreed," she said, her voice low. "I'm sure—"

"I did."

"And you knew what had happened."

"I did."

Lilah blew out a breath. "And now a whole festival of people will claim you are wed."

Liam nodded. "Because we *are* wed." He turned to face Clara straight on. "I did not plan for this to happen, but we are here now. Let us figure out how to go on."

Figure out how to go on? She had yet to understand what had happened. One thing was clear, though, he had lied to her, and the fury at that built like a fire behind her eyes. She held it in. She wasn't ready to let it burn through her. Aaron, on the other hand, had no trouble expressing his fury.

"Go on?" Aaron bellowed. "She'll go back to London with me. And if I ever see your face again—"

"You'll what?" Liam shot back. "I allowed you the one blow, Aaron. You'll not get another."

"You're not fighting!" Lilah said sternly. "Don't be ridiculous. We are a civilized people, and we shall act as such."

Aaron didn't change his stance by one inch. "You'll not get a penny of her dowry."

"Then I will see you in court, and it shall be a lengthy, expensive process which you will lose."

"You'll not have my sister!"

"He already has!" Clara said loudly. Fire burned in her throat, and she wrapped her arms tightly about her middle. She hated being in the middle of something she didn't understand. Worse, she hated being lied to by one of the few people she'd trusted. And now… She clenched her teeth and gestured at the flapping bedsheet. "According to that sheet, I am wedded and bedded." She looked hard a Liam. "Do I understand that correctly?"

He jerked his chin down in a nod. "Yes."

"Then you have won my dowry." God, it hurt to say those words, but she forced them out nonetheless. She'd been duped by a fortune hunter. She pressed her hands to her aching head.

"That's what he wants, Aaron. Give it to him and let us be gone."

The word "gone" clanged in her head. Gone as well was her hope of an independent life, even as a demi-rep. She had no money now since she couldn't win in court. Even if she proved she was still a virgin, the wedding vows had been spoken according to Scottish custom.

"Clara—" Liam began, but she held out her hand to stop him from speaking. She didn't want to hear anything. He continued nonetheless. "What if I have a different proposal?"

"Be damned with you—" Aaron growled as he wrapped an arm around her.

Far from making her feel better, the touch irritated her, and she pushed him away. "Aaron, pray shut up," Clara snapped. She needed to think. She needed to breathe. And she needed her damned head to stop pounding.

Liam crossed quickly to the basin and poured her a glass of water. He held it up, offering it to her silently, and though she was loath to touch him, she needed the drink. It soothed her parched throat, if nothing else. And when she finished her drink, she lifted forced herself to look at the man who had betrayed her.

"What are you thinking?"

Liam squared off with her, pointedly turning his shoulder to Aaron and Lilah. "Your dowry is mine. You can fight it in the courts, but you will lose."

"Don't be too sure—" Aaron grumbled, but he cut off his words when Clara made a curt gesture at him.

"What is it that you propose?"

"Stay and spend your money."

She frowned, not sure what he meant.

He gestured around him. "You're a brilliant woman. You have knowledge on subjects I never even heard of. Look around at my castle, at my people. Make all that knowledge useful by doing something with it here."

"What would I do?"

"What do you want to do?"

He stepped forward and touched her arm. She was too angry to allow him to touch her, so she jerked her arm back. But he remained distractingly close. "When we first met, you were talking about modern plumbing in a castle. Why not start with that?"

"That was Mr. Russell's idea. He has a fascination with such things."

"Hire him. Bring him here to build his ideas."

She shook her head slowly. "That would be expensive."

"I'm told you have a large dowry."

She did. Well, it was large enough to pay Mr. Russell. "You say that now, but I know how this works." Indeed, she had tried it several times at her parents' home. During her adolescence, she had talked her parents into all sorts of improvements only for it to go disastrously wrong. "You will pretend it is the most exciting project until it comes time to implement it. Then the money will need to be spent elsewhere. The townspeople will reject innovation. Workers will grumble because workers always do, and your determination to stand up against all that intransigence will disappear."

"Leave my people to me."

To the side, Aaron snorted. "You cannot control your father or his men. They hold the power here."

"They do not have the coin. I do."

"Not yet you don't—"

"Aaron, stop," Clara snapped. Or perhaps it came out more as a growl. "I am negotiating, not you." A bold statement from a woman who was lousy at hiring her servants and routinely made a mess of the practicalities of life. She turned to Liam. "So I am to bring in Mr. Russell to refashion the water in this place. What then?"

"What do you want to do?" He tilted his head. "You could teach the children. Create a school for them."

She nodded. She had already thought of that. Indeed, Clara had already thought about Deirdre's brother and sister running naked through the fields without anyone to care for them or teach them. But she was not the woman for that. Her education was in esoteric topics and her patience with children was never high. She shook her head. "I would be a very bad teacher."

"But you would be able to supervise a curriculum for the children, yes? You could hire someone to teach them letters and figures."

She snorted. "I would train the girls equally to the boys. There would be no difference between the sexes in their education."

"Done." He spoke the word firmly enough that it echoed in her head. How many times had she decried the lot of women in this world? Uneducated and unskilled, they were trapped in bad marriages with no way to escape. Even worse, the cycle continued with their daughters. Generation after generation with no way to thrive.

"I would teach the women how to handle money, how to work and live without a man."

He nodded. "So be it. If a man cannot prove his worth to a woman, then he does not deserve her as a wife."

She snorted. He was giving her lip service, telling her what she wanted to hear. If she agreed to stay, he could change his mind at any moment. Unless she forced him to put his name to it.

"Would you sign a paper to that effect? That you will use my dowry as I direct to bring good water to the castle and to let me run a school as I choose."

"I will."

"But it would not be binding because you are not the laird," inserted Aaron.

"It would be binding on me because I will sign it. Because I will control the money, not my father."

It couldn't be this easy. It couldn't be within her grasp to put into effect all the ideas that she had talked about with her friends. The things that ought to be but never were. The idea intrigued her enough to distract her from her sore head.

Up until now, everything she'd ever talked about was theoretical. *This is what ought to be, someone should do this, or it's unfair that someone has to suffer that.* As a child, she'd fought with her parents and the vicar about all sorts of things. When she was young, she wanted to learn about subjects they thought inappropriate. But as she grew, she also fought for better homes for the crofters or that women and children should be allowed to manage their own coin. At best, her parents pretended commitment, only to delay with excuse after excuse. At worst, they told her to play with her dolls and leave the management of things to other people.

In the end, they'd won. She'd left for London and stayed there where she had no chance to change anything.

But now Liam was looking at her with his arms folded, and his brow quirked in that challenging way. Damn it, he knew that expression always drew a rise from her. It did now as she remembered all the things she'd been stopped from doing throughout her life. He seemed to be offering her carte blanche with his castle and his people.

"You won't do it," she finally said.

"I will. I will swear it." Then he touched her chin, lifting it up until they stared into each other's eyes. "Do you doubt me or yourself? Because you know that I will do everything I can to see your work in place."

She hated to admit that there was some truth to his words. She'd created a comfortable life for herself lost in her books without ever putting her ideas to the test. Every argument she'd ever heard about how her ideas wouldn't work, that she was naïve, or that there were Godly reasons women were subordinate to men came back to haunt her. The last thing she wanted was to prove those people right.

Liam's expression softened as they looked eye to eye. "Clara, I agree with you on most things."

"And on things we don't?"

He grinned. "Then we shall have a rip-roaring good fight

about it. And who's to say who will win?"

"You will," she said as she stepped back from his intoxicating presence. "As my supposed husband, you'll have the law on your side."

He nodded, but then he spoke slowly and very clearly. "You have your virginity, Clara. One that can be proved by a doctor's inspection."

To the side, both Lilah and Aaron gasped in surprise.

Liam ignored them as he continued. "What do you care if a village in Scotland thinks you married? You could return to London at any time. Claim you went on a holiday with a paid companion. Whatever you want. None of my people will tell tales in London. They'll never venture past the twenty square miles of the village." He lifted his hands in an open gesture. "You can leave at any time if I do not honor my bargain."

"But you'll still have her money," Aaron groused from the side.

"Aye, but I have that anyway."

"This is all nonsense," Aaron asserted. "Clara, pack up. We will return home immediately. This entire disaster can be swept under the rug. I will do everything in my power to see that you are not harmed by this—"

"And what will you do then, Clara?" Liam pressed. "Waste your time at lectures learning things that you will never use? Get fitted for a new dress to go to a party with people you despise? Or will you sit around the house feeling like you are a burden on your brother and his new wife?"

She winced at his words. He was right. He was right about all of it. Then he said the one thing that struck at the core of her soul.

"Do you truly have so little faith in your ideas?"

She did believe in herself. Damn it, how many times had she prayed for just this kind of power when she was younger? And how stupid was she to turn it down just because she had a sore head and was married to a liar?

She straightened her shoulders and felt strength gather with every breath. "Aaron," she said before she could change her mind. "I want control of my entire dowry. Put it in an account in Edinburgh."

"I will have to sign for it," Liam said. "As your husband, I will have control of it."

"And if you interfere once with my use of the money, then I will leave immediately for London. And I will name you a liar."

He smiled, the expression filled with triumph. "You cannot hold all the cards, Clara. We do this work together or not at all."

She frowned. "What does that mean?"

"We must agree—the both of us—on the money you spend."

"Absolutely not—"

"You can stop me from what I want to do as equally as I stop—"

"Why would I care what you spend on your people?" she huffed.

He seemed to think about it for a moment, and then he nodded. "Half, then. You may spend half however you want. I spend the other."

Aaron folded his arms. "And then she will be impoverished by the year's end."

Liam arched his brows. "Or she will have built a life here that she can be proud of." He looked back to her. "The other choice is that you go back to London, and I have all your money to spend as I wish. You will have nothing but an empty existence in your brother's shadow while you wonder if you could have accomplished something special here."

"Here in *Scotland.*" It was the last of her arguments. She resented the fact that against her will, she was now trapped here.

"Here in Scotland," he echoed, "where there is opportunity for a clever woman to make a difference."

He wasn't wrong, and somehow, he had fired her up for the challenge. She lifted her chin and struck her bargain.

"Agreed."

CHAPTER THIRTEEN

S HE SAID YES.

Liam felt a weight the size of the castle roll off his shoulders. Unfortunately, it landed in the pit of his stomach. She'd said yes—and he believed her—but the moment she understood the magnitude of the problems at his home, she was likely to run back to London in terror. He fought that particular fight daily, and this was his homeland.

"How would you like to start?" he asked. The quicker she became invested in doing something here, the more mired in Scotland she became.

The door pushed open from behind with nary a knock. "Start with making her ladyship presentable," came Mairi's dry voice. Knowing her, she'd probably been listening at the door waiting for the right opportunity to burst in. "You've got the Aberbeag and others to greet for the wedding breakfast afore they depart. They're eating through our larder, so the sooner you bid them good-bye, the sooner we can work on filling it for the winter." She cast a critical eye at him. "An' she's not the only one who needs a bath."

He gotten used to Mairi's sharp tongue when they were children. He'd deserved it, of course, because he often used her dolls as target practice. But today was about securing Clara by his side, and a harsh female was the exact opposite of what was needed.

"Mairi MacAdaidh, you will knock before entering my lady's chamber," he snapped.

"It's not her chamber, you dolt," the woman snapped. "It's yours."

"And when have I ever given you leave to enter without permission?"

He watched Mairi open her mouth to argue, but she wasn't a fool. They both knew the tone he took when he had run out of patience. And the last thing he needed was a former lover ruining life with his wife. Which meant he needed to take control before Mairi figured out a retort.

He took Clara's hands in his. "What say you? Do we bathe and then see our guests away?"

Uncertainty flitted through her expression. She was not a woman who wanted to play hostess. And while she hesitated over her response, her brother spoke up.

"I have a different bargain," he said coldly. "I will sponsor your whisky to the prince regent. You'll get your royal mark, and you'll never say one word to me or my family again." He took a menacing step forward. "That's what you wanted, isn't it? That's why you got me so drunk last night." The turned to his sister. "Damnation, Clara, I failed you. When I most should have—"

"Oh, stop the dramatics," Clara said as she disentangled her hand from Liam's. Then she abruptly laughed, though the sound was high and brittle. "Imagine that. Me telling *you* not to be dramatic."

Aaron wasn't impressed. "We will leave. I'll get him what he wants, and we'll say no more about any of this."

She nodded slowly, and in that moment, Liam thought she would renege on everything they'd just promised one another. She turned to him. "Did you plan this? Get Aaron drunk? Make me into a ghost bride?"

"You know I did not."

She didn't know that. She had yet to sort out who had done what, but the challenge he had issued still burned in her. He'd called her brilliant and told her to put her ideas to the test. No one else—liar or not—had ever said as much.

She turned to her brother, her tone growing stronger with every word. "Dearest brother, you've been telling me to grow up for years now."

"I wanted you to take care of the servants, not harry after a Scotsman!"

She snorted. "That's rich, given that you have supported his courtship until now."

"Clara—"

"You are free, Aaron. I cut our ties, I end your responsibility for me, and I bid you go off and have a delightful life with Lilah. Only give me control of my funds and you need never worry about me again."

He threw up his hands. "Good God, there is no reasoning with you. Either of you!" He pointed at Liam. "He wants a royal warrant for his scotch, and your dowry."

"And I want to take a bath," she responded calmly. "Before I meet the guests." She arched a brow at Liam. "I am to pretend to be your bride, yes?"

Liam sighed. "You *are* my bride, Clara."

"Yes, well, I shall not consider it truth until I am no longer a virgin."

"Clara!" Aaron exclaimed.

"Rather like waving a red flag in front of a bull," Lilah murmured, and Mairi released a short burst of laughter at that.

Meanwhile, Clara continued as if no one had commented. "Please, Mairi, would you show me to the bath house. There is one, is there not?"

"Not for years," Mairi said. "I've got a tub set for you in Miss Rees' chamber."

"I'll run to the stream," Liam said, "and meet you when you're ready. We'll go into the great room together."

Clara nodded, then Liam added an extra command so that none would have a question as to Clara's status in this house.

"And while we are doing that, Mairi, have my wife's clothing brought into this bedchamber."

There was silence for a long moment as everyone absorbed the meaning of that. Then Mairi dipped into a half-mocking curtsey. "Right away, my lord."

"Lilah," Aaron said. "Why don't you go with Clara. See if you can talk sense into her."

Miss Rees snorted. "Clara walks her own path. Always. Do you honestly think—"

"Just try!" he said, and his fiancée dipped her chin in agreement.

A moment later, the three women left. Which meant it was time for the man to man reckoning. Already tired on what was to be a difficult day, Liam did his best to dispense with the confrontation as quickly as possible. He gathered soap and a razor, barely giving Aaron a sidelong glance.

"Tell me what it's to be then. Duel? Fisticuffs? Murder while I sleep? I know you're angry. So am I. But if you want to kill the culprit, then slap my father with your glove. I've been courting your sister honorably."

Liam waited, his shoulders tense. If he were Aaron, he'd be looking for a pistol. Instead, the man remained stubbornly silent. And when Liam finally turned around to face his new brother-in-law, he found the man staring at him with a dark expression. He waited, silently willing the man to get on with it. And when that didn't work, he poked some more at the man.

"I'm equally skilled in sword and pistol, so it matters not to me," he said. "Otherwise, get out of my way."

Aaron held out his hand. "Stop. Think for a moment."

Liam paused, his mind slowing as he focused. "You have my attention."

"Really think how much money you want. You're a reasonable man with an eye to the future. If you get the royal warrant for your whisky, that would go a long way to adding coin to your coffers. Five thousand pounds right now would be enough to set your home to rights. Then you could pick a woman you want. A wife who will love you and serve you as a man deserves. My sister will never be that. She's prickly and determined. She goes off in odd starts, and she's already said she doesn't want to live here."

"She just said she would."

"Because you lied to her, and she thinks there is no other choice. How many men do you know who are trapped in horrendous marriages with a woman who despises him? Do you know the misery of that? Even worse, imagine the expense of keeping her away from here just so you can have a measure of peace."

Scores. Indeed, the people in unhappy marriages far outweighed the good.

"You could have a future with a woman who loves you, as I have found with Lilah. We are in love." Aaron straightened to his full height. "I believe you have some fondness for Clara. Do not doom her or yourself to a miserable future just for money. Especially when I can get you funds another way."

It was tempting. Indeed, it was exactly the solution he had been looking for, but hadn't expected. No man in his position—a future laird of a poor county—could expect to marry happily. His future was inextricably tied to the future of his people. And they needed food in the winter, education for the future, and modern plumbing right now. That all required money which Aaron was offering. Right now.

"Five thousand pounds," Aaron pressed. "What could you do with that coin?"

A great deal. Liam found his hands clenching as if to hold on to the very idea. Liam tried to keep his expression flat, but Aaron was no fool. He understood better than many the pressures of a lord who paid attention to his responsibilities.

"Five thousand pounds," the man repeated. "You can have that without constantly having to negotiate with Clara. You know how unreasonable she can be, how demanding and pricklish about the oddest things. I love her to distraction, and that is exactly where I have been with her year after year: tearing out my hair because she is completely unmanageable. That is not the future you want."

No, it wasn't. Certainly not how he described it. "For a loving brother, you take a very dim view of your sister."

"Am I wrong?"

Looking now at Aaron's honest face, Liam certainly remembered every single frustrating moment he'd had with Clara. She was not one to try new foods easily, and he'd had to coax her to taste common Scottish dishes. She became impossible when absorbed in one of her hobbies. She'd once talked for hours about African animals and how they differed from English creatures. Plus, small things could upset her for days. Back in London, she'd discovered that registry offices often exploited their ignorant customers. She'd learned it from Lilah, of course, but her outrage had lasted well beyond when a typical person would have moved on.

By all reason, he should leap at Aaron's offer. He thought about the most irritating aspects of Clara's personality and extended those moments into the years of his life. Horrible! She didn't even like haggis.

"No."

"Then—"

"No, I will not throw her over. No, I will not release her back into your indifferent care."

"Indifferent!"

"She is mine, my lord. As is her dowry. Do not ask me again or I will be forced to toss you unceremoniously from my land. And my lady wife would not like that."

Aaron folded his arms and sighed. "You love her. Or you think you do." His tone made it sound like he'd just been bitten by a poisonous snake. Which was an odd sentiment from a man who professed to be blissfully in love with Miss Rees.

Nevertheless, the words gave Liam pause. Among Scotsmen,

he was considered a thoughtful man who planned, but all Scotsman had a passion that burned through their blood. His father's was fucking, no better way to say it. If it settled the fire in his loins, then he pursued it. Mairi's passion was for organizing everything to her liking. The kitchen, the people, even the weather seemed to bend to her command. Perhaps that was why he had a fondness for Clara. Her passion for learning often controlled her, but without purpose, her passion would burn uselessly to the detriment of everyone. Like his father's did.

Liam's one failing was that he had no passion and no purpose beyond what he had set for himself at a very young age. He meant to see his people prosper. And to that end, he had gone to school, made influential friends, and spent many nights ferreting out the best way to bring education to this remote corner of Scotland. With education came ideas, and good ideas made money. Plus, it gave everyone something else to do beyond rutting or fighting.

A woman who genuinely enjoyed learning would, of course, be attractive to him. Make her an heiress, and he had spent the better part of a year in pursuit of her. To attach an emotion such as love or even passion to that pursuit was beside the point. He wanted her. He caught her. And now, he needed to use her to bring about the future he'd planned for since the day—at seven years old—that he'd seen the body of a child who'd died of starvation.

"Call it love if you want," he said brusquely as he shouldered his way past Aaron. "She's staying with me."

Aaron grabbed his arm. "Do you honestly think you can make her happy? That either of you can be happy?"

He would be happy if no one in the county ever died of starvation again. "Clara will be happy because I will see to it," he said. "And if you and Lilah leave."

"What?"

"She needs to accept her new life here, and she won't do it if you're constantly offering to take her away."

"I am—"

He rounded on Aaron. "Do you really want to make me—her husband—the villain in all this? She has agreed to try. You have to let her do it without constantly offering her something else." He lifted his chin. "Now do I throw you out or do you respect her and leave as she asked?"

"She didn't ask me to leave," Aaron huffed.

"A fact that makes no difference."

He could see Aaron struggle with his thoughts. The desire to protect his sister warred with the certain knowledge that this was the best future for her. A place where her educational passion would be valued, even if it was in the wilds of Scotland. At least that's what he told himself.

He knew he'd won when Aaron fell back on the most ridiculous reason to stay behind.

"I cannot travel with Miss Rees alone. We're not yet married."

"You have a maid and valet with you."

"It's not enough."

The hell it wasn't. Especially since Miss Rees was an acknowledged bastard who ran an employment registry office. Her reputation was already ruined among the elite. Traveling alone with her fiancé would do nothing to harm it one way or another.

"If you cannot think of a way around that, then you are the stupidest man alive."

CHAPTER FOURTEEN

CLARA STOOD AT the doorway into the great room and felt her stomach twist in a knot that she might once have labeled terror. And yes, this new Scottish adventure of hers was certainly terrifying. But something else was affecting her more strongly than the idea of facing an entire castle's worth of people.

Liam.

He stood before her resplendent in his kilt as it wrapped around a loose-fitting blouse. It was his full regalia as befitted the son of the Laird, but she'd seen that before. Indeed, she had accepted it as his standard attire once they'd crossed the border into Scotland. Something else about him drew her stomach into knots and heated her skin to a prickly fire.

As was her wont, rather than focus on her reaction, she decided to pick apart what was different about Liam as he joined her at the door to the great room. He appeared to stand taller than before, his shoulders seemed to broaden, and his chest was puffed up to display his full strength. He was clean shaven, which was always nice, but why did he seem to be physically larger than ever before? Especially since she'd seen him half-naked while throwing a tree across a field?

She found her answer in his first words to her.

"Are you ready, *my* Scottish lady?" His eyes twinkled as he spoke, his smile was warm, but there was a warrior feel to his body that seemed to transmit from him to her. It was all in the emphasis of the word "my." Suddenly, he owned her. Everything about her—including her nationality—had changed to be his. And he dared anyone—everyone—to defy his claim. Including her.

She ought to be outraged. She had worked too hard to become her own person to easily give it up now. But in this, she was a perverse creature. Instead of being angry, she was excited. He touched her as if she were a crystal sculpture. She felt the callouses on his fingers as he pulled her hand to rest on his forearm, and then he set his other hand a top hers to anchor her there. She could have escaped. Strong as he was, he couldn't hold her immobile if she wanted to twist away.

She didn't. He'd invited her to use her knowledge to a practical purpose, and the idea had taken hold in her heart. She held in her head the memory of Deidre's siblings. What could she do to make those children's lives better? A bath house would be nice for her. Literacy would help them. She was a firm believer in the ability to educate oneself if one knew how to read.

She had plenty of other ideas, of course. She'd thought over every aspect of the last thirty-six hours with an idea to improvements. What ideas she had! Thanks to Liam, she could implement them all. And so she took up the challenge she saw in his eyes. She lifted her chin and squared her shoulders in an echo of his stance. And she grinned when he smiled in appreciation.

"You're beautiful," he said as he gazed down at her.

She felt it. Better yet, she felt her body respond to the light in his eyes. She understood the basics of arousal, but the experience of it was still novel. She'd never expected the emotions to be this intense, never dreamed that the sight of a man would make her belly grow liquid or her nipples tighten. Her skin flushed, and she stretched up on her toes. He obliged her by leaning down, and soon their lips met. Her mouth opened, their tongues entwined, and the air around them burst into sound. Cheers, guffaws, and many lewd comments.

Absorbed as she was in his kiss, she tried to block out the sounds. But he pulled back from the kiss and turned to grin through the open doors of the great room.

When had they opened? In the middle of the kiss, obviously, but how?

She looked to the side where Mairi was gesturing two boys back to their seats. They'd opened the door, but how awkward about the timing. Her cheeks burned as the comments turned downright disgusting. She started to withdraw, but Liam held her hand tight.

"Steady," he said under his breath.

"And here he is!" crowed the MacCleal from the head of the table. "Raise your drinks to my son who has made us all rich by plowing the Sassenach!"

Several people screamed, "The Sassenach bitch," in response. Others just drank to being rich. Clara looked around, shocked into immobility by the crudeness of it all. She'd never been called a bitch in her life, much less any of the other things they said. And here everyone was saying it as if it were a lovely thing.

"Don't listen," Liam said in her ear.

She could hardly stop her ears. And even if she did, the gestures alone would make their words clear. Fortunately, she had something else to focus on as Liam's father came forward with outstretched arms. Beside her, Liam stiffened, but she understood her duty. The laird wanted to greet her, so she gently disentangled herself from Liam and dropped into a curtsey.

A roar of approval went up from everyone in the room. Just how much had they already drunk this day? And then when she stood up, Liam's father embraced her. He wasn't as large as his son, but he had bulk in his belly and his arms that he used to great advantage. She was quickly smothered beneath him and then shocked as his hands roamed down her back to cup her arse with a full grip.

She squeaked in alarm, but the man held her firmly as he pressed himself against her. She was surrounded by his bulk, his smell, and his… Oh damn. His cock pressed against her belly. She tried to wriggle free. She tried to position her knee, but he was too big and—

He released her. She stumbled backwards while the crowd roared in delight. She turned instinctively toward the door, planning to run back to England as fast as she could. Instead, she ran straight into Liam who had a grip on his father's wrist as he bent the man's hand at an uncomfortable angle. No one but her could see this. Her body blocked their line of sight. And she heard true violence in Liam's voice as he spoke in an undertone.

"Touch my wife again, and I will kill you. Make no mistake." His brogue was at full strength and Clara shivered at the menace in his tone.

"If you cannot be a man wi' her, then I'll—aieeeee!"

Caught between the two men, she heard the full agony in the Laird's cry, but she had no time to react as the MacCleal stepped back. Or maybe he'd been thrown back. She was too busy trying to regain her balance. Liam steadied her with one hand, but his eyes were hard on his father's who held his right hand cradled against his belly.

"You dare—" the MacCleal began, but Liam cut him off.

"A hunt!" Liam bellowed as he turned to the crowd. "The Laird has declared a hunt in honor of my new bride!"

The reaction was immediate. Men throughout the Great Room banged their fists on the table as they cheered. Liam had to wait until the roar died down to be heard over them.

"Let the Laird and his men prove their mettle to the new MacCleal lady!" He pointed to six men in the crowd, naming them loudly as they stood with pride. "You are the great hunters here, the ones who are honored to be spared from the daily toil of the keep."

"Laird!" each bellowed as he stood.

"Bring us game for the table. A great stag—"

"Wolves!" cried a young man from the back. "Kill the wolves that menace our sheep!"

"Aye!" others responded. "Kill the wolves!"

Soon the whole place was cheering. Good lord, there were a

lot of people here. Clara distracted herself from the whole thing by counting the throng. She thought thirty-five at most, but then the little ones were hiding or running about, so it was hard to tell. Either way, they made a great lot of noise.

"A hunt is for a younger man," the Laird said. And one with a leaner waist. Clara doubted this man had been away from his bed in a decade.

Liam's brows rose. "Do you retire your sword then?" he asked sotto voice, but not so quiet that the nearest men couldn't hear. Indeed, they were the very ones who had stood up a moment ago. Barrel-chested with arms as thick as their beards, they were of an age with the laird and would not take well to being put to pasture. "Do we cancel the hunt?" Liam asked. "I must remain here to collect my wife's dowry."

Everyone saw the wisdom of that. They needed her coin in their hands, and if that required Liam at home, then they would bar the door to him if he tried to leave. But a hunt was clearly an exciting thing. A needful thing too if their sheep were menaced by wolves.

"You want to stay laird?" Liam challenged, this time quiet enough that only she and his father could hear. "You'll need to prove your worth at something other than drinking and rutting with a willing woman."

His father turned to him, his expression hardening. And as he glared at his son, the great hall slowly grew quiet. In the end, the MacCleal spoke four words.

"I am laird here."

In response, Liam smiled. "Do you remember the warning I gave you ten years ago when I left for England?"

All around them, people drew breath. Some in a gasp, others in a slow shudder. Clara was the only one to be entirely clueless on what had transpired between father and son.

The MacCleal curled his lip in scorn. "You were a boy, wet behind the ears, that I could best with one hand.

"Maybe. Maybe not." Obviously, Liam wasn't giving his

father any quarter. "But I told you then that I would return here with money and a plan." He looked around at those gathered. "I have both now—"

"A woman ain't a plan, boy," his father said.

"This woman has the plans," Liam countered as he smiled at Clara.

A shock went through her body as she began to see the magnitude of what she had just agreed to do. He was putting all his faith in her ability to do what? Feed and educate his people? Turn poverty into sustainable wealth? He couldn't be serious, and yet the challenge in his eyes told her he was.

"I told you then," Liam continued, "that you would have to prove your worth to the clan or step aside."

"I'm not—"

"Think carefully, Father. Every MacCleal works for his bread." The challenge was clear as was the implication that Liam's father did nothing for his own people. Clara could see a few of the younger faces were on Liam's side. They clearly resented shouldering the burden while the elders grew fat and lazy. "Why not go hunt a wolf with your cronies?" Liam pressed.

"And leave you to the running of the clan?" The MacCleal snorted. "The castle thrives because I set it that way. Once the rock is set upon the hill, even a lackwit can keep it here."

"It's summer," Liam challenged. "Food is everywhere, and the grass is soft. Do you say you canna hunt a wolf who menaces our sheep? That the heath is too cruel for your old bones?"

"Summer is for boys to learn."

"Then take them! Teach them!" Liam folded his arms. "Show them how to be men of Scotland."

Mothers and boys cheered that statement. The boys because they wanted to leave, the women because they had plenty of work without the youth underfoot. And worse, the Laird's men also cheered. It was something they wanted to do. Which meant the MacCleal was caught.

Typically, he made a show of it. He planted his fists upon his hips and strode forward. "We go hunt!" he bellowed as if it were his own idea. Everyone cheered, and the man grinned. "And when we return with meat for all, I will show my son his place."

There was a whole lot of commotion then as plans were made. Liam led her to the head table where he held the chair for her, then sat down beside her. Mairi brought them food with a dark look. "You should have warned me of your plans," she said as she thumped down a pitcher in front of Liam. "The women and I are run ragged for your fair day, and now we're packing them up? We're run off our feet, already."

Liam frowned as he looked over the room. When he spoke, his tone wasn't exactly loud, but it could be heard if one cared to listen. "Are the MacCleal men cripples then that they canna pack up their own gear?"

"Can and will are two different things," Mairi groused. "You know it's the women who—"

"Coddle their men? Everyone works in this castle. Every single soul or I'll hear why they're a burden to the clan." Then his voice lowered. "You work more than ten women, Mairi, with more piled on every day. You've made them lazy, and I won't have you weaken us anymore."

"I weakened then?" she said, her voice rising until it squeaked. "When I have near killed myself—"

"Aye. You did their work, and now they expect it."

Her jaw dropped open and her face flushed a bright purple. And then she threw down the basket of bread as if it burned. "Verra well," she said as she glared at Clara. "I'm done. See if your Sassenach bride can do better." Then she stomped away, and not toward the kitchen. She went right out the main door, throwing it open with a hard shove of both hands.

Everyone watched her stalk out of the room, the quiet growing in her wake. Then one by one, they turned to stare not at Liam who had created the mess, but at her. She was the lady of the castle now, and with Mairi gone, she would have to see that it worked and worked well.

"What have you done?" she rasped. "I'm hopeless at running

a household!"

Underneath the table, he gripped her hand tight while he turned to her. His expression was nothing short of besotted, and his words were clear to everyone. "I promised you a free hand to do as you will here. No one to interfere with your plans, no one to naysay you but me."

She gaped at him. "I know nothing about running a castle. Mairi is the one who managed everything here." Her voice was growing stronger as outrage filled her. "You've doomed me from the start!"

"Nonsense," he said with a grin. "I've given you the challenge of your life." He looked around the room. He had everyone's attention, that's for sure. "Is what my lady said true? Is one woman—a MacAdaidh, no less—the only one who can manage here? Can the men not pack their own gear without her telling them what to do? Can the women not cook without her direction? Should we all change our names then to MacAdaidh?"

That was like pouring oil on a ready flame. The hall exploded into denials. Men and women alike were on their feet, chanting the MacCleal name as if it were the answer to their prayers. Liam grinned as he grabbed a handful of bread. He then filled his flagon with wine and lifted it to the room. There was a collective pause as everyone waited to hear his words.

"I thought not," he said. He stood up, his chair scraping loudly behind him. "We are MacCleal," he said. "And we will work until we thrive."

She did not think it could get any louder in the hall, but she was wrong. Every voice cried out, even his father's. There was clapping and stomping of feet. There was drink consumed in Liam's honor. In Clara's honor. And, of course, in the MacCleal name. It grew even louder as Liam took her hand and pulled her up to stand by his side. She smiled, of course, and tried not to look sick.

"I hope you enjoy that bread," she said in an undertone. "God knows, it's the last decent food you're going to get with me in the kitchen."

CHAPTER FIFTEEN

"**A**RE YOU INSANE?"

Liam turned to hear Aaron's low growl. He'd been standing with Clara at the top of the Great Room while people finished their meals and headed to work. It was late in the day for that, but there was a great deal to do before the men left on their hunt. His father had made a great show of pulling the men and boys away. After Mairi stomped out, several of the women had followed. That left his brother-in-law, Miss Rees, and a small contingent of Aberbeag men including Connall who watched everything with amused eyes. It was always fun to see a rival clan descend into chaos.

Meanwhile, Aaron and Miss Rees lost no time in expressing their concerns.

"You've made a right mess of it!" Aaron continued.

"Yes, he's touched in the head," Clara agreed grimly. "I've never been good at running things."

"Not true," Liam answered. "You've never tried."

She rounded on him with her mouth agape, but he cut her off before she could start shouting at him.

"You left the running of the house to your servants and barely put any thought into who you hired." He arched a brow at her. "Clara, if you can learn advanced mathematics, you can learn to run a home."

"This is a castle," she snapped.

"It's *our* home," he retorted, using the emphasis to remind her that she was in this with him no matter what.

He could see the skepticism on Clara's face. Worse, he saw Lilah snort in disgust. She was the one with the knack for running a household and if she thought he was doomed, then he became very concerned. Especially as the lady spoke up. She was kind with her words, but he heard the message nonetheless.

"You must make amends with Mairi," she said. "She's the one who knows what must be done. Convince her to come back."

"Absolutely not." Liam spoke forcefully. "Clara, you'll never make your mark here as long as she's around to countermand your orders."

"But she could help—" Miss Rees pressed.

"And then whatever happens will be her doing, not Clara's." He brought Clara's limp hand up to his lips and pressed a kiss there. "You know how to do this. You figure out the system, then improve it."

She shook her head. "I… It's too much. I can't—"

He arched his brows. "Never did I think to hear you say that you wouldn't even try." He smiled reassuringly up at her. "I'll help. Whatever you want."

Clara swallowed. "No. Lilah can show me—"

"Lilah cannot. She and Aaron are leaving today."

"What?" Clara jerked her hand back. "They won't abandon me!"

The terror on her face was real, as was the shock on Miss Rees' face and the chagrin on Aaron's. But at least her brother seemed to understand why.

"We can help you get started. We'll stay a few days, but he's right. If you're to make a go of this…" He shot a hard look at Liam. "You need to start as you mean to go on."

"You can't stay," Liam interrupted. "You're English."

"So is she!" Aaron shot back.

"No, she's the new wife of the MacCleal heir," Miss Rees said sadly, showing that she understood the way hatred showed up.

"If Lord Loughton makes a great show of backing whatever she does, then they won't go against him. But if we stay, we're emphasizing that she's a foreigner."

Aaron shook his head. "We could draw their wrath away from her."

"That never works," Miss Rees said.

Liam agreed. It would only give his people two more people to complain about. "Clara, they have to go. You have to stand on your own or it won't work." He turned her away from her family to look him in her eye. "You threw in your lot with me. Don't lose faith now before you've even begun."

That was the crux of his wager. Make or break—the two of them together—with his clan's survival at stake.

"I will handle the glass and whisky. All you need do is—"

"Make a castle livable and educate the children."

"Yes," he said with a smile. "Preferably before my father comes back from his hunt."

Her mouth dropped open on a gasp, but he was quick to speak over whatever objection she had.

"We just have to keep it from falling apart. That's what my father wants. He'll take every healthy man and boy away from here because he thinks that women can do nothing without him."

Clara and Lilah both snorted at that assertion.

"Excellent," he said. "Now prove him wrong."

Lilah squeezed Clara's arm. "If anyone can do it, you can. You will."

Clara did not look so sure. Indeed, she looked downright terrified, but he would not let her fail out of fear.

"I will help you."

"You can't," Aaron said darkly. "It'll never work without the coin. And that you have to get in person."

"No!" Clara cried, but he shook his head.

"Your brother can make the necessary arrangements first. I'll follow later. It won't be but a day gone and back to get the coin."

"And murdered by highwaymen on the way, no doubt,"

Clara said with a grimace. "And if that happens, then I'll leave every single one of your people to rot. I'll walk back to London if I have to."

He smiled. "It's a deal. If I am killed by highwaymen, you may walk back to London with my blessing. I'll even suggest you take a horse."

She sighed, but he could see his joke worked. She wasn't panicked anymore. Merely resigned. "I don't even know where to start," she said.

"By writing a letter to your friend, the engineer with grand ideas about plumbing."

"Mr. Russell? Yes, all right. And Juliet Adams. She loves children, even the reprobates, and would make a great teacher." She dropped his hands and took a deep breath. "I'm going to offer them a lot of money to come. A really, really big lot."

He pressed a kiss to her nose. "It's your money to spend. Mairi will show you where the paper—" He cut off his words. Mairi was gone. Fortunately, Lilah was still here.

"I saw some. Come on, Clara. Let's start by making a list."

The women started to move away, but Aaron held his fiancé back for a moment. "This is madness," he said, "but I'll help for my sister's sake."

"Thank you."

"And one other thing. Just to keep to propriety's sake." He looked at his fiancé. "I, Aaron, Lord Chamber, do state publicly, that I love Lilah Rees to distraction and have therefore married her right here, right now. We are married, yes?"

Lilah's eyes widened and her cheeks flushed pink. "Have you gone native then?" she asked. "We're doing this the Scottish way?"

"If that's what it takes to get you into my bed on the ride home, then yes, it is. We can have a proper wedding as planned, but—"

"Yes, my lord," she said. "We're married."

"And I witness," Liam said, pleased beyond measure that

these two had found happiness.

"Well," Clara said, "it seems there is some good come from your Scottish customs after all. I witness it, too." Then she kissed her brother and embraced her new sister-in-law. Happiness surrounded the new couple, and Liam took a moment to bask in the moment. But it was all he had as Connall and his men got to their feet with a whole lot of bluster and noise. They were about to leave, and Liam had some things to say first.

"Go get started," he said to Clara before he gestured at Connall. "I'll find you as soon as I can set things to right here."

Aaron snorted. "Then I'll see you in five years at the earliest."

"Done."

"What?"

"A bet, brother-in-law. Five years to see a complete change here."

Aaron frowned, his expression sour. "I just want my sister happy."

"That, too. A case of fine Scottish whisky if I'm wrong."

Aaron nodded. "Against a case of brandy."

"French brandy? Och, you English can't even make a good spirit."

"We make good women," the man returned as he fell in step with the women.

"I canna argue that," Liam said.

"I can," Connall said as he made it to Liam's side. "You're a fool to throw over Mairi for that one, heiress or not."

Liam turned. "Mairi's a right fine woman," he said. "And if you see her worth, then why haven't you put a ring on her finger?"

"Because it's always been aimed at you."

He shrugged. "Not anymore." He looked at his oldest friend. They had been best friends and rivals from the day the bawling brat had been born. Liam was older by a year and, by all accounts, had been unimpressed when they'd first met. And though Liam had looked beyond Scotland for answers to his problems, Connall's faith had always been right here in their homeland. Liam respected the choice, even if he disagreed, and there wasn't a finer woman than Mairi. "I suggest you get courting afore she turns her head elsewhere."

Connall laughed. "When I need your advice on women, I'll have my head examined." Then he sobered. "Truth, Liam, but you've cocked it up for sure. There's no way that lanky Sassenach can set this place to rights." He looked around. "Not with all the men gone and the women set against her."

"Be damned to the lot of ye," he said, abruptly losing his patience. "Not a one of you can see the use of a woman beyond your cock, and that's a right shame."

"It's not the woman that's the fault. It's the English in 'em," Connall said.

"Done. Your copper against my whisky, that she'll outshine us all. Give me one year."

Connall grinned. There was nothing the man liked more than a good wager. "Done." Then he chuckled. "I hope she swives like a goddess because you'll not have your whisky to console you when it's done."

"And I pray that a pesky Sassenach turns your brain inside out." That was, after all, exactly what had happened to him.

Connall and his men had a good laugh at that. They took their leave soon afterwards. Proper manners required the man to voice his thanks to Clara, but Liam knew that was best forgotten. Whereas his own clan had gladhanded with the English for survival, Connall's people had fought bravely at Culloden and died. He'd been reared on a hatred of the English much darker than anything Liam had known, and so his prejudice ran deep. It was best if Connall and Clara never met until she'd proved her worth.

And now the hall was empty except for him. Even the dogs were gone and the mess that remained would bring vermin and stench. He had a mile-long list in his head about what changes he wanted to enact here. None of them included cleaning up the dining hall. But a man started with what was in front of him, and so he rolled up his sleeves and began to scrub.

CHAPTER SIXTEEN

CLARA DIDN'T WANT her family to leave, but she understood the reason they had to go.

Aaron was equally torn. "I want to protect you," he said as he pressed a kissed to her forehead. "But the sooner I get to Edinburgh, the sooner I can get you the coin you need. It will buy you good will—"

"At least for a while," Lilah said as she looked up from the list she was making. "Plus take my dresses and give them away. There must be a seamstress here."

"I wouldn't go changing things too soon," Aaron continued. "Learn how things are going and change one thing. Just one."

"You have to keep everyone fed. The kitchen is most important."

"And hide your coin someplace safe."

"Carry it with you."

"In a lockbox in the wardrobe."

"Lord Loughton ought to carry it. They won't attack him."

"He can't take everything!"

The two continued to bicker while Clara dropped onto Lilah's bed and set her head into her hands. This was never going to work. She could never do this. Not without them. Her mother was right. She was terrible as a housekeeper. Horrid when it came to managing people. And was, in truth, completely hopeless as a woman.

She was so steeped in self-pity that she didn't realize that the room had gone silent until Lilah wrapped her arms around her shoulders.

"This is hard," her brother said as he set his hand on the top of her head. "I want to fix it for you."

Lilah squeezed her tight. "Maybe we can—"

"No." One word and it was hard to get out. She didn't want to face her future. Her hands itched to grab the nearest book and drop herself straight inside the words. Nothing upset her there. But that was the reaction of a child. She was an adult and, apparently, a married woman. Which meant she had to take the reins, create her future, and…and…do the damn work. "I'll never get it done if you're here to coddle me."

"We're not coddling," Lilah said. "We're helping." So saying she handed Clara a list of things to do when setting up a household. Good God, there were a hundred tasks written in tight letters. She didn't even know what some of them meant. She'd never heard of a spit-boy, ewerer, or gong farmer. "How do you know about all this?"

"You know my sister Gwen had a great many passions growing up. We spent at least a month pretending to be princesses trapped in a castle. She learned all sorts of bizarre things about it."

"Then you should be the one here, not me."

Lilah had no response to that, except to squeeze her tighter. "Write me with any questions. There must be some sort of post around here."

"I wouldn't count on it," Aaron said grimly as he held up Clara's letters to Mr. Russell and Miss Adams. "I'll post these for you in Edinburgh."

Both ladies looked at him with equal expression of horror. The idea that she couldn't get regular posts left her shaking.

"But you won't need it," he hastened to add. "Think of it as one of your projects. Throw yourself into it. You'll be fine."

He didn't sound certain of that at all, but Clara knew better than to press for the truth. Aaron was the one soul in her life who had always allowed her to try things and fail with no recriminations. She straightened up and looked grimly out the window. It was already mid-afternoon.

"If I'm to have any kind of dinner for people, then I'd best get to the kitchen."

"Maybe I can stay—" Lilah began, but Clara was done with all this dithering.

"You need to head to Edinburgh while there's still light." Then she leaned down and picked up her favorite dress. It was comfortable with soft fabric and a minimal amount of decoration. And it was the best gown she could give Deirdre to replace the one that had been shredded last night. "I'll try to send up a footman..." She hadn't the first idea where anyone was. Fortunately, Aaron had it well in hand.

"I'll take care of it. You've only got a few hours left to learn how to bake meatpies."

She nodded. "They must be very easy, right? Meat, dough, and an oven."

Lilah opened her mouth, probably to give cooking instructions, but in the end, she just pasted on a bright grin and said, "You'll figure it out. And Lord Loughton will help."

"Of course, he will," Aaron agreed. Then they both shooed her out the door as Lilah finished packing.

Clara heard them speaking in low tones to each other as she left. She didn't try to make out the words. It was hard enough to stop her tears.

She had only a vague idea where the kitchen was. It had to be off the great hall, right? She made it down there to find that someone had cleaned the tables and set the room to rights. That had been a great deal of work for someone. She'd have to find out who and thank them.

She found the kitchen sure enough, but there was no one inside. Not a soul except for a small boy tending the fire.

"Hello—" she said, but the child took one look at her and dashed away. "Wait!"

He didn't. So without any other idea, she scrambled after him. If she couldn't catch him, he'd surely lead her to other people. Or so she hoped. It was awkward rushing along the twisting, cluttered corridors while carrying the gown for Deirdre, but she managed as best she could.

Fairly soon, Clara realized she'd travelled into an older part of the castle. A second keep with rough stones, tight corners, and—hallelujah—the sound of people speaking. Girls, by the sound of it, laughing as they scolded the boy.

"Davie! What's got into you?"

"Who's tending the fire?"

Clara knew that voice. It was Deirdre, the very girl she'd been looking for. "No one, I'm afraid," she said as she tried to make a friendly entrance. Unfortunately, she stubbed her toe on something and stumbled into the room.

"Bugger," she cursed, as she twisted around. "Damned stupid place to put a... a..." She frowned as she realized that she'd tripped over an uneven stone in the path. "Someone made a mistake there," she said as she looked at the architecture. The problem was where the old stonework met up to the newer. None of the stones fit correctly, and the result was a hazard to anyone who crossed the threshold. "As if they couldn't be bothered to cut the set the things properly."

There was no condemnation in her tone. She found it an oddity, nothing more, but when she turned to the girls, they looked like they were going to burst with outrage.

"Oh dear. I'm terribly sorry. I didn't mean to insult..." Her words faded away as the two girls covered their mouths as they tried to hold in their laughter.

Not outrage, then.

Careful of her steps, she set the gown on a nearby chair and then turned to the girls. "Go ahead and laugh. It will serve you well in the coming days. And tell me what I said that was so funny?"

"Nothing, my lady," Deirdre said with a rushed curtsey.

"Nothing at all," said the other one.

"Now none of that. I mean to hear the truth of my ridiculousness. Out with it." She turned to Deirdre who she'd tried to befriend yesterday. "Please."

The girl blushed. "That's exactly what Mrs. Owen used to say. Every day. It made us giggle, is all."

The other girl nodded as she lowered her very big brown eyes.

"Ah, well, it's a remarkably intelligent comment, I would think." Then she took a look around. This was obviously the old kitchen, used by the less important workers in the castle. Better yet, she could smell the scent of bread baking and, if she didn't miss her guess, there was stew in a huge pot over the fire. These two girls were making food! Or rather, the second one was. Deirdre, she now saw, was working on a gown. A young seamstress, then. Better and better!

"Do you have a gown for me to fix, my lady?" Deirdre asked.

"What? Oh, no. This gown is for you. To replace what was destroyed last night." She pointed to where she'd dumped the thing on a chair. She really had to start being neater with clothing. "I know it won't fit now, but you're a seamstress, yes? You can fix it."

"Oh no, my lady. Nothing so fancy as that. I just sew things when things are needed."

"Well, that's a seamstress, Deirdre. And this is yours now." Then she turned to the other girl. "And what's your name?"

"Rhona, my lady."

"And you must be the baker, yes? That's bread I smell?"

"Aye, my lady, but it's rough bread. Not at all fit for your table."

Clara snorted. "I've had black bread before, and it's plenty fine for me." She looked around. "Where is everybody?"

The girls exchanged a look, but it was left to Rhona to answer as Deirdre was busy stroking the fabric of her new gown.

"They've gone to send off the men."

"Of course. But they'll be back this evening to make supper?"

"Er, no my lady. Most'll go back to their homes. Fair day was a lot of work, and most just want to rest afterwards."

That made sense. "They'll be back in the morning, then?"

"Not likely, mum," Deirdre said, her voice low. "They won't get paid this eve with Mairi gone. And they'll not come back without coin."

"I see." She would have to find the castle lockbox and sort out who got what. She hoped Mairi kept good records. "So why haven't you two gone?"

Deirdre gathered the gown into neat folds then set it in the corner atop what looked like thin bedding. She looked up with a guilty shrug. "We sleep here," she said.

"It's warm," added Rhona, "and we share the work."

And probably safer given that they were two girls just growing into their looks. "Well, I am very pleased to meet you." She peered into the bubbling cauldron. "Is that enough to feed everyone who will be here tonight?"

"Maybe…" Rhona said. "But we haven't enough bread for everyone."

"Then I guess we'll have to make more."

"Yes, my lady," both girls said together, but neither did anything more than that. Nothing but stare at her as she pulled on an apron that was hanging on a peg.

"Well?" Clara said as she turned back. "Come on, how do you cook bread?"

It was a simple question, but they both gaped at her.

"I know I'm an idiot because I haven't learned how to do that. I think even my mother knew how, though she hated going into the kitchen. But we've no choice now. I've got to learn how everything works here, and this sounds like a good place to start."

"Uhm…" Rhona began. "I…"

"Start at the very beginning. Assume I know nothing. In fact, pretend I'm Davie and I want to learn how to cook." She smiled. "In fact, for right now, refer to me as Davie."

Well, that broke the ice. Both women giggled at the idea of the boy trying his hand in here. Clara grinned. "That's better. Now let me help you. Say, Well, Davie, the first thing we do is…"

Rhona looked exquisitely uncomfortable, but she dutifully responded. "Well, my lady Davie, the first thing…"

And so began the most exhausting afternoon of Clara's life. It wasn't just the pounding, kneading, and unfortunate burning. Clara was determined to understand the way everything worked in the castle, and the two girls had a wealth of information on who did what and why. But it was so much information! And as clever as Clara was, she couldn't understand it all. Not at once, and not while trying to pull bread out of a hot oven. Which is why, when evening came, Clara was a frazzled mess. And Liam looked even worse when he finally found her well past time for the evening meal.

CHAPTER SEVENTEEN

LIAM PULLED UP short, barely missing the trip stone as he entered the old kitchen. He wasn't surprised when Clara hadn't appeared to wave the hunting party off. With all the people gathered or going, it felt like a second fair day. Especially since his father had taken most of the food as provisions for his excursion. Clara had endured more than enough people yesterday. He expected her to be in his bedroom writing lists of things to do. Or hiding in a book because the task was too overwhelming.

But she wasn't.

It was a surprise to him when he discovered Miss Rees' room bare of luggage. And with Aaron equally absent, he feared that Clara had changed her mind and left while he was occupied with his father.

Which meant he tore about the empty castle looking in every corner for his bride while his gut clenched in fear. Without her money and her education, all his plans were for naught. He'd almost given up when he heard giggles coming from the old part of the castle. Finally! Someone who might know what had happened. He rushed there only to find his bride covered in foodstuffs with her hair askew and a fierce scowl on her face as she pounded her fists into dough.

She'd never looked more adorable.

"I do hope you're not imagining anyone I know," he drawled

as he watched her punch with an awkward fist.

She looked up with a start then grinned. "I am actually. It's quite fun."

"Then, I hope it's not me," he drawled.

She frowned at him. "You look quite done up. Would you like some dinner?"

He straightened in surprise. "There's food?"

"Of course!" She sounded very proud of herself for that. "People have been coming in for stew and bread. I've been meeting them." As if on cue, a boy too young to be part of the hunting party slipped inside. He sidled over to the table where hot loaves of bread were cooling. "Davie!" she said with a smile. "Are you here for a third helping?"

The little boy looked up with huge eyes. His belly was distended from all he'd already eaten, but he still tried to stretch his hand up for another loaf of bread.

"Ack," said a young woman as she waved her apron at him. "You've had plenty—" she began but Clara stopped her.

"He can eat if he's hungry," Clara said. "We have enough, don't we?"

"There's enough with the new bread," said one of the two young women.

"But he's not hungry," said the other. "He's giving it to them that are too cowardly to face you."

Clara straightened up from the dough with a frown. "Do I really look that frightful?"

Trust Clara to look for the fault in herself before considering that his people were rude. "You look wonderful," he said. Then he squatted down in front of Davie. "How brave you are to face the scary lady!" He tweaked the boy's nose to make him smile. "Will you tell the others that there's plenty of food, but they have to be as brave as you. They have to show themselves."

The boy nodded and scampered off while the two young women exchanged looks that meant…something. He had no idea what and was too tired to it figure out. Now that relief at seeing

Clara was washing through him, he felt every knot in his body begin to ache. He pulled out a stool and sat while Clara made a happy show of serving him a bowl of stew. It was hearty Scottish fare, and he tucked into it with relish. And he enjoyed the sight of Clara accidentally brushing flour across her temple and into her hair.

"Tell me what you've been doing today," he said. "Other than making bread."

"Well, that's enough, don't you think? It's an exhausting process." She punched a small fist into the dough.

"I'll finish it, my lady. Have some dinner."

Clara held up a finger. "No, no! I'm Davie right now. I still have questions."

"Davie?" Liam asked. "Is that an English expression?"

"It should be. It means I know nothing right now, which means I can ask every question I want even if they're stupid."

She could ask any question she wanted anyway, but he could see that the two young women were playing along with good cheer. That meant something. Indeed, given that the castle was virtually devoid of servants, it meant a lot that Clara could charm these two.

"Well then, Davie," Liam said. "Sit down and tell me about your day."

Clara pulled out another stool and sat down with an audible sigh. "Thank you, Rhona," she said as the girl began to knead the dough. "Rhona, Deirdre, and I have become good friends," she said as she accepted a bowl of stew. "They've been telling me all about how things work here. I'm learning how to cook, then tomorrow, Deirdre is going to teach me how to sew."

His brows rose. "That's quite a lot for two days."

"I am told I'm quite clever."

Of course, she was, but sewing and baking were not her tasks. "Perhaps your time would be better spent becoming the lady of the castle. I thought you wanted to start a school. A...a Davie could not do that."

"How would you know what it takes to start a school?" she asked, her voice tart. "Have you ever thought on it?"

"In fact, I have. And not once did I imagine it involved learning how to make bread."

"That depends on the school. Cooking is an important skill."

"But the MacCleals already know how to do that. Clara, I brought you here to teach us things we don't know. Not to learn the things we already do."

She lowered her spoon slowly, her eyes narrowing as she looked at him. He hated to see her expression darken, especially since she'd been so happy a moment before. But she had to understand her place here, and it wasn't working as an apprentice baker.

"You said I could do as I wanted. You said I could spend my half of the dowry doing as I saw fit." She spoke slowly, but he could hear the anger growing underneath. So could the two girls as they curtsied and slipped away.

"This isn't spending money on improvements." He brushed at a smear of dough on her forearm. "This is playing at being a peasant."

"I'm playacting now?" She thrust her chin out in stubborn display.

"Don't look so offended. We both know several women who run around pretending to be shepherds like Mary with her little lambs." He grabbed his empty bowl and added it to the pile of dirty dishes. "You once called them silly creatures with empty heads."

"Yes, I did." She straightened up to face him nose to chin. "I cannot believe you think I'm doing the same thing."

"Aren't you?" He tried to reach for her, but she jerked backward. "Whyever would you need to know how to bake? Every woman here knows how."

"Because every woman here knows how. It is not helpful if I can't do—"

He cut her off. "There are hundreds of things the women

here can do that you will never master. They won't accept you just because you try." He shook his head. "Indeed, they'll gossip about how bad you are at it."

She didn't say anything, and he thought for a moment that he had hurt her. No one liked to be wrong, least of all a woman as clever as Clara. But she needed to start on the right foot, and neither of them had time to waste.

Still, he felt bad for the pain he'd caused her. "Clara—" he began, but she cut him off.

"You want me to come in as a lady and order everyone around. You want me to throw money at them and demand that they follow my commands. And anyone who disobeys won't have a job. Yes?"

Yes! "You need not be mean about it."

"I won't be," she said firmly. "Because that is not how I intend to go on."

He blew out a breath. "Clara, I'm trying to help."

"You're trying to tell me what to do. You want me to be just like my mother." She shoved him in the chest hard enough that he took an involuntary step backwards. "If you had wanted that, you should have married her."

"I've upset you."

"Go away, Liam, before I throw the crockery at you."

"What are you going to do now?"

"I'm going to wash the dishes! That is the next thing that a scullery maid does."

Of all the infernally stupid ideas. "You're not a scullery maid!"

"I am the lady of the castle—"

"Yes!"

"Then I shall do as I please."

He was tired. It had been a frustrating day. He saw now just how little respect he had here at home when he had spent every waking moment trying to find a way to make their lives better. The last person he thought he'd have to fight today was Clara. And certainly not about crockery!

He caught her arm and pulled her around to face him. "Clara, listen to me. This is not the way things are done."

She arched her brows. "So you know the way things are done, then?"

"Yes!"

"You know how to wash dishes or bake bread? You know who sews what and why?" She jerked backwards from him. "You understand how people are paid to do their work? Who is the gong farmer here and how is he chosen? Better yet, how often is he needed?"

He gaped at her. "Clara, make sense."

"I am! I am learning the systems that are in place, from the lowest task to the highest. If I haven't done it, then I don't understand it, do I?"

"You're not going to muck out the latrine as a gong farmer!"

She shrugged. "Maybe not, but I've been learning a great deal about how it's done while I've been baking bread." She dropped her hands on her hips. "Do you know that Deirdre has an excellent memory for numbers. Must be how she remembers all those stitches. But she also knows what everyone is paid."

"She couldn't. She's not—"

"Old enough? The chatelaine? Believe me, the quiet ones hear everything." Then she turned him away. "And those with a good head remember it."

He watched as she dragged out a washtub filled with brackish water. She groaned as she moved it. He rushed around the center table to help her, but by the time he got there, she already had it where she wanted. Then she squatted down just as if she worked in the laundry and began washing the bowls one by one. The sight horrified him. She was a noblewoman, educated and brilliant. To see her thus was to waste her talents, and yet he could see the stubborn jut to her chin and the tight hunch of her shoulders.

"This is madness," he said.

She shrugged. "I have been called worse."

What could he say to that? She was determined in her course, and he…well he was starting to respect that she had thought things through. At least better than he had. Which meant he had better join her since he sure as hell couldn't fight her. She was too determined.

He grabbed a bowl and began to wash it.

"What are you doing?"

He smiled at her. "What does it look like? I'm joining your madness. Now tell me. What did you learn from Rhona and Deirdre?"

She looked at him for a long moment. And though he was acutely aware of her inspection, he kept his head down as he continued to wash dishes. And then he smiled when she began to talk.

"It really was quite interesting," she said, her voice tentative.

"I'm listening," he said. And he was.

CHAPTER EIGHTEEN

CLARA HAD ALWAYS talked through her problems. At first, she'd spoken to her dolls. Later, she worked on paper using steps and arrows as she thought through whatever annoyed her. The amount of coin spent on paper for her was the truest sign that her parents had loved her. Of course, she had tried to talk to people about her thoughts, but Aaron had little time or patience for her tortured ramblings, and her parents had even less. So she had learned to mumble to herself or write it all out.

Until Liam had said he was listening. While they cleaned the kitchen together, she talked through what she'd discovered. He said little at first, but soon he added to the conversation. And his thoughts were on point, which made him the rarest of creatures—one who listened and could think. It made sense. He'd grown up here and knew the general workings of his castle home. The people had changed over the years, but the systems by which everyone functioned remained the same.

Or so he said. Rhona and Diedre agreed when they returned to help clean. And before long, Clara had a good idea of how each day passed in a general sense. She guessed it would take several weeks more to understand the details, but the basics were clear. She hoped.

By the time the kitchen was clean and the last loaves of bread set out to cool, she ached from head to toe. She desperately wanted a bath, but would never require anyone to fill a tub for her. Which meant—

"I can take you to a place to bathe," Liam said. "The water is cool, but it's a warm night. And you'll be safe with me."

"Bathe in a stream? Outside?" Certainly, she had done such a thing before the masquerade, but that had been at Beitidh's rough insistence. Plus, Clara had been fuzzy with drink. Now Liam was suggesting it as if it were appropriate. "Are you sure it is proper?" Such a thing was never done in London. And though others had done it in the countryside where she grew up, she had never been allowed. Her nanny had told her to stop imagining such a thing, much less try it. And her mother had been so scandalized by the thought that she had constantly cited Clara's desire as the purest example of why Clara would never be a true lady. "I expect you still want to bathe in the stream like a heathen," was a common refrain. So to discuss it now felt very daring indeed.

"It's a secluded place," Liam coaxed. "No one will go there but us."

Us. As in Liam and herself in the water. Naked. The thought revived her aching body enough that she pulled off her apron, but she still couldn't believe it was proper. Especially since Rhona and Deirdre kept their eyes downcast when Liam continued to coax her.

"I used to do it all the time as a boy," he said.

"But you want me to act as a lady, and I doubt—"

"Do you want to get clean, Clara? This is the best way."

She did. She'd worked hard this day. She glanced at the two girls. "How scandalous is this?"

The girls exchanged awkward glances. "No one will know, my lady," said Rhona.

"Them that would find out are all gone with the laird. And any others will be sleeping now," added Deirdre.

"That won't be true when they return," Liam said as he held out his hand. "Tonight's the night."

Whatever she thought of his words, it was the gleam in his eye that convinced her. She knew what he was thinking, indeed what she was thinking. They could do all sorts of illicit things together in the water and under the stars. She had just discovered how he made her body feel, and she could not resist the temptation of experiencing it again.

She clasped his fingers with the tips of hers, and allowed him to reel her in. Soon he was escorting her though the dark, stepping around rocks and physically lifting her over obstacles that she could not see. The night was lit with a three-quarter moon. Enough that the world seemed limed in silver. But the shadows were still thick except for the whites of his eyes and his Cheshire cat smile.

"How do you know the way? I can barely see."

"Growing up, I spent more time outside the castle than inside. I know every inch of my home."

Obviously true since he walked with confidence beneath trees and around outbuildings. "Was it a happy childhood here?" she asked.

He frowned as if that were a strange question. "As the son of a laird, I was allowed to do whatever I wanted with no one to gainsay me except my father. And my mother, of course, while she lived."

He tugged her close, slipping his arm behind her back as he supported her onto a fallen tree trunk. She walked along the top of it with him scrambling beside her on rougher terrain, and she wondered at the image of it. How often did he manage difficult things just so another could have a smooth way?

She slowed her steps as he leaped across a muddy patch. "How did you become like this?" she asked, unable to express her thoughts clearly. "Helping everyone else? Making plans for your people?" Marrying her for their benefit?

"What else would the son of a laird do?"

They made it to the far side of the muddy creek—what she had walked safely across on the tree trunk—and so she jumped down to face him on level ground. She did not mince her words. They were too unformed for her to find them delicately.

"Your father is a boor." Surely he knew that. "In my experience, sons emulate their fathers. So how are you so different from him?"

He did not shy away from the question, but neither did he speak quickly. He held her gaze and spoke with weight as if her reaction to what he was about to say meant a great deal to him. "The MacCleals were collaborators. We did not fight in Culloden. We were too small a clan to have fierce warriors or great pride. When all our neighbors were being slaughtered, my grandmother hid in a cave with a handful of others. And when the English came, my grandmother claimed this land and the title for herself and the Englishman who wanted her. My father was raised fiercely Scottish by his mother, and yet damns himself for his English blood. He wed a Scotswoman from a dead clan and birthed me. Every day I heard that only the living can revive Scotland. A dead man might be honored, but he is useless to getting the day's food. And so I grew to value staying alive."

"There is a great deal of difference between living and thriving. You…" She couldn't shape her thoughts, but he had obviously thought hard about this.

"I plan to thrive," he explained. "My father sees no more than the food in his belly and the woman plowed by his cock. That will never be enough for me."

She already knew that. He had talked often of his plans for his clan, but those weren't the essence of him and that is what she wanted to know. "What happened to make you so different from him?"

He entwined his fingers with her, speaking in a wistful way as if remembering a time long gone. "My father used to think beyond his cock. He taught me a great deal, but he began to drink when my mother died."

"When was that?"

"I was fifteen when a sickness took my mother, sister, and two younger brothers. It also killed more than half the village."

She gasped. "I'm so sorry."

His expression shuttered as he tugged her back to walking beside him. "I survived as did my father. And yet…"

"The joy has gone out of him."

I nodded. "Yes. I left because to remain here was to steep in misery. I became educated. I saw that there was more to the world than drinking and rutting. And then…"

"Yes?"

"Then I met you."

She snorted. "You made plans for your clan that required money. Then you found me."

"And courted you—"

"And tricked me—"

"And married you."

She had no retort to that. All her resentment had boiled up. For all that they were sharing a romantic moonlit stroll, she had still been tricked into her situation. Though he might not have created every detail of the experience, he was culpable for the planning. And his choice to marry her.

He must have sensed her withdrawal. When he spoke, his voice was gentle as if he were calming an angry beast. "Long before I met you," he said, "I made a list of the things I needed in a wife and the things I wanted. I needed a large dowry."

She nodded. Thanks to her status as an eccentric bluestocking, her parents had raised and raised her dowry as an inducement to overcome her oddities. It hadn't worked. She'd had suitors, but except for her first indiscretion as a teenager, she had not been tempted by any of them. Not a one until Liam.

"That is all I needed in a wife," he continued. "As to what I hoped for in a woman. I wished for someone who enjoyed music."

She frowned at him. "I am indifferent to music. I enjoy it, of course, but there are so many other ways to fill my time."

"Yes, I know. Though I do hope you will indulge me when I wish to attend a concert."

She nodded. She had enough interests of her own. She would

not prevent him from enjoying his loves.

"I wanted a woman who delights in the land. One who enjoys growing things and appreciates the storms as well as the sun."

"The weather is an annoyance to me. And though I delight in the science of things that grow, I have never found interest beyond the truth of it."

"I am aware," he said, his voice dry.

They were nearing a bubbling stream. She could hear the rush of water as he tugged her through the trees.

"I also wanted a biddable woman, one who would take my direction. She would follow my instructions and not argue over small things. That, perhaps, was my fondest wish. It was a key reason why Mairi and I never fit. She was always telling me what to do, never rested even when exhausted, and she...well, she is not a quiet person, and I wanted a restful wife."

She stopped, her mouth ajar in shock. "You thought I was a *biddable* woman? Perhaps you could be forgiven for not understanding my indifference to music and growing things. But...but..."

"Clara, you are the least biddable woman I know. Your dowry is the bare minimum of what I require. You think three times as fast as any person I've ever known and at least half your ideas are unworkable and yet you fight for them with a passion that would exhaust any normal soul."

"Of course, half are unworkable!" she all but bellowed. Damnation, how many times had she had this exact argument with her parents and Aaron? "They are ideas! I would guess ninety-five percent or more would be utter failures, but that is the point. One has to test them to discover what is feasible and what is not. If you are not willing to fail, then how do you imagine you will ever succeed at anything new or innovative? You will be doomed to repeat what your parents and grandparents and everyone else before you has ever done. And if you are not willing to think for yourself, then what good are you?"

He had one hand raised, gripping a tree branch. And as she

ranted at him, he relaxed against the tree trunk while his smile grew ever wider until she finally sputtered to a stop. Her outrage could only last so long while he relaxed there. His face was touched by silvery light, his smile was wickedly tempting, and everything about him read glorious happiness.

"Whatever are you smiling about?"

"You," he said. "That. What you've said."

"That I am not biddable? That I am willing to fail? That you understand nothing about how to try a thousand failures in order to find the one success?"

"Yes. Exactly that. It is what I want you to teach my people." He touched her face. "It is what I want in my life." His palm flattened across her cheek while his smallest finger curled under her chin, tilting her face up to his. "I found my biddable woman with a huge dowry and a love of herbs. I arranged for a meeting with her at a ball. She was even a beautiful woman who worked hard to be pleasant." He shrugged. "I hated her. I wanted you."

"Who was this woman?"

He shook his head. "It doesn't matter. It was at a ball, and instead of dancing, you were arguing with Mr. Walsh about Roman bridges. I stood nearby and listened, completely entranced. From that moment on, I had no interest in anyone else."

"Mr. Walsh? You met me with Mr. Russell when we talked about castles."

"I saw you well before then with Mr. Walsh. Specifically, when you told him he was an idiot."

She shrugged. "Well, he is."

"Undoubtably."

Her face tingled where he cupped her. But more, her belly tightened, and her chest seemed to squeeze tight in an intriguing way. His words warmed her. The idea that she had appealed to him for more than her dowry made her think he knew her as more than a bank account.

"I am nothing that you want," she finally said.

"And yet you are everything to me." He kissed her then. As

always, he was not tentative but swooped down to claim her mouth. He was ever bold in his attention to her. Yet she knew that if she withdrew, he would let her go. Such was the contradiction in him. He claimed her, then released her. He wanted her, and yet she knew he would let her have her own mind.

And nothing was more seductive to her than a man who respected her mind.

She opened her mouth to him, she let him thrust inside as he stroked every inch. The brush of his tongue spurred her to taste and duel back. She clutched his shoulders as she went up on her toes. She would have climbed his body if she could so that she could dominate him as much as he bent over her.

Then he pulled back. His eyes were dark wells of shadow, but she felt his need in the rush of his breath and the heat from his cock against her belly.

"The stream is right over there. Shall we get clean?"

"No," she said. "Let's take off our clothes and touch one another in the water."

He grinned. "Never change the way you speak, Clara."

"What?"

He bent down to her and teased his lips across hers. "Nevermind me, Clara. You have addled my wits."

No more than she'd lost hers. She rushed to unbutton her gown, but he was there before her. His fingers were clever as he undid her buttons. She fumbled with his shirt, but his kilt was easy to lift away. And then he tugged her dress down, pinning her arms to her sides. He untied her stays and pulled it away, leaving her in her lightest shift with her dress caught around her wrists and ankles.

"Trapped," he murmured with a grin.

"Hardly," she retorted. She could rip her hands free or step out of her gown. But the way he looked at her had her waiting to see what would happen. Especially as the sight of him was so delightful. The muscles in his chest rippled as he stroked his hand across her belly. The breadth of his shoulders was outlined in moonlight, but the hard thrust of his cock drew her.

She stretched her hands toward it, but she was constrained by her gown. And by the fact that he ducked away from her. "Not yet," he said. Then before she could react, he swooped forward and scooped her feet out from under her.

She gasped, then freed her wrists such that the gown dropped away. Finally, she could touch him, but he was lifting her high as he walked. He wore nothing but his boots as he carried her confidently through the brush before setting her on a large rock. Then he knelt before her to take off her shoes and stockings. His hands were large as he pulled at her footwear, and she marveled at the feel of his rough caress.

She felt safe in his hands. She felt safe with him. So much so that when he looked up from tugging down her stockings, she stripped off her shift. Now she sat naked before him and completely unconcerned.

"Finally," she said as she stroked the corded sinews of his arm. "I can dance in a stream."

"Dance!" he said surprised.

She shrugged. "I was told once that if I danced naked in a stream at night, the water sprites would join me."

"We have much the same tale in Scotland."

"And will the boy fairies carry you away to fairyland?"

He grinned. "Not me." Then he turned and made quick work of his boots. They were naked, the both of them, and she had no interest in the water.

She caught his face and kissed him as he had kissed her. She thrust her tongue into his mouth, she tasted all she could while he coiled around and around, and he...

He scooped her up and carried her to the stream.

CHAPTER NINETEEN

L IAM CARRIED HER to the stream and welcomed the cool slice of water across his overheated body. She gasped when he lifted her, but quickly threw an arm around his shoulders and laughed when he stumbled across a sunken branch. He might have dropped her then, but she braced them both with a quick hand on a nearby rock.

Perfect. Because as he lay her body in the wet, she was already open with one hand down and the other gripping him. She had to brace her legs given the bumps in the stream while he set his knee between her thighs and set to work caressing every part of her body.

She laughed as he splashed water over her breasts, and the sound mixed perfectly with the sparkle of waterdrops on her flesh.

"I can wash myself," she said as she struggled to sit upright.

"But I'd much rather help you," he said, as he gently pressed her down. "Lie back, luv. Feel the sweetness wash over you."

With his help, she lay back and the water quickly sorted her hair out into long streams beside her. She closed her eyes and sighed with true delight.

"It's like everything is washed away," she murmured. "The aches, the cares, even my thoughts." She flowed her fingers through the current. "I want to stay here forever."

So did he. Her nipples were tight, tempting nubs. Her belly

rippled in the moonlight. And her mons was dark, wet, and so accessible to his fingers. But most of all, he appreciated the way her legs moved around him, coiling up thigh to thigh, or teasing her toes along his calves. She was ready and open to him, and yet so at ease that he smiled.

"I like you this way," he murmured. His fingers traced the dappled shifts of moonlight across her belly. And when he continued the motion to her breasts, she exhaled as if she had been waiting for just this moment.

He indulged himself with the shaping of her breasts. He loved how they fit in his hand, adored the sounds she made as he tweaked her nipples, and the taste of them made his body thrum with hunger. She arched into his mouth as he suckled her. Her legs became restless as she alternately squeezed his hips or scraped along his calves. Her hands came up to grip his head, burrowing into his hair as she pulsed with need.

So fast, so hot, so welcome. She was a responsive lover and he had been long denied. He lifted off her nipples while she clutched him in her impatience. He stretched up her body to kiss her, tasting the freshness of the stream on her lips. She met him taste for taste, and his whole body tightened when she thrust her tongue at him.

"Is it always like this?" she gasped when he pulled back.

"With you, it is."

Unable to resist touching her, his hands had found her breasts again. He watched her stretch beneath his touch and when her hips lifted, he stroked downward. Both his thumbs slid between her nether lips. He pushed at her in every way possible, opening her wide, pushing upward to hear her cry out, and then inside. She wanted everything he did, every touch and press, and he marveled at her beauty in the moonlight. She pulsed with unfettered enjoyment.

He settled her legs on his shoulders, then lifted her up so that he could taste her pleasure.

He licked her. He thrust his tongue deep inside her. And he

coiled his tongue over and around her nub. He watched her the entire time. He saw the way her body shivered, the way her breasts thrust to the sky, and he saw her mouth open on a soundless cry.

He tongued her slow, then fast. Then faster still. She writhed in pleasure. And when he thrust hard against her nub, she shattered like a bow pulled taut and then released. Not once, but time and time again.

He kept at her as long as he could hold her. He would see her pulsing like this for hours if he could. But neither of them could sustain it for that long.

In time, she wiggled out of his grip. She collapsed backward into the stream. Her arms and legs were akimbo. Her skin was flushed red. And her mouth curled in such womanly delight, that he felt proud that he had brought her to such a place.

He stroked the outside of her thighs as she still quivered. He pressed a kiss to her belly as she gasped. And he widened her legs as he set his throbbing cock at her entrance.

"Say it, Clara," he urged as he pressed his tip to her wet entrance. "Say it and be mine."

"What?"

"I have courted you as I have no other woman. I want you as I have never wanted anything before."

Her expression softened as she touched his cheek. "Liam," she whispered, and he gloried at his name on her lips.

"Clara, you have caught me as a man on your hook. I am yours."

"Yes."

"Yes," he echoed. "You are my wife. And we will flourish here as will our babes."

Her eyes widened as he spoke, and she frowned. "No babies," she said.

He should have thrust inside and been done with it. She'd said yes and they were wed by Scottish law and her own admission. And yet, he could see the denial in her eyes.

"Clara," he growled. "Be mine!"

She gripped his hips with her thighs. "Take me. I give you leave."

She wanted him inside her, no more than he needed her. But he heard the denial in her words. He knew what she meant. She was not his wife, but his mistress, and that was not something he wanted for either of them.

"Clara," he gasped, trembling as he held himself back. "I want a wife."

She smiled at him, but the expression had steel behind it. And rejection. "I want you." She pressed her mouth to his, but he wrenched himself back.

"You will not commit to me?"

"I am here now."

"Now?" he said, anger burning up his spine. "Just for now?"

"Just for now," she responded.

There was no compromise in her tone, and so he gave her none with his body. She was begging him to impale her. She'd wrapped her legs around him, she'd angled her body for his taking. She even pulled at his arms, urging her higher on her body.

He shook them off.

Then he pressed her knees down and open as he positioned himself not inside her, but along her folds. He would not enter a woman who would not claim him. And so he thrust upward, between her folds. He felt her slick along every ridge. His hands fell off her knees and into the streambed. That gave him better leverage to move against her.

She cried out at the feel of him, hard against her nub. He ground himself down to maximize what she felt.

It worked. She cried out as she gripped him tighter.

He ground down even as he thrust. Harder. Faster. The fire that pulsed through his whole body concentrated. It boiled down his spine as he thrust. He heard himself grunt as he punished them both with every thrust. She growled back as she tried to adjust his position.

"Take. Me!" she commanded.

"Take. Me!" he retorted, meaning something very different.

Neither relented as he drove himself against her.

They both lost as sensation overpowered.

Fire gripped his loins and burst through him.

He slammed hard against her as she released.

Wave after wave of ecstasy.

He rode her without filling her. He released into the heated flesh between them. And he cried out in frustration and joy. No other woman had consumed him so. And no other woman could make him so angry as he pleasured them both.

He collapsed to the side, grateful for the water that bubbled and gurgled steadily around them. It washed away his despair. He'd done everything in his power to claim this woman, and yet she remained blissfully herself.

Apart.

"Clara," he sighed. "What have you done to me?" He was a Scotsman and a future laird, and yet right now he felt as raw as a young boy denied food in a harsh winter.

It was a while before she recovered her breath, but when she did, she returned his question with one of her own.

"Why can't you be satisfied with what I offer?"

"It's not enough," he said.

"It is for me."

He rolled up onto an elbow. She stretched out beside him, as beautiful as the moon and just as remote. "Is it? Truly, Clara?"

She sighed. "I have given you more than I have to anyone else. It's not just my dowry, but you've got my attention, my work, and my body."

"For as long as I can hold it," he grumbled. "I am a powerful man, Clara, but even I have limits. I do not want my wife to wander back to London if I spend a day making whisky or a night in rest instead of pleasure."

"Do you think me that fickle?"

He didn't know. Her interests were many. How long before one of them took her away from him? "I want a wife."

"Then you should not have looked at me. I told you I would not marry you."

How could he not look at her? How could he not want her? "How can you be so stubborn?"

She pushed herself upright, taking her time as she twisted the water out of her hair. And even frustrated with her, he saw the grace in her body that came from strength. She was lanky, angular, and yet so confident in every way that it mesmerized him.

"Clara—"

"It has been one day, Liam. I learned we'd married this morning and I have forgiven you that treachery."

"I didn't do it!" he snapped.

"I don't care," she retorted. "You have cornered me in every way. You have everything from me. Why do you demand more?"

Because he wanted her commitment. More, he wanted her love. And though he knew she had affection for him, he feared that any one of her intellectual loves could pull her away from him. "I am a man who holds on to what he has."

She dropped her forehead to his. "That is why I will not let you own me. If you do, what will be left of me?"

Her words made no sense to him. She would be herself always, no matter if she agreed to stay with him or not. But he could see that she believed them, so he schooled himself to be patient. And he was well aware that she had already given him her dowry and her attention, both of which were formidable.

"I am greedy," he finally admitted. "I want your love." How hard it was to say that. A man did not admit that he needed a woman in such a way. But for her, he said the words.

She nodded, but she had no comfort for him. She kept herself apart from him as she stood up from the stream. Water sluiced down from her body and he touched her rounded buttocks. It wasn't a sexual caress, but a comforting one. With one hand, he steadied her in case she fell. He warmed her if she needed his heat. And he admired her because she was her own unique soul.

"Tomorrow will be better," he said as much to himself as to her.

"Tomorrow will be better," she agreed.

Then together, they dressed and headed back to the castle.

CHAPTER TWENTY

H E WANTED HER love? What man talked about love except in the most derisive terms? Or as lies to tempt her.

Such had been the case with her first and only teenage indiscretion. The boy had spoken in such glowing terms about love and adoration. He'd read her poetry and drawn her likeness with a moderately talented hand. But he had been a fortune hunter—bribed to leave her alone—and she had survived her broken heart by burying herself in her books.

Liam already had her fortune, so what use for him to speak of love? None, of course, except the need to own every part of her. She'd given him everything else. She would not surrender such a thing to him.

And yet, perverse creature that she was, she gloried at the idea that he wanted it. She was secretly pleased that he required her to sleep beside him. And as she curled against his heat, she smiled that he still needed something from her. How awful to have him take her dowry and be done with her. Instead, he had given her a challenge that interested her and begged her to love him.

That gave her a sense of power, not over him, but over herself. As if what she did and who she loved mattered. She liked that. She liked that a lot.

She snuggled tight against him and smiled when she felt his arm curl possessively around her middle. And she slept while listening to his rumbling snore.

She woke when he did, timed with the sun. According to Deirdre, most would want the bread they'd made yesterday for their morning sustenance before starting their day. But the castle workers would expect dinner tonight, and that had to be more than the stew she'd provided last night. Since she had no idea how to run a kitchen, she had to get the cooks back. And the best way to do that was to bribe them with higher pay.

"How long until I get my dowry coin?" she asked.

Liam glanced over at her from his place at the washbasin. He was shaving, and she enjoyed watching him run the razor over his stubble. It was a distinctly masculine thing to do, and she had lately come to appreciate manly things. Or at least one man and the things he did.

"A week or more."

She winced. "Then I need to get the coin from Mairi. Do you know where she is?"

"Yes. And I thought we could go together." He glanced out the window. "She's always up before dawn and is probably bored to tears without the castle to run."

Clara bit her lip. "Should I ask her back? I cannot do what she—"

"Absolutely not. You must establish yourself now." And at her panicked looked, he crossed to her side. He still had cream on half his face, but he looked rugged as he touched her arm. "We do this together."

"My way?"

He frowned. "You just said you don't know how to run a castle. What way do you think—"

"I have a plan. But it needs coin."

He nodded, but she saw doubt in his eyes. It didn't matter because as soon as they finished their morning ablutions, he tugged her out the back way toward the glass factory. It felt cowardly not to stop by the kitchens and face the lack of activity there, but Liam was adamant.

"You need keys and coin to be mistress here. Mairi should have given them over to you yesterday, but since she hasn't, I mean to wring them out of her. She'll respect you or feel my wrath."

That was a statement filled with rancor, and she slowed her steps as they crossed through the bailey. "There's history between you—"

"Naturally—"

"And I don't want to know about it."

He stopped and turned to her. "I didn't marry her. I married you. You've no cause—"

She held up hand. "I said I don't want to know." She took a breath. "And I don't want to stand like an errant child while the two of you bicker. It's awkward and embarrassing."

He frowned. "There will be no bickering. I will—"

"Say something forceful, and she'll fight back. And then you'll snipe at her and—"

"I'll be very diplomatic."

She doubted it. Though she'd seen him measure his words, she doubted he'd do it with his childhood friend. "Let me go by myself." The idea terrified her, but if she was to have any respect here, then he couldn't spend all his time standing beside her.

"No. I will speak to her—"

"Please—"

"—And then I'll leave. A few words, nothing more."

Her skepticism must have been clear because he held out his hand to her. "Trust me," he said, and she had little choice but to comply.

As it turned out, she needn't have worried because Mairi wasn't going to let either of them get a word in edgewise. The woman was sitting on the railing eating an apple while she watched her father shape glass. Her face was flushed from the heat, but her mood appeared pensive. At least until she spotted them.

Then she leaped off the railing and rounded on Liam as if

they'd been in the middle of an argument.

"So I'm to be given away like an old, shriveled apple, am I?" She tossed her apple core into the furnace with a powerful flick of her wrist. "The high and mighty Liam doesn't want me, so he gifts me to the neighbor. I'll have you know, Liam MacCleal, that I can pick my man without benefit of you. And that man—whomever he be—will be damned grateful for me." She shoved her hand hard against his chest. "And do' you forget it!"

She ended with a finger pointed straight at his face while Liam stared over her shoulder at Mairi's father. "Wot the devil—"

"The Aberbeag came calling this morning," her father said between blowing into a copper tube to expand the glass. "He had apples and fancy words—"

Mairi interrupted. "And he said you sent him! As how I wasn't pining after you anymore, that left room for him to come pluck me. That's what he said. *Pluck me!*" She dropped her hands onto her hips and glared at Liam. Her body quivered with fury, and it was clear she expected a response from Liam. An apology, most likely, but what she got instead was a low whistle.

"I'll be damned. Connall's got less skill with women than his horse."

"Aye," said her father as he pushed the glass back into the furnace. "Scotsmen are damned mutton-headed around women, as a rule, but Connall's a bit stupider than most."

Apparently so, if that was his idea of courting. But then Clara had rarely understood men and their idea of courtship. Mostly because she hadn't paid any attention to it before Liam. So rather than allow the woman to go off onto another rant, Clara raised her hand to get the woman's attention.

"I've come to get the keys," she said. "And the coin for the castle. I've a need to pay the servants, and I'm told you've kept good records."

"Records?" the woman sniffed. "I've watched every penny and know the coin which I've given to every soul around."

Clara's brows rose. "Without writing it down?"

"Paper's expensive. Why would I mark what I can remember?"

"So I can know it."

Mairi stared at her, and she looked back. No one—not even the men—did more than that. Clara knew that this was the time when Mairi would either submit to Clara's new authority or fight everything and everyone. And who knew what damage would come from that?

Clara wanted to say something to ease the tension, but that had never worked well for her. Whatever she said inevitably made things worse. She held her tongue and her breath while she waited. Finally, Mairi conceded.

"You'll be wanting the keys then."

"Yes."

"I've told them all that they will work for you as a good Scot—with pride in a job well done. They'll not be slacking off because I'm not there. I told them that, every one. And those that don't listen, you've got coin to tempt or turn off. I'll not be having you blame pisspoor work on me." She lifted her chin. "I've done my duty."

"When I have the keys and coin, you have. And I'll be having what's in your brain, as well."

"What?"

Clara gestured to Mairi's head. "You said you remembered it all. Is that true?"

"Of course, it is!"

"Then tell me every bit of it."

"As if you can remember what I do!"

Clara shrugged. "I'll use a ledger."

Liam nodded. "There should be one from when I kept it."

"I have it," Mairi said, her voice flat. She took a breath. "They'll fall in line if you're fair. All except Mrs. Boyce, the main cook. She's hated me since my twelfth birthday and I turned her son's head. She's off with the laird's men now, seeing to their bellies. When she's back, you tell her you've sent me away, and she'll kiss your feet."

"I'm not sending you away," Clara said firmly.

"Of course you're not." Mairi cut a hard look at Liam. "And if you think to fob me off like an old apple, you've got piss for brains. I'm off to London, I am. I'm done with idiot Scotsmen."

Liam reacted as if he'd been struck. "London? What is there for you?"

Clara snorted. "A very great deal, I should think. If you help me now, I'll write to Lilah. I'm sure she will sponsor you. And if not her, then one of her sisters."

"That's a terrible idea," Liam said. "You don't know how they treat Scotsmen in London."

Mairi frowned, but Clara dismissed it with a wave. "Similar to how they treat spinster bluestockings, I imagine. She'll be fine."

Liam winced at that, then changed tactics. "She hasn't the money either."

To which Mairi sniffed. "What do you know of my money?" she asked. "I'll teach you everything I can, Lady Clara, and I'll thank you for the introduction—"

"It will be my pleasure—"

"—And be damned to you, Liam MacCleal, and your cock-sure Aberbeag."

CHAPTER TWENTY-ONE

L IAM WAS PLEASED to see that Mairi was as good as her word…in that she helped Clara and roundly damned Liam. He didn't mind. So long as Clara's way was made smooth, then he would suffer whatever his old friend dished out.

It took Clara two more days to get the castle functioning again, though on a very restricted meal diet of stew, more stew, and stew after that. Still, two days to get most everyone doing their job was a tremendous accomplishment.

With his support and Mairi's guidance, she wrote out everyone's tasks and their pay. Then she required them to sign the first letter of their name as way of marking payment.

"Literacy is the first step to advancement," she declared to anyone who would listen. "What cannot be taught person to person can be found in a book."

No one cared what she thought except that they wanted to get paid. Many grumbled, argued, and complained, but she was uncompromising and a little insulting to those who refused.

"If you are too stupid to learn how to draw a single mark, then you are too stupid to do your work. Is that true?" And if the unfortunate soul persisted in their refusal, she added an extra kick, delivered in that flat tone of a bored aristocrat. "I have heard all my life how dumb the Scots are. Are you saying that the idiot English are correct? You cannot learn to make three strokes with a pencil?"

It made the daily task of paying people go on forever, but by week's end, everyone had memorized the shape of the first letter in his or her name. Then she gave an extra penny to anyone who learned the next letter. And a twenty pence prize when the entire name was written by hand.

His people might be stubborn, but they knew the value of money. By three weeks, every soul could sign as a literate person.

To any who wanted more coin, she declared they must write the entire alphabet for more treasure, and after that, read a page in a *Bible*. No one had accomplished that so far, but several souls were working on it, and that impressed Liam. He'd privately thought his people were incapable of such a thing in so short a time, but he was wrong and so he told her at night when they made their way to their private corner of the stream.

And she let him applaud her efforts in all sorts of delicious ways. So long as he didn't require a lifelong commitment from her, that is. Which meant he refused to consummate their marriage, though they did everything else.

That left him frustrated, annoyed, and blissfully happy all at the same time. He had a woman who drove him mad even as she slowly set his house in order. He had the time free of his father's interference to play, bully, and order his people to follow his dictates, and yet nothing was going as quickly as he wanted. No word had come from Aaron that he had a royal warrant for his whisky which left the market for his goods uncertain. Winter would come faster than he wanted, and the coin to build up their food stores was equally unclear.

He needed to go to Edinburgh to demand Clara's dowry, but he was loathe to abandon her for even a day. For all that she had thrown herself into "learning and fixing the castle systems" as she called it, her authority flowed from his unflinching support. Who knew what would happen if he disappeared for even a day?

And then something happened that made him feeling even worse than before.

Her friends arrived.

They rolled up looking disheveled and grumpy. Clara leaped from her desk in their bedroom and ran outside with more glee than she'd shown since leaving England. Liam had just returned from working at the distillery and was looking forward to a quick trip to the stream with his wife. Instead, he hastily dragged a wet rag over his body before joining the squeals of delight in the bailey.

Mr. Russell looked as sour as an exhausted man could. Of average height, average looks, and average stamina, he appeared done in as he struggled to maintain his grip on a sketchbook while being embraced by Clara. Miss Juliet Adams was older than he expected, appearing to be in her thirties, with a soft face, soft eyes, and what likely started as a tight bun of black hair but was now an untidy mess of straggly curls. She had no problem embracing Clara, but her gaze took in her surroundings with unabashed curiosity. And clear dread.

"Well, this is quite a place," she said after the introductions were made.

"It's as bad as it looks," Clara declared with glee. "But Mr. Russell is going to fix all that." She squeezed the man's arm. "You're to make us a bath house."

"So you said in your letter," the man said, "but it's not as easy as snapping your fingers—"

"I know," Clara interrupted. "But you've always wanted to be taken seriously. Now's your chance." Then she grinned at Miss Adams. "Yours, too. They're a clever people, these Scots, but they need education. That's your job."

"Clara, you're quite overwhelming," Miss Adams said in a dry tone. "As usual."

"I'm excited to finally have company!" she cried. "Come take a tour while there's still light. Mr. Russell, you can overlook the stonework while I show Miss Adams what's to be her school-room. Then we can discuss what's to be done."

"Stop, stop!" Miss Adams said with a strained laugh. "We haven't had a proper meal in days and I should like to use the privy, if you don't mind."

"Right," Clara said, her voice dropping into a chagrined note. "That will be much more pleasant once Mr. Russell is done."

"I cannot wait that long!"

"Of course. This way."

Clara tugged at both her friends' arms, all but dragging them inside with a happy giggle. She was already peppering them with questions about mutual acquaintances and events in London. She'd missed an important lecture on Roman architecture that Mr. Russell had attended. Miss Adams was privy to whether someone's baby was a boy or a girl. She wanted all the details while Liam was left in the bailey to order the disposition of the luggage. He did his best when he had no earthly idea where her friends were supposed to stay, but it added to the irritation when he heard Clara apologizing—again—about the shabby state of their home.

It was a castle, for God's sake, not the King's palace. Just what did they expect?

It got worse when he realized that they only had one decent guest room. Why hadn't Clara thought ahead and prepared for her friends? They had the chambers, of course, but none of the bedding had been refreshed since Aaron and Lilah had used the rooms. He could direct a servant to the task, but what few were on hand were busy with cleaning after the main meal or carrying the luggage. That meant he bent his own back to the task, and by the time he was done, he wanted a proper bath.

He went instead to find his wife.

He found her in the great hall inspecting Mr. Russell's sketches and making quick computations on a piece of foolscap. Their two guests were scooping up mutton stew with hard bread—the same meal everyone had had for weeks now—while alternately nodding or shaking their heads in response to some question from Clara. Neither looked happy to be there while Clara seemed completely oblivious to their discomfort.

"No, no," Clara was saying as she wrote over one of Mr.

Russell's drawings. "This should be here. And this part is all wrong."

"Clara," Liam interrupted. Then he had to say it louder to get her attention. "Clara! I believe our guests would like to rest."

She looked up. Her hair was askew, her mouth was pursed in a confused frown, and her mind was clearly on whatever computations were running through her head. And she looked blissfully happy.

The realization hit him like a punch to the gut. She had her friends and an architectural puzzle to solve. Forget the management of his people, forget the fact that her friends right now wished to be in a bed, forget that he had given her physical bliss every night of the last few weeks. This right here was what consumed her. And Mr. Russell, as well, as she went to adjust another one of his designs and he all but spit out his food to correct her.

"You cannot do that," he said sharply. "The stresses on the pulleys would be too much, not to mention the protection from the elements."

"Oh?" she asked, as she turned back to the design. "Are you—"

"Sure? Of course, I'm sure." Mr. Russell set down his bowl and took away her pencil. "You'll not be touching another sketch until I see the entire castle."

She blinked. "But you said you were hungry."

"I am hungry!" he snapped. "And tired. And you know nothing about—"

"Perhaps," interrupted Liam before the man lost his temper. "I could show you to your rooms now. You can plan on a thorough inspection in the morning."

"Oh," Clara said, obviously disappointed. "But I have so much to discuss with you both. I've made plans."

"And we've made plans," Miss Adams agreed. "And we can discuss them in detail in the morning, can't we?"

"Yes, I suppose." Then she brightened for a moment. "If you've written them down, I could look them over while you sleep." She held out her hand as if excited for a treat. Liam caught her hand and wrapped it firmly in his own.

"Plenty of time in the morning," he said. Then he gestured to the old kitchen. "Besides, everyone is waiting to be paid."

She looked at the darkened windows as if she had no idea what time it was. And indeed, she probably didn't. "Very well," she finally said. "I'll get the lockbox and my ledger." She might as well have said, I'll get a gun and shoot myself.

He wanted to take the obviously unwanted task from her, but it was the only leverage she had over his people. She controlled the coin. If he took that from her, then she would lose what gains she had made with them.

Still, one night couldn't hurt...could it?

"Clara—" he began, but she cut him off.

"Come with me, Juliet! You can see what they've already learned. I've forced them, you know, to remember their letters and some have really taken to it."

"Clara—" he tried again, but Miss Adams held up her hand to silence him.

"Very well," she said. "My lord, if you please help Mr. Russell, I'll learn what I can from Clara." She rolled her shoulders as she stood up. "The sooner I get to know my charges, the better."

"Exactly my thought," Clara declared as she linked arms with her friend, her words flowing quickly as she all but skipped away. "It's been a task, I tell you, getting them to learn a few letters, but in figuring, they're very accomplished. Basic arithmetic has been instilled from birth, and a few can do complex..."

Liam watched the two women go. He had no idea she'd been testing his people's ability with mathematics, and yet she'd obviously evaluated them. Meanwhile, Mr. Russell was gathering up his papers.

"You've caught her, that's for sure," the man grumbled. "But keeping her is another problem altogether."

"What?" The word came out sharper than he intended. The last thing he needed was this Sassenach criticizing how he handled his own wife. Unfortunately, the man hadn't been born with the brains to hear the warning in the word.

"You forced her hand, didn't you? You've got her dowry now and felicitations. But you won't hold her here. Not for long. She'll get bored and come back to London."

"Where you'll be waiting with open arms?"

Mr. Russell shook his head. "I'm not one to bed another man's wife. But I'll take her time. I'll take her attention and her ideas. She's brilliant, you know. And it's a damned shame that you've trapped her here in this dark hole of the world."

"My home is not a dark hole," he said with a growl.

"It will be to her." He pursed his lips. "I give it three months. It'll take that long for her to figure out how things are done here, meddle in them until she has it running how she likes, then…poof." He popped his fingers open. "She'll leave you for people who can think."

"The hell she will. She's my wife!"

"As if Clara ever paid attention to that."

He wanted to punch the man in the face, but even he knew that would be childish. After all, the man was correct. From the first moment they'd met, Clara had defied convention, declared that she would never marry, and—now that he'd forced the issue—had decided she was a demi-rep. He was the one who kept her innocence intact. And he was the one who would tie her to his bed rather than let her abandon him for better—more educated—company.

"She will not get bored with me," he declared firmly. He said it like a vow, but two hours later, he realized he'd already lost her.

CHAPTER TWENTY-TWO

CLARA WAS HUMMING as she headed to her bedroom. She often hummed when sorting through calculations in her head. She wasn't trying to find fault in Mr. Russell's designs. It simply amused her to run through the numbers while she walked. It took the tedium away from travelling through this great monolith of a home.

She smiled when she opened the door to see Liam standing naked as he looked at papers on the desk she had set there. She'd never known a man who was so casual about nudity. If it was a Scottish custom, she heartily endorsed it. As a student of anatomy, she appreciated the way God had combined muscle and bone for optimal function. As a woman, she gloried in his masculine beauty. Thick muscles, long limbs, powerful hands. One night, she'd pleased herself by naming the muscles that wrapped his torso. She'd barely made it to his serratus anterior before he was awake and reaching for her again.

She vowed to make a game of naming his leg muscles soon, but right now she was more interested in what he was reading so intently.

"What do you have there?"

"Mr. Russell's plans."

She leaped forward. "You got them from him? How did you manage that? He's normally so protective—"

"I gave him no choice. Since I am paying for the changes, I

expect to be included in every decision."

She caught his cold tone and wondered what had set off his mood. She'd been hoping they could visit the stream tonight, but she quickly revised her expectations. She also suppressed her annoyance that he'd claimed to be paying for the changes. It was her dowry that would finance this, and he had given her leave to handle things how she wanted. But she knew better than to challenge a man when he was being prickly, so she sought a shared interest.

"I'm so happy you want to be involved," she said. "What do you think?"

He was silent for a long moment, but she could hear the hard push of his breath in and out. For some reason, staring at it was making him angry.

"Oh dear," she said as she sidled closer. "Has he done something awful?"

"How should I know?" Liam shot back. He rounded on her, his face twisted in frustration. "I'm an educated man, Clara. I studied hard and can learn quickly—"

"I never said you didn't!"

"But this," he said, flicking the sketch with a single calloused finger. "This is beyond me."

"Oh, well, I shouldn't worry about that. No one understands Julian. Not even Julian, sometimes."

"Julian?" The word came out with a hard growl.

"Yes. Mr. Russell. We use given names in private." She waved her hand in dismissal. "He was my first dance at my come-out ball, after my father, of course. We've been friends ever since."

"And you use given names with each other."

Why was he focused on such a minor thing? As a rule, he was never one to stand on formality. It was one of the things she most liked about him. "Well, yes. My father hoped for a match between us, but Mama ended that because he's a younger son. Not even a title for him for all that he's a grandson of a duke. I didn't care, of course, but that holds sway with Mama."

If he was angry before, his face darkened now with fury. "Would you have married him? If your mother had given permission?"

She dropped her hands on her hips, confused and angry now by his attitude. "I don't know. What does it matter? He'll not have me now that I'm bound to you."

He stepped up to her so fast that she unbalanced backwards. She didn't fall, though, because he gripped her arm such that there was nowhere for her to go. "You'll not be having your leave with him under my roof. In Scotland, you're my wife!"

"I'll not be having my leave with him anytime! If he tempted me, then I would have become a demi-rep years ago." She jerked her arm out his grip. "What has gotten into you?"

He didn't answer, but there might have been a softening in his face. It was hard to tell especially as he turned back to the sketches and stabbed his fingers down at where she'd overdrawn Julian's sketch. "Why was this wrong?"

"What?"

"Why did you change this?" He bit out every word.

She peered down at it. "Oh, well, Julian has lately enjoyed creating fountains of a sort. A well that can be pumped into a pleasing display. He's made some money fashioning them, and so he puts them everywhere." She shrugged. "I thought it unnecessary."

"Because it isn't worth making my castle beautiful?"

"What? Of course not. But why would you set a servant to pump water just so it can spray about? It only works if there's a cistern somewhere and pipes to carry the water." There was a great deal more she could say about pumps and piping, but she barely understood it. What she knew came from listening to Julian through the years. But Clara could not believe her normally unflappable Scotsman was upset about a fountain. "What has happened?"

He didn't answer at first. He glared at the pages and where his thumb was planted atop her marks. In the end, he turned from her to stomp aimlessly about their room.

"You are happy with your friends."

What did that have to do with anything? "Of course, I am. They're my friends."

"And you understand that." He gestured to Julian's sketches.

"Only at the most rudimentary level."

"That is more than I comprehend."

"Well, I don't understand glasswork or whisky, so you have me beat there."

He turned, his brows raising. "Do you want to?" There was hope in his tone.

"Not really. Do you want me to? I thought that was what you loved."

"It is. And the money it will bring us."

She nodded. "So why do you want me to learn it? I have plenty to do, I assure you."

He grunted. "Yes, with teaching letters and denying fountains. And knowing who has a talent for numbers—"

"And learning how to cook something other than stew and being sure that Deirdre's twins aren't bullied."

He frowned at that. "What?"

"Did you know that people here think twins are a sign of a curse?" She shook her head. "Children are never a curse. It's backwards thinking, I tell you."

"It's Scottish thinking," he growled.

"And you brought me here to change it. So I am."

He rounded on her. He was on the far side of the room and still gloriously naked. The lamplight touched his body with gold as he stood there in all his strength. "And is there nothing here that you would love?" he pressed. "Nothing that will hold you once you have remade my home to your liking?"

His words seemed distorted to her ears. She could never think clearly when she saw his body. But even more, they made little sense to her. "What do you want of me?" she asked. "I have given everything I have to the task you set for me."

"You have worked very hard," he concurred, but it didn't seem to appease him. He took a step forward, but only a step. They were still separated by several feet. "Do you want to go back to London?"

"Of course, I do! I miss Lilah and Aaron. I miss my friends and the business of London. I am always at a loss here, set back on the wrong foot. I didn't mind when that happened in England. I had found my place. But here..." She made a gesture of confusion. "Sometimes I cannot even understand people's words, much less the meaning." Then she dropped her hands on her hips. "Aren't you tired of stew?"

"Yes!" The word came out with an exasperated shout. But for all that he seemed to agree with her, he appeared at a complete loss. For her part, she had no understanding at all of what he was about.

"I do not understand," she finally said.

There was a plaintive note in her voice that he responded to. His gaze softened, but not in kindness. It looked more like despair, and she could not comprehend why he would be so upset about fountains and stew. He came forward and touched her face. His stroke was gentle, and she lifted her chin into his touch.

"I want you to be happy here," he said.

She sighed. "It has been three weeks, Liam. Did you think I would find happiness so soon?"

"Aye," he murmured, his brogue thick. "I did."

"Then you do not know me at all."

He touched his thumb to her lip. He stroked his thumb there, bringing a tingling that began at her mouth but quickly spread to her body. Her nipples tightened, her belly grew warm and wet. She yearned for him, but she didn't close the distance. His mood was so strange, she wasn't sure of her reception.

And yet, in this, he was as he had always been. He took her mouth slowly, but with a thoroughness that undid all her thoughts. Soon her body was pliant as he helped her out of her gown. He burrowed his hands into her hair, tossing aside the few pins she had left until the weight of it all tumbled down. And as she let her head drop back, he cradled it as he kissed her chin then neck. She twined her arms around his shoulders and was ready when he scooped her up.

He carried her to their bed, kissing down to her breasts and belly. Her legs dropped open. Her hands found his cock. She wanted to guide him to be inside her. She wanted to squeeze him in the way he had taught her. She wanted to see the hunger in his eyes as he took her.

He spread her legs and let his hips drop between them. She was so ready for him, especially as he spent time suckling her nipples. She lifted her hips to him, she arched her back, begging for his penetration. But he lifted his head instead and asked what he always did in this moment.

"Be my wife." It was a question, a plea, and an order.

She answered as she always did. "Take me."

He did not. He rolled his cock along her folds. He thrust against her while her pleasure built. And they writhed together until madness overcame all. She climaxed with a cry. He spilled his seed upon her belly. And they kissed one another as if mere passion could overcome the growing distance between them.

Later, he helped her clean up. She remade their bed and pulled the covers over them. He held her tight, and she closed her eyes.

This felt good, pressed as she was against him. She liked his smell. She liked the sound of his breath and the beat of his heart. And she wished she had the words to understand why he'd been angry because she knew he was still at odds with her.

"Do you want a fountain in the bailey?"

"No."

"Do you want me to learn about distilling whisky?"

"No."

"I have tried to learn how to cook something other than stew. It hasn't gone well."

"I know."

"Maybe Mrs. Boyce will come back soon and take charge of the kitchen. She's been at your father's camp, but has sent boys back and forth for supplies."

He lifted up his head. "How do you know that?"

"Rhona told me. And what she doesn't know, Deirdre overhears." She lifted up to see him more clearly. "Did you know?"

"Yes." He dropped his head back. "My father is growing tired of romping around the woods. He'll be back soon."

"Have they killed the wolf?"

"No. But he'll kill a stag or something and pretend it was the wolf."

"But won't everyone know?"

He shrugged. "They know what they want to know." Then he sighed. "I have to get the money from Edinburgh. I need the coin here before my father returns. Without it, I fear they'll follow him no matter how much he lies."

"That doesn't make sense."

"Loyalty runs deep in Scotland."

"But coin runs deeper?"

He snorted. "It doesn't hurt."

"Then you should go. Maybe I'll have learned how to roast a chicken by the time you come back."

He smiled and pressed his lips to her forehead. "If Mrs. Boyce won't do it, then cast her out. I like your stew well enough."

"Actually, it's Rhona's stew. I just do what she tells me."

"Either way."

She quieted, relaxing more because they had made up, of a sorts. He still wanted something from her that she did understand. Or perhaps, if she was honest, she didn't want to understand. It was much easier to pretend ignorance than face anything beyond her tasks for tomorrow. She let herself relax into his side as she listened to the steady beat of his heart.

She thought he'd fallen asleep, but then he spoke. His words were whispered, but she heard them clearly enough.

"I saw it this evening," he said. "I saw that you have given up your friends and your studies. I realized what little there is here for you and how happy you were to have a piece of it back."

She had given up a lot, but she had gained some things, too. She liked the challenge of learning how a castle ran. It was a like stepping back into a fairytale of old and she wanted to see if she could improve things or if it all was exactly as it ought to be. She'd found teachers, too, in Rhona and Deirdre. She didn't much care who she learned from so long as they showed her how things were done. And she'd discovered that some talents eluded her no matter how she tried. Cooking would always bore her, she feared, but she liked spending time with the women as they discussed their lives here. Plus, she'd heard some very good ghost stories that way, and that always intrigued her.

"I've asked Mr. Baird to tell stories tomorrow night. Deidre says your father's run him out of his cottage up north. I can't understand half of what he said when he came for dinner today, but Rhona says he tells the best tales."

"He's not Mr. Baird. He's just Baird. It's another word for storyteller."

"Then he's well suited to the name. And Juliet has brought a guitar. She sings beautifully."

"Sounds like the day is well planned then."

They remained silent for a long time while she struggled to find something to say. In the end, there was nothing, except perhaps a question. "When will you leave?"

"Very soon." His brogue was coming back. A sure sign that he was feeling something deeply. Or perhaps he was falling asleep. Either way, she had no more ideas of how to connect better with him for all that they were pressed hip to hip, chest to breast.

She slept.

CHAPTER TWENTY-THREE

L IAM LEFT THREE days later. He didn't even wake her when he left because he'd pleasured her until nearly dawn. She had no idea if he slept at all and so worried about him as he travelled first to see the Aberbeag to order copper pipes, then to Edinburgh for her coin, stone, and skilled masons. While he was gone, she was to help Mr. Russell finalize his plans, organize for the incoming workers, and find the reason for her restlessness.

That was an odd question to plague her. She was generally a restless person, her mind hopping from one academic pursuit to another. She dabbled here, then grew bored and dabbled there. It defined her life in London as she wandered from one lecture to another in search of…

What?

Friends? She had found many, but they drifted into and out of her life with regularity. Intellectual stimulation? Yes, of course. But eventually endless studying grew irritating, and she ended up wandering into a new field of study simply because she decided to attend a new lecture by someone previously unknown to her.

What did she want? And had she found it here? That was the question Liam kept asking her. Did she have a good day? Was she happy? Could he make her life easier here?

He had given her purpose. It was a fine challenge to run a castle, but already she was tired of the work. Endless meal preparation, cleaning, and then coaxing of children and adults to try something new. It was incredibly hard to get them to learn the alphabet, and she'd tied it to their pay. And though a few people were inspired to learn, several more grumbled at every turn. It was exhausting and she already knew such a life would destroy her.

And yet, she wasn't ready to leave. Instead, she grew more and more irritated as she went about her day. Without Liam around to distract her at night, she was restless, short-tempered, and unable to work in any coordinated fashion. Fortunately, she had a great deal of people to distract her.

The Laird was returning.

She learned that when she was standing in the newer kitchen discussing a new oven with Julian and Rhona. The first had no more idea what would work in the large kitchen than she did. The latter was even less help since her every answer was to shake her head and say, "Mrs. Boyce is verra particular."

"Then Mrs. Boyce should have shown up to work today!" she snapped.

"She's gone to help the Laird. She's got two middle boys with him—"

A strident voice cut in. "And I'll not have them drinking their brains to pudding while they're playing with knives."

Clara spun around to see a woman with salt and pepper hair, a wide face, and a sturdy frame stomp into the room. Her face might be appealing if it weren't pulled into a sour frown as she inspected the people here.

"What are you—" the woman began, but Clara cut her off.

"You're Mrs. Boyce, aren't you? Thank God you're here."

"—doing in my kitchen? And who's he?"

Not a woman to be interrupted, it seemed, but Clara was annoyed enough to get her answers any way she could. She glanced at Rhona. "Is that Mrs. Boyce?"

"Yes, my lady."

"Wonderful." She turned to the woman who was looking more mutinous by the second. "We're putting in a modern oven.

I thought it should go there." She pointed to the far side of the nearest wall. "Looks like it would be easiest to get things in and out of it without moving things too much. But Mr. Russell thinks it must be here for best use of the pipes that will transport the water to the bathhouse. Your opinion would be valued."

"An oven? Why do you think we need a new oven? I've managed just fine—"

"Well, of course you've managed. I thought you'd want one. And since we're doing repairs now, this is your chance. We won't be at it again for…" She shrugged. "Ever, I should think."

"Repairs? What repairs? You won't be mucking about my kitchen, interfering with the feeding of good people. Not while I'm here, you won't." She dropped her hands on her hips and glared at them.

Clara looked back and considered her options. She wanted a better cook than what she and Rhona had achieved, but she would not fight a woman who was contrary just to be contrary. She turned back to Mr. Russell.

"Mrs. Boyce does not want changes to her kitchen. That means we shall be upgrading the old kitchen with the new stove. You have made plans for that possibility?"

Julian grimaced. "It'll be a great deal more expensive. And the walk will be long from there to the great hall."

"Can you fix that trip stone? I cannot tell you how many times I've nearly knocked myself unconscious just from walking into the room."

"Of course, I can. But as I said, it's far from ideal. The old kitchen is much smaller. I thought you meant to move this oven into there and bring a new one here."

"That makes logical sense, but Mrs. Boyce has refused it. If she wants to make meals with a smaller, less effective oven, then I shall give Rhona here the better kitchen." She rapped her knuckles on the sketch. "Done. Now let us go to the other kitchen and see what's to be managed there."

She turned to go, gesturing Rhona ahead of her, but Julian

held her back. "Lady Clara, be reasonable. That is not the logical choice."

She stopped and looked at him. "I do not have time for people to fight me. We must have a finished design by the time his lordship returns. Mrs. Boyce said no, and therefore we go to the next choice. Unless..." She frowned. "Are you suggesting I sack a woman who has served the clan so faithfully all these years?" She rubbed her finger across her chin. "I am loathe to do that, but time is short."

Mr. Russell sighed. "Time is not that short. We have an hour to explain the details to Mrs. Boyce. She might change her mind."

"An hour! We have a thousand decisions to make this day alone. We have yet to discuss the provisions for laundry, and then there is the schoolroom."

Julian held up his hand. "Half an hour? It would save me time if I did not have to redo all my work from last night."

Clara took a moment, then turned back to Mrs. Boyce. "Well? Can you make decisions in that time? Do you wish to listen to Mr. Russell's logic? Or do I give the new oven to Rhona?" Then she lifted her hands. "Or you could quit and leave with my blessing. It is entirely up to you."

"Quit!" the woman gasped. "Why would I—"

"Are you out of your mind?" came another voice. "Why would you put children next to a glass factory?" Mairi burst into the kitchen with her hair askew and her eyes blazing. She wore a simple dress burned in several places, and she had heavy gloves in her hand—not on them—that she whipped about as she gestured. "There's space enough in the castle, the bailey, in the barn even. Children love horses! But to put them next to molten glass is beyond insane! I canna believe even a Sassenach could be that stupid."

Clara sighed. Another fight she had not wanted to have right now. And for them to come upon her together was exhausting. She was still sorting through her options, though, when Julian lost hold of his composure.

"Good God, are all Scotswomen like this? Uncivilized, screeching creatures with less decorum than a wild horse?" He rounded on her. "Clara, this...this overflowing emotion is not to my liking! Not in the least!"

Clara was dumbstruck. She'd never seen her friend so exercised in all her life. His face was flushed, his hands were fisted above his sketches, and he looked like he wanted to throttle the entire room. But he never got the chance as Mairi pointed her finger straight at the man's face.

"And who are you to bluster at me? What idiot puts children next to a hot furnace?"

"One who wants to keep them warm in winter. And if you would look at the design, you would see that there are walls. Big, heavy walls all the way to the bailey between them and the fire." He lifted his chin. "What woman would allow her children to freeze to death when there is heat and comfort to be had?"

"Children get everywhere," she snapped.

"As do idiots and fools. Can you not keep track of your own?"

"Have you never had a child underfoot?"

His breath caught, and his face paled. It was obvious to everyone, including Mairi. Clara knew, of course, that his younger brother had died under tragic circumstances. She'd never gotten the details. He never spoke of it. But she knew he thought it was his fault and he'd never forgiven himself.

Fortunately, Mairi had hold of her temper enough to stop her verbal assault. She softened her voice and dropped her hands on her hips. "The school cannot be attached to the factory. It's too dangerous."

"The school is in the castle," he said firmly. "But sometimes they need a warm place to go. Sometimes the girls need to be in one place and the boys in another. Or does it never get so snowbound that everyone must survive together for weeks on end?"

Mairi was startled into silence, as was everyone else. Julian was normally a soft-spoken man, but when he allowed his emotions through, he could be ruthless with his logic. And now he turned that weapon onto Mrs. Boyce.

"The stove will go there," he said pointing. "It is the most efficient place to distribute the heat. You'll have hot water flowing through a pipe behind it to come out here." He pointed. "It can be high enough for a table or lower down to the floor for washing."

Clara shook her head. "The laundry will be done as part of the bathhouse."

Julian nodded. "If it's high, I can get you a sink that drains away with the sewage. Mind that it doesn't get clogged. I'll not come out here in the dead of winter to unstop an ugly mess."

Mrs. Boyce grunted. "I know how to keep a sink clean."

"Are we agreed then?" Mr. Russell asked as he pinned everyone with a hard stare. It was a cold look, but it sat well on his face. It gave him an air of authority that was normally absent, and for the first time she could see his aristocratic ancestry in every line of his body. If he had been born to his uncle, he could manage the stature of a duke, she thought.

So too, apparently, did everyone else. Mrs. Boyce nodded. Rhona and several others who had come to spy upon them also dipped their heads. But Mairi was not so easily cowed.

"I would see these plans for the children."

"Why?" he challenged. "I heard you were off to London."

"This is my home and my people," she said. "I'll not abandon them to an English folly."

He folded his arms as he stared at her. "And what education do you have to challenge my plans? Have you studied mathematics, architecture, or the engineering of wells and pipes?"

Clara almost had sympathy for Mairi. No woman had the credentials that Julian had. Certainly not in his chosen field. But apparently Mairi was not intimidated by years of study.

"Och," she said, rocking back on her heels. "I know the running of this place and the temper of the Scots. We're born with a contrary side and what makes sense among you milksop

Sassenach will no' work here."

He crossed his arms. "Not milksop. We're civilized."

"Not civilized. You're mutton-headed."

He snorted. "I pray I am there at your come-out ball, Miss MacAdaidh. I should enjoy watching as you realize the English are completely uninterested in your coarse manners."

"And I will enjoy dazzling your chicken-hearted compatriots. Every man loves a woman with spirit."

He looked at her a moment, then shook his head. "Not if they're a rude, impertinent busybody." He turned to Clara. "If we've made the decisions here, we should address the matter of the laundry now."

Clara nodded as she turned to Rhona. "Can you send Deirdre to us, please? This is her area of expertise."

"Yes, my lady," Rhona said as she dashed away.

Then Clara turned back to Mrs. Boyce. "Are you able to manage dinner here now? Or do you require help?"

"I am well able to do my duty," the woman said stiffly. "The MacCleal sent me ahead to do just that." Her brows rose in challenge. "He'll be here by tomorrow's evening meal."

The laird and his rowdy companions would be here before Liam returned. That made her gut tighten with fear. She was not prepared to face them alone. but she knew better than to let the panic seep into her features. "I'll leave you to it," she said.

She turned to go but caught sight of the fierce defiance that blistered across Mairi's features. What had happened, she wondered, to carve this woman into the firebrand she was now? She didn't know, and truthfully, she feared that Julian was right. The English she knew would not appreciate a woman who spoke her mind so forcefully.

"Mairi," she said gently. "There is society in Edinburgh. Perhaps a London season is not the right choice—"

"I will be a sensation in England!" she declared with a determination that startled Clara. Mrs. Boyce, on the other hand, seemed to be well-versed with Mairi's temper. She shook her head as she spoke.

"You've too tart a tongue for a Scotsman, Miss Mairi. It'll cost you more in England, and well you know it."

Instead of a response, Mairi gathered her pride about her like a royal crown. Clara had never seen anything like it. If the woman were clad in rags, she still projected the bearing of a warrior queen. She didn't bother to defend her case. She simply pinned them both a withering glare before walking away.

Clara had never been one to focus on the social whirl. Truthfully, she hadn't been strong enough to hold her head high despite all the sniping and whispering around her. But Mairi was a different sort of creature. If anyone could thumb her nose at society and win, it would be her. But to what end? And what man would value her strengths over her rougher aspects?

She didn't know, and she had her own troubles to handle anyway. She had sent the letter of introduction to Lilah. It would be up to her sister-in-law to navigate Miss MacAdaidh's marital prospects. In the meantime, she had a rowdy laird to welcome, and without her husband to help. That was challenge enough.

CHAPTER TWENTY-FOUR

L IAM RODE IN silence, his head and his back aching from lack of sleep. Hard enough to get the coin from the bankers, even with Aaron's letter and cheque. Harder still to order the stone and hire masons to help rebuild his home. But the worst task of all was riding with his once best friend Connall, future Laird of the Aberbeag, as the man teased him mercilessly about following a woman's plans. He was a man, damnit, and a man knew when to listen to an educated soul, even if she be a woman.

But it was madness to try to restore a castle starting in mid-summer based on the designs of a man he did not know.

"Why aren't you selling your whisky to the Sassenach?" Connall asked. "It's good enough for them."

"I am!" he huffed.

"No, you're waiting for your wife's brother to push it to the Prince Regent. Why not just sell it in London to every nob who—"

"Because a royal warrant triples the price, and well you know it."

"True, true," the man said with a waggle of his brows. "But what if it doesn't, eh? What if your brother-in-law isn't as close with the Prince Regent as he claims."

"It's not Aaron, it's his cousin who orders the royal food—"

"Yes, yes, but what if doesn't work? Where will you be then?"

"Home in a newly built castle with my wife." He hoped.

"But what if I were to take your whisky there myself? I'd get you a good price, tease it to a few of my friends."

"You have no English friends. You hated English school and left the moment you could."

"I did, but I made friends with a few. And perhaps it's time for me to find a wife." His gaze slid away. That was clue enough, but then he began to whistle a low tuneless sound that scraped along Liam's nerves.

"For heaven's sake, Connall—" Liam began, but he was interrupted.

"I could sell your whisky, and mayhap I can escort a certain lady to London at the same time."

Liam twisted on his horse and glared at his friend. "Is that why you insisted you follow me to Edinburgh? Is that why I've been cursed with your infernal whistling all this time? Just so you could fabricate an excuse to court Mairi?"

"I had tasks in Edinburgh," Connall retorted.

"Trivial matters—"

"And I enjoy the trip more with company."

Liam snorted. "Not with my company."

"True enough, but I had no idea you would be so surly the whole time." He shuddered. "Slit my throat if I ever moon over a woman the way you are."

Liam cut his friend a hard look. "You're creating an excuse to go to London with Mairi. That's lovesick enough."

"I'm offering to help you before you're broke and on my doorstep begging for crumbs. Though…" he added slowly, "it would be useful to have an excuse to work with Mairi. If she and I together were tasked with finding an English market for your whisky, then I might use the time to know her better."

"Why not just court her in the normal way?" He looked up with his first smile in two days. "Oh, yes. I heard you tried that, and she sent you packing. What did you say? Something about apples and how you would pluck her." He chuckled when he remembered her outrage. "How I wish I'd been there to see it in person—"

"That's not how I meant it," his friend grumbled.

"It's not how any man with a brain would mean it." He shook his head. "You and Mairi have been oil and water since the first time she outran you in a footrace."

"It's not me. It's her being so prickly. Which is why I need a reason to be around her. If we've a task to do together, then she'll have time to realize I'm not a monster."

"She's known you all her life. She doesn't need more time—"

"She thinks I'm still a boy. Will you help me or no'?"

He wanted to say no, just to annoy his oldest friend. But he had to admit that pinning all his hopes on Aaron was not the prudent path. "If you'll sell my whisky honestly—"

"You know I will."

He did. His friend might be ham-handed when dealing with Mairi, but he was honest to the bone. "But you can't go just with Mairi. Haven't you a female cousin to bring along as chaperone? Someone who might also want an English husband?"

"I do. I've already spoken with her."

"Then I'll see if Mairi will consider helping with the job." The relief on his friend's face was enough to make him chuckle. Connall had a way with every woman but Mairi. Whatever happened between them, he was sure the trip to London would be a fine tale one day.

But now he had to finish his own story. Two days away from Clara had told him how much he wanted her. He hadn't chuckled at a clever turn of phrase since he'd left her side. He hadn't marveled at anyone's education or been astounded by her lack of practical knowledge. Just last week, the woman had been shocked to learn that the Scots could make fine soaps. Sweeter ones, indeed, than she had used in London. The memory of her expression—so excited by the discovery—had him smiling a week later.

That's what she did for him. She made him smile. When all felt heavy in his soul, she would say or do something that made everything in him settle.

And now, two days away from her, he was very much unsettled.

He kicked his weary horse to a faster trot. They were nearly home, and he wanted to gallop to her side. She'd likely be eating more of that terrible stew while making notes on a new way to mix soap for laundry.

Except the nearer they came to his home, the more he saw that he'd been away too long. His father had returned. He saw it in the blazing lights, in the horses that were still being tended near the barn, and the many souls dashing about the courtyard. They were children, mostly, set to one task or another. Which meant—

"Your father has killed his wolf," Connall said.

"More likely, Beitidh grew tired of the camp and convinced him to come home." He looked at the bright stars. "The weather is fine. He should have stayed away for a week more."

"Unless he killed the wolves and has come home triumphant."

It was possible, he supposed. His father had once been a good hunter. His stamina might fail him, but his tracking skills could still be sharp. But if that were true, then Liam faced an early power struggle against his father. Neither he nor Clara had established themselves here. Hell, he'd only now returned with coin.

"Bloody hell," he cursed as he kicked his horse. "I need to get there now."

Connall matched his pace, his keen eyes scanning the castle for clues. Neither of them found any, and so when they clattered into the bailey, the man grabbed Liam's reins.

"I'll take care of the horses. You go see to your wife."

CHAPTER TWENTY-FIVE

CLARA SCRATCHED AT her best gown as she stood at the top of the great hall to greet the MacCleal. It was too hot to wear this heavy thing, but she wanted to honor the man with her best attire. As did Beitidh, apparently, who rushed to stand beside her in a scarlet gown that had seen better days. Apparently, she'd made it back early with the rest of the women so that she could prepare for the celebratory feast. Not that Beitidh had done any of the work.

"Step aside," the woman said as she elbowed Clara. "You can stand there when Liam comes home, but this is my place when the laird enters."

"You've married, then?" Clara asked. "Should this be a wedding feast?"

"What? Get on with you. I'm the laird's lady, and this is my place."

Not without benefit of a ring, but Clara didn't have the time to argue. The noise was growing as the laird threw open the doors and stomped into the castle. He was surrounded by his men who hooted and cheered like every man returning from a successful hunt. Women and children followed or were streaming in from other doors. The mayhem was deafening, especially with the dogs that barked underfoot.

The smell was intense as well, and Clara mentally counted the days until the bathhouse was complete. At least they'd gotten part of it working. But for now, she clapped and cheered with everyone else.

"Welcome—" Clara began, but Beitidh had her own greeting.

"My great hunter returns!" she squealed as she launched herself into the man's arms. He caught her quickly enough, but Clara noted that he winced as he did so. Perhaps his aging body didn't appreciate three weeks without a soft bed. It didn't stop him from bending Beitidh over as he kissed her. Then he straightened up and slapped her hard on the bottom.

"That's the way to welcome a man home," he bellowed. Then he turned to Clara. "Is the meat ready? My men are hungry."

Clara clapped her hands. "The meat has been cooking all day in anticipation."

It had arrived courtesy of five teenage boys who had lugged the beast into the kitchen with as much fanfare as the older men wanted now. Thankfully, Mrs. Boyce knew what to do and set her sons to cleaning the beast. It looked like a stag to Clara, and everyone agreed. The boys said that the laird had killed the wolf earlier, but they had feasted upon it days ago. Clara declared it one and the same and left them to their work.

"The food will be ready as soon as you return from cleaning off the smell of the hunt."

"What?" the laird said with a laugh. "You would have us muck to the stream now?" He leaned forward. "That is not the way to treat a man in his own home!"

"I have great news, then!" she cried as she clapped her hands. It was generally a noisy place with each man greeting his family, but at her tone, most everyone quieted. Even the dogs settled. "Mr. Russell has fixed the pump that ran to the bathhouse." She smiled. "We rushed the work for your return. And now you may be the first to use it!"

She put all her enthusiasm into her voice, but it fell on uncertain faces. It was clear the laird, at least, did not like being sent to the washroom like a dirty boy. But he didn't argue. Instead, he frowned. "How did you repair it?"

"That is a question for Mr. Russell—" Clara began, but Beitidh apparently disliked the discussion. She stepped between Clara and the MacCleal with an airy wave.

"It is English foolishness," she cried. Then she kissed the man boldly on the mouth. "I think you smell fine."

Clara shook her head. "I know Mairi would send every one of you to wash off your dirt. And now we have water right through the north bailey. Don't you want to see it? It will be beautiful when all the work is done, but right now it is merely functional." She couldn't imagine *not* wanting to inspect a modern convenience, especially one so badly needed.

Beitidh pitched her voice high and hard. "Och, the Sassenach wants to beautify the castle. She thinks we've not got beauty enough here with our strapping Scottish men." She grinned as she squeezed the laird's arm.

Clara shook her head. "You are arguing merely because it is my idea." She pinned the MacCleal with a hard look. "Have you married her, then? Does Beitidh make the rules? I swear Liam learned to wash from someone and it wasn't her. Not with the stains in her skirts or the mud in her hair."

It was a risk pointing out the lack in Beitidh's appearance. She was, after all, the laird's woman. But Liam had said his father was different before, back when Liam's mother still lived. And there had to be a reason that the laird had not yet wed the woman.

"You're a good man who loved a good woman," Clara pushed. "What would your wife have thought of her?"

She saw the moment the man's thoughts turned. He looked at Beitidh's mussed hair and dirty dress. He probably didn't realize that he'd done half the damage when she'd leaped into his arms. It didn't matter. She did not look like a respectable woman, and everyone here could see it. Beitidh, too, must have felt the mood turn against her. She bared her teeth and her nails as she launched herself at Clara.

"Bloody Sassenach!" she screamed.

Clara jerked back. The change had been so sudden and so violent. Part of her couldn't credit that it had happened. Which meant that she was slow. She brought up her arm to block—too late—but before the woman's nails raked her face, something worse happened.

She stepped on a dog's tail.

The creature yelped, Clara stumbled, and Beitidh sliced down with her nails. She never touched Clara, thanks to the dog and the laird's quick reactions. The MacCleal gripped his woman's arm and jerked her away. Then he cast her back to fall onto yet more barking dogs.

What a disaster. Especially since Clara had fallen with a bruising clatter. But before she could recover, a roar of fury exploded from the base of the hall. From her vantage point on the floor, Clara couldn't see who was coming. Truthfully, the sound had been dark and guttural, but she had a guess. Or perhaps she had merely wanted him by her side so badly that she imagined him.

He was real.

Liam burst through the laird's men to rush up to her side. She had little time to react. He looked at her, his face a dark mask of fury. His teeth were bared, and his hands fisted.

"I'm fine—" she began, but he didn't wait.

Liam rounded on his father, and he punched the man straight across his face. "You would dare hit my wife?" he bellowed.

The MacCleal's head snapped back, and he stumbled back. His men were no help in catching him, and the dogs began to bark in true fury now.

"Wait!" Clara cried, scrambling to get her feet under her. "Liam! Wait!"

"I didn't touch her!" the laird bellowed.

Beitidh was faster than Clara. She was already on her feet and pointing at Clara. "You see what she has brought into your home? Son against father! It's a disgrace, and it's her fault!"

Clara had had a long day. Rage was not her usual temper, but these last days without Liam had frayed her nerves. And the last thing this situation needed was a low-class tart screeching over the barking dogs.

She pushed up to her feet, knocking Beitidh's arm out of the way. That was all she meant to do as a high-pitched whistle called the dogs back. But the woman was not one to be pushed aside easily. She surged forward and Clara did what she'd been taught. It wasn't even a conscious thought, but a reaction to someone coming straight at her face.

She threw her fist upward as hard as she could. Her fist caught Beitidh's chin, snapped her head back, and sent her flying. It would have been more satisfying if her hand hadn't immediately started throbbing, but she appreciated the sudden silence nonetheless. Especially as Beitidh appeared to drop unconscious from the blow.

"Ow," Clara said, as she shook out her hand.

Then she peered closer at Beitidh. Had she killed the woman? To her relief, the lady breathed. Once. Twice. And then she began to blink hard as she came back to awareness. This time Clara was the one who pointed her finger.

"Stay quiet," she said, and her gesture included the woman and the dogs.

Then she turned to Liam who stood before his father with both his fists raised.

"It wasn't your father," she said. "Liam, I tripped over a dog." She touched his arm and felt the muscles quivering with emotions.

"He didn't hit you?" Liam rasped. "I saw his fist raise. I heard you fall."

"It was a dog. And Beitidh."

"His woman." He spat out the words.

Meanwhile, his father glared at his son. "You thought I would hit her? Your wife?" The outrage was clear in his voice.

"You have done as much before in your cups."

"Not your *wife*." There was emphasis on the last word that told her the man had respect for the title if not the woman. It was enough. Especially since he had acted to save her from Beitidh.

Meanwhile, Clara tugged Liam back from his father. "Well, isn't this lovely?" she tried with a false cheer. "Everyone's home now. We can have a proper celebration…after everyone's washed up, of course." She raised her eyebrows in a hopeful expression. "Julian got a pump working in the bathhouse. There's water there now. Isn't that wonderful?"

Liam looked at her, his expression slowly softening from fury into bemusement. He touched her cheek and she felt herself relax into his palm. "You aren't hurt?"

"Just my backside from tripping over the dog."

"I'll banish them from the hall."

She looked past him. "I think they're already gone." Someone had indeed taken them outside. And while she watched, the women began ushering or chiding their men toward the bathhouse. There would be a long line as everyone cleaned the worst of the dirt off, but they wouldn't argue with her about it.

Meanwhile, another man sauntered up with a cheeky grin on his face. She recognized him as Connall, the future laird of the Aberbeag. He stopped next to Beitidh, who was only now starting to sit up.

"Never knew a Sassenach could have such fire," he said in a cheery tone. "Laid her out with one blow, and you a woman, no less. I'd wager Mairi could have done no better."

Mairi would likely have seen this fight coming and found a way to prevent it. But Clara had done what she could, and it had worked. She saw respect in everyone's eyes as they filed past her. That was nice, but nicer still was the way that Liam kept looking at her. His eyes were burning with intensity, and he had yet to release her. She pressed her lips to his palm.

"I have so much to tell you."

"Yes?"

"I've made charts of every job in the castle. I know how things work here now."

His brows rose. "Do you now?"

"And Mr. Russell and I have figured out what can be done before winter, and what should wait. I know you went over most of it with him before you left, but—"

"You have suggestions."

"Not just me. I've talked to everyone I could. Even Mairi."

Connall chuckled. "I bet she gave you an earful."

She frowned at the man. "She was very helpful. And don't you think you should go wash as well? Dinner will be coming soon, and you don't want to miss it."

The Aberbeag gave her a courteous bow. "As you please, my lady." But he glanced down at Beitidh before he left. "Should we do something with her first?"

"I'll take care of her," the MacCleal said in a heavy tone. "Go to my chamber and don't leave it until I say," he ordered.

Beitidh's eyes widened at that, but she knew better than to argue. With a nod, she made it to her feet. Her steps were steady and before long, her chin came up. But she didn't argue, and Clara was happy to see the back of her.

"I will wash as well, my lady," the MacCleal said. Then he looked back at his son. "We will feast tonight, and then you and I will speak."

Oh dear. That did not sound like it would be a good discussion. Apparently, Liam agreed because he spoke in a hard tone.

"You're not able to discuss anything in your cups, Father. We can speak in the morning."

The man's eyes narrowed, but he agreed with a short grunt. And then he joined the Aberbeag as they left the great hall. Clara heard a few of their words as they left. Something about copper pipes and whisky, but the meaning of it was lost on her as Liam caught her mouth with his.

She'd been watching his father leave, but he swiftly brought her attention back to him. His mouth was demanding as he moved over her, and she opened to him with a sigh of relief. Liam was back. She could rely on him to explain things she didn't understand. And they could resume the nighttime activities which she so enjoyed.

She gripped his arms, pulling herself closer even as he arched her backwards with his demands. She felt the tension in him, and she didn't know if it came from fury, worry, or desire. It didn't matter. She responded to him as she always did. Her heart sped up, her belly grew liquid, and her ever-churning thoughts quieted until all she thought about was him.

Until he pulled back.

"Clara," he whispered. "Be my wife."

Always back to that, and for the first time, she hesitated before denying him. "Can we talk tonight?" she asked. "Afterwards?" Even though she wasn't looking, she could already hear the platters of food being brought into the great room. They weren't alone, and this wasn't the time to rehash their nightly argument.

"Tonight," he agreed. "But no later."

She straightened, but as she looked into his fierce expression, she heard herself say the first thought that came into her head. "I don't know how it will be different."

"*I* am different." He touched her lips. "And I think you are, too."

She bit her lip, feeling the tingling swell of her flesh. Her first thought was to deny that anything had changed between them. Three days apart was not long enough for new revelations. And yet, she could not disagree. Part of her had thrilled when he'd rushed to her side to defend her. The sight of his fists raised as he protected her set her heart beating in a purely carnal way. And three days apart had told her that she disliked his absence intensely.

But was that enough?

"It's too soon," she said. "We've only just begun the work here."

"There will always be work, Clara. Things to do, systems to change, people to educate. Will you be my side as I do them? May I be at your side as you remake everything around me?"

"It's just the bathhouse."

"I heard something about a classroom."

"Well, of course. And I thought about your bees."

"Our bees?"

"I have some ideas there as well."

"Anything else?"

She nodded. "A great deal, actually. But I know we can't do it all at once."

"It might take a lifetime."

It might. "I miss London."

"We can visit." He dropped his forehead to hers. "Do you want London more than you want me? Do you want it more than you want the work here?"

She didn't answer. Not out loud, at least. Her heart was already thumping away with her choice. It said, *Liam. Liam. Liam.*

"We'll talk tonight," she said.

"Tonight."

CHAPTER TWENTY-SIX

HE DIDN'T TALK to her that night. Liam was too busy managing his father's friends, two of whom needed help to find their homes. By the time he made it to his own bed, Clara was fast asleep, no doubt exhausted from managing the feast. Or perhaps it was the laundry. Or maybe it was the details of the schoolroom. She had those papers strewn about their bed and was quietly snoring beneath them.

He gathered up the debris of her thoughts and set them aside, then climbed into bed beside her. She felt soft and womanly as he tucked her against him. She sighed happily in her sleep, and he couldn't help but agree.

This felt good. This was right. And so rather than wake her for an uncomfortable discussion, he pressed his lips to her neck and whispered, "Good night." Then he let every ache in his body, every worry in his heart, dissolve against her steady heat.

He slept.

She slipped away at sunrise. He wanted to pull her back, but she said something about the privy. While she was gone, he fell back into slumber, though his arms ached for lack of her presence. By midmorning, he had to face his father. The laird had been prudent in his drinking the night before, so his head did not throb today. Better still, he had seen the havoc his friends had caused as they drank whisky the clan needed to sell, broke platters as they wasted food, and required help to find their beds safely.

One night of this was simple indulgence, but such things could not continue on a regular basis.

Fortunately, the laird had a head for numbers, especially when Liam showed him where they could earn coin—from sale of their whisky—to how much was consumed by his men. Then Liam did what he had never attempted before. He explained everything to his father. He had plans not just for the whisky and glass factory, but also their crops and herds. He put bread, plates, and cups on the table to indicate the clan's holdings and people. And he told his father everything that had been brewing in his mind since he first left home.

It took hours.

And it felt wonderful, especially as his father listened without complaint, commented without bluster, and ended with his father staring at Liam in a whole new way.

"How did you think of all this?" The laird frowned. "Never say it was that Sassenach woman."

"I have been working on these plans since I was a boy."

"You were never this clever as a child."

He shrugged. "Mother taught me to plan—"

"Aye, she was good at that."

"The numbers, I learned in school."

"Sassenach school."

Liam nodded. "And now, Clara and Miss Adams will teach it to our people here."

His father wasn't convinced. "A schoolroom is a foolish way to spend her dowry."

"Is it?" Liam challenged. "I hear young Egan Jack has ideas about our bees."

The laird snorted with derision. "That boy thinks honey should go in everything, even whisky."

"Imagine if that boy learned how to sell honey for English coin. It tastes different, you know, depending on the bees and where you set the hive." He lifted his open hands. "Do you know aught about bees? I don't."

"But your wife does?"

"Aye. And a lot more."

The man grunted. "We've survived well enough without all this."

"We have. But there's a lot of space between survive and thrive."

His father didn't argue as he stared at the assortment of things on the table. "It's ambitious," he said, "but you've never lacked for that."

Liam waited, trying to measure his father's mood. He knew full well that he had more patience than his father. Eventually he was rewarded as the man dropped his fist on the table with a heavy thud.

"Do it, then," he said as he pushed up from his seat. "See to it with my blessing, but I'll not stay here and suffer through the noise and upset."

"What?" Liam asked as he stood up to match his father's height. "Where would you go?"

"Do you know why we came back when we did? The weather couldn't be finer, but down we come back here, where your woman demands we bathe." He snorted as he picked up an empty flagon. "And now you won't even let us drink the whisky."

"I have no idea why you came back. I thought you'd be gone at least another week."

"And so we would have. The young ones were taking to the woods well, and Mrs. Boyce cooks fine meat over the fire." He grew quiet. "And there wasn't so much drink that I couldn't think about the way things had gone between us."

There was the key. His father had been sober for long enough to look at his life. "So why did you come back?"

"Beitidh." He blew out a breath. "I always knew she aimed to be a laird's wife, but she made a bad choice with me. She wants a soft bed and food that doesn't have to be plucked or skinned by her hand."

"She insisted you come back."

"Aye. I indulged her because I wanted to see what you're up to." He gestured to the table. "Now I know." He looked out the window. "But I found I liked it up there. Reminds me of who I was as a boy listening to the wind and the birds." He scratched at his beard. "Don't have to trim this for a lady's fancy and I can piss anywhere I want."

There was a story there, but Liam didn't want the details. "You miss Mother," he said softly. She'd loved walking the land with his father, was as good a tracker as he was, and a fair hand with a knife for cooking or killing.

"I'm going up to the tower," he said, as he thumped his tankard down on the farthest corner of the table.

"The tower? But that's Aberbeag—"

"Spoke with Connall about it last night, and he's amenable. He's got young boys who need to be taught the ways of the land. And a few girls, too. Ones like Mairi who know how to stab a man who gives them grief."

"You're the one who taught her that."

"Aye. And I'll teach it to the Aberbeag girls, too, and any of ours that want the learning."

"Will you take anyone else? Your men, perhaps."

He nodded. "The ones who'll give you the most trouble when your woman makes them wash. I don't care so much about such things."

"And Beitidh?"

His father shrugged. "That's up to her. I'll welcome her in my bed, but if she stays here…" His voice trailed away.

"She'll have to work like everyone else."

The laird grunted. "Never saw her so clearly before last night. Screeching like a banshee as she tried to rip your woman's eyes out."

Liam's jaw clenched. He hadn't witnessed the attack itself, but the knowledge was enough to make him want to toss Beitidh out on her ear. Apparently, his father was taking care of the problem for him.

"You've got plans," the MacCleal said. "It's best if me and a few others leave you to them."

"There's always a place here for you," Liam said.

"Course there is. I'm the laird!" He narrowed his eyes. "And don't think that I won't be checking on you. This plan of yours can fail any number of ways. And that wife of yours will need a strong hand. You've given her too much freedom here—"

"I can handle my wife," he said flatly.

His father took the rebuke with a knowing smile. "I suppose you'll try." Then his expression sobered. "I spent too much time in drink since your mother died. Took going out hunting for me to start thinking." He held out his hand. "But I'm steady now, and I'm seeing you as a man instead of a boy." He made an expansive gesture. "You set this place to rights. Then I'll come back and see how you've done. I want to see this *thriving* you're bragging about."

"You'll see it."

"Aye, or we'll be trying something my way, won't we?"

Liam smiled. "Then you'll bring us back a fat stag to eat, and we'll talk it through again."

"And maybe I'll wash in the new bathhouse just to try it out."

They had more talk. Good, companionable discussion as they walked together to see the construction that was already beginning. It was healing in a way that hadn't happened since his mother died, and Liam had left for England.

He had Clara to thank for this. Not directly, of course. No woman could force a father and son to reconcile. But Liam had needed to protect her, and so he'd pushed his father out into the woods. That had led directly to this moment, and for that, Liam was grateful.

He planned to tell her exactly that. Indeed, he managed to say thank you as they climbed into bed, but her attention was on other things he could do with his mouth. And he was more than willing to accommodate her.

But in that moment when he would have thrust inside her, at

the time when he demanded she say they were wed in truth, he lost himself to fear. She was here now, and he was all too aware of what she brought to him and his clan. Her money, her intelligence, her drive to conquer whatever challenges were set before her.

He didn't ask, but he also didn't take her. He would not risk a babe with her until she promised to remain with him. And he would not bed her until he knew she was his.

So he thrust upward rather than inside. And he took her cry of delight into his soul, holding it as proof that he gave her something. She could want him for a reason. And when she tucked herself tight to his side, he forced himself to wait.

Clara made her own choices in her own time. All he could do was wait and hope that she wanted him with a fraction of the fierceness that he had for her.

CHAPTER TWENTY-SEVEN

ONTHS PASSED.

Clara barely noticed while summer turned to fall, and fall hinted at winter. Her focus was on her twin goals of finishing the bathhouse and making sure the school was well-established.

The first month had been horrible. Clara spent every day wondering if they had tried to do too much. Liam spent night and day with Mr. Russell, controlling the workers, setting his hand to the mechanics, and even resetting the stone when needed. He collapsed exhausted every night, and she was little better as she and Miss Adams tried to press knowledge into children who had too many other tasks as well. It was summer and flocks needed tending, crops had to be watered, and so much more.

If it hadn't been for Liam holding her tight every night, she might have turned tail to run. But he kept her close, and she found rest in his arms. Enough, at least, to face the next day.

The second month passed much as the first, except that the walls of the bathhouse grew with speed. She could see the shape of the building with a roof soon to come. The children enjoyed school now. Or rather, they appreciated not doing the labors demanded by their parents. At least for a few hours every day. Plus the coin she paid to every child for completing a study helped ease the pain for the parents.

Tragedy struck in the third month. Mr. Russell had news of a sickness in his family. He rushed home to England while the leaves were still turning gold. Fortunately, between herself and Liam, they understood the final tasks. At least well enough for winter. They now had hot water for a full bath inside the castle. The laundry was not finished, but it had enough done that they could complete it in the spring.

Success. At least with the bathhouse.

The children were a constant challenge, but Miss Adams was determined. She had whipped up a course of study for each and every child. Even Deirdre's brother and sister attended in new clothing. Clara would never have managed to get them there if Liam hadn't demanded it of his clan. Every child, he ordered, would come without fail. Thanks to his firm hand and Clara's pennies for good work, every child could read some words. And many had interest in learning more.

That was a glorious change, and she declared it a success as well.

Victory in the two outcomes she'd set herself at the outset. And now that the roof was in place, the pump and the pipes in good order, and the children dutifully scratching out their studies, she found satisfaction in herself. A contentment that steadied her when something went wrong. That was joy like nothing she'd ever felt before.

If only Liam shared her happiness.

While her heart had gotten lighter and brighter as the building neared completion, Liam had withdrawn. It had been weeks since they'd snuck away to their quiet corner of the stream and longer still since they'd spent the night talking through plans beyond tomorrow.

It wasn't hard to guess why. They both knew that now was the time for her decision. If her time in Scotland had been nothing but playing, then she should leave before the first snowfall. She'd set her tasks, completed them, and now should head back to her true home. London waited for her. She longed to hear Aaron mutter about the government, and Lilah had hinted in her last letter that she might have interesting news regarding their nursery. She missed daily lectures about unusual topics and evenings with the friends who were not Miss Adams.

Sometimes she yearned for that while she sat discussing beehives with Egan Jack or listening to Mrs. Boyce take credit for the new oven. She wondered if she'd rather be in her London bedroom filled with books where no man snored or wrapped himself tightly around her body.

If she was returning to London, it was time to leave. They both knew it.

But rather than speak of it, Liam grew sullen. He touched her with desperation, even as he refused to take her virginity. And cruel creature that she was, she let him take her to the heights of passion while denying him the one thing he wanted.

Herself forever bound to him.

The very idea made her itch. She would become his property in a very real sense. He would have the legal right to beat her, if he chose. He could lock her away in an empty cage and none would stop him. He could do anything he wanted, and she would be helpless against him. She had seen it happen to other women. What started out beautiful became ugly, and the husband held all the cards.

But she didn't want to leave.

She had thoughts on other building projects. And no one believed a few months of education would save the MacCleal clan for generations. There were bright children here, but half had barely begun to read.

But most of all, she wanted Liam. She'd even started dreaming about what their children would be like. Would they be clever and strong? They might be willful or silly. For certain, they'd have every advantage of a mother who could educate them and a father who rarely lost his temper. Even when she'd tried to manage the laundry and boiled his tartan to threads.

She knew that if she was determined, Liam would let her leave for England tomorrow. But if she imagined his face as she rode away, her heart broke into a thousand pieces. He would clench his jaw with pride, but agony would burn in his eyes.

Her breath caught as her belly hollowed out. Hard enough to imagine Liam's face as she left. Worse still to feel what might tear through her. She was fond of telling Liam how she was growing on his clan. Barely anyone grumbled about washing before meals. The servants rolled their eyes, but they didn't fight her when she declared a new way of doing a task. They harumphed loudly but allowed her to try a new method of boiling a shirt – they were right, she was wrong – or thickening their cock-a-leekie soup – she was right, Mrs. Boyce was wrong.

So they had adjusted to her, but the opposite was also true. They had grown on her. She'd spent many nights entranced by their tales, and not just the ghost stories. Deirdre had lately talked with her about ways to make cloth, and she itched to try it during the hard winter months. And Rhona wanted a stillroom to mix poultices and other medicines.

Liam's people were stubborn, particular, and as individual as she was. They might have different ways of expressing it, but the core was the same. She appreciated their unique qualities and felt secure in allowing her own to shine. And if one thought to chastise her, Liam was always there to keep her safe. No man lay a hand on her, and no woman spread mean gossip about her.

It was the safest she had ever felt. And the freest.

That was saying a great deal given that she had spent all her adult life in Aaron's home with little responsibility and no restraint. Here she had safety, freedom, and purpose. What more could a woman want?

The answer came every time Liam kissed her awake in the morning or pulled her tight to him at night. "G'morn, love," he would say in his gravelly brogue as he kissed her awake. "Sweet dreams, love," he would murmur as his body fitted itself to hers.

Love.

He'd offered it to her morning and night for months now. He declared himself freely from the beginning. He'd courted her with honor, admitted the truth when she'd been tricked, and held to their bargain despite how desperately he wanted her.

And he gave her his heart.

So what was missing? Why couldn't she give him the commitment that he wanted? Why wouldn't she risk her own heart when he had given her every reason to trust his?

Such were her thoughts as she stared at the newly complete bathhouse and twisting her fingers in her dress. What was wrong with her?

Then Liam's gentle voice surrounded her, chasing away her tortured thoughts. At least for a moment. "Are you dreaming of a bath with your fancy soap?"

"I am," she lied.

"You've done a good job here. None could do better."

"It wasn't me, and you know it. It was Mr. Russell and all the workers. It was you standing face to face with the ones who wouldn't do what I said, and you putting your back to the job when they wouldn't."

He touched her chin and pulled her around to face him. "Without you pushing every day, nagging the men and holding back the mead, then it would have gone half as quick and not be done by winter."

Maybe. Probably. She smiled as she looked into his eyes. "Will you share the bath with me? After dinner or later, after everyone else is abed."

He teased her lips with his. "I'm not hungry," he said as he nibbled along her lips. "Are you?"

Not now she wasn't. At least not for food. "They'll know what we're doing."

He chuckled. "They'll know either way, lass."

That was probably true. And she was in desperate need of a distraction. Her thoughts had gone in the same circles for days now, if not weeks. She took his hand and tugged him toward the bathhouse. He lagged behind for less than a second. Very quickly, his longer steps had him pulling her along.

They stepped into the bathhouse together, then barred the

door. She pumped the hot water while he opened the valve for cold rainwater to drain in from the cistern above. He built up the fire while she opened her one bar of sweet gale soap and set it within reach. Then she felt his hands on her gown as he quickly stripped it off her body.

She laughed when the cool air hit her because she knew nothing came off more quickly than a kilt. Soon he was as naked as she as they sank into the tub together.

She thought he would stroke her then. He loved to shape her breasts, and soap made everything slippery. She set her hands on his shoulders and offered herself to him, but he held himself back.

"What were you thinking, love?"

"What?"

"When you were staring at the bathhouse, your thoughts weren't on soap and hot water. What were you really thinking?"

He knew her so well. Ridiculous of her to try to hide her thoughts from him. She leaned back against the edge of the tub and tried to find the words. In the end, she blurted out the truth.

"Why can't I love?"

His body stilled and his face blanched. When he spoke, his words came slowly but she felt his pain even though he never expressed it. "You don't love me?" he asked.

"I don't think I love anybody."

"What?"

"I love learning, and I love what we've built here." She gestured around her. "I love to smell the heather in the air, and I love it when Rhona cooks a meal as well as Mrs. Boyce."

"But you don't think you love…me?"

"I hold my brother in affection. Lilah, too. And I cannot wait to see their baby, if Lilah is indeed pregnant."

"That's not the same kind of love, Clara."

She nodded. "I know." She touched his arm. "And when I look at you, I feel warmth. Happiness, even. I feel safe and valued." She took a deep breath. "I have a place here in a way I never did in London."

He grinned. "That's very good, love." His accent was thick, as often happened when they were naked together. He stroked along her jaw. "But you don't think that's love?"

She shrugged. "Is it? I feel more for you than any other man, but that doesn't mean its love, Liam. And you deserve someone who loves you more than the sun and the moon."

His expression turned wry. "You leave what I deserve to me. Tell me more about what you don't feel."

"If you locked me away and took away my books, I would hate you. I'd despise you!"

"I wouldn't dream of taking away your books." He sounded shocked that she'd even thought of it.

"That's because you're wise. But doesn't that mean I love my books more than you?"

"Ah. We're measuring feelings then. You could despise me, so you can't love me?"

She nodded. "That's it exactly."

"What if I swore to never take away your books? Write it on a paper, and I'll sign it."

She chuckled at the absurd thought. "I'm serious, Liam. I don't think I'm capable of love. Not the kind of love you deserve." Her expression fell. "Which means I should leave soon. I should let you find a woman who worships you as you want."

"Worship! Good lord, woman, if I wanted worship, I would have become a priest."

She blew out a breath. Maybe he was right. Maybe he didn't want that mindless doe-eyed adoration that young girls gave, but that was a far cry from the blandness of her feelings. "I'm milquetoast, and you deserve haggis."

He chuckled. "I have no idea what that means."

She dropped her head back, letting her body go limp as she steeped in her misery. "I want to love you," she said. "I want to feel everything for you, but…" She raised her hands then let them splash back into the water. "I'm milquetoast." She winced. "A bland, spiritless Sassenach."

"Where have you gotten these ideas? Have you not run me ragged all through England and Scotland? Wasn't it you who paid a man to throw knives at me?"

"That was the ghost of your grandmother."

"That was a fake séance done badly by carnival folk."

It was.

"And wasn't it you who pretended to be the ghostly bride of Bride of MacDhubhthaich in little more than your underthings?"

"Beitidh insisted on the dress."

"You were right convincing with your, *Ooooh, aie, where's me husband?*"

She smiled at the memory. "I was rather good at that, wasn't I?"

"You took my breath away."

When she didn't respond, he tugged on her arm, pulling her into his lap. His cock stood hard and proud between them, but he made no move to use it. Instead, he tucked her against his shoulder and spoke in a gentle tone.

"You have spirit, Clara. You have fire and a brain that thinks and thinks, until I near scream at the workings of it."

"It makes me want to scream sometimes, too."

He pressed a kiss to her temple. "So if it's not your spirit or your mind that's the problem, then it must be your heart."

Her breath caught. That's exactly what she'd been thinking. She had no heart. Or at least not one that could love as normal people did.

"Liam—"

"Clara, it's not that it can't love. You've got plenty of love for Dierdre and her kin. Rhona's caught your heart as well, plus all the little ones."

"That's not the kind of love—"

"Listen, Clara. You're afraid to love a man. You're afraid to trust yourself to a grown man because who could take care of you better than yourself? Letting yourself love me means that you put your heart in my hands as surely as you've got hold of mine."

She shuddered, fighting his words even as she tried to hear them.

"You trust your body to me, don't you? That I'd never hurt it."

She was sitting naked on his lap. She'd seen him protect her in a thousand ways big and small. "Of course, I do."

"And you trust your thoughts with me, don't you? I let you remake my castle, didn't I? And I heard something about a new stillroom?"

"For Rhona. Near the old kitchen," she said.

He grunted but would not be distracted.

"So now you've got to trust me with your heart, and that's a frightening thing."

She curled tightly against him. "I don't know how."

"Course you don't. Your mother didn't teach you. She wanted to change you and so picked at you until you were both mad. Your father and brother love you, but they didn't know what to do with you. They let you go your own way and braced for whatever disaster befell."

She winced. There had been several disasters over the years.

"And then there was your first love." His voice deepened at that.

"He's not important. He was a fortune hunter. He's gone."

"And he broke your heart, so there was no opening it again."

She lifted her head. "But you're not him. You're you. And I want to love you."

"But you don't feel it?"

"I don't."

He smiled. "Let me help you." He took her hand and pulled her fingers to his lips. "Your body's safe with me."

She nodded.

"Say it, love."

"My body's safe with you."

"Your thoughts are safe with me."

"My thoughts are safe with you."

"Your heart is safe with me."

"My heart—" Her throat tightened, strangling the words. Her eyes widened in shock.

"Aye," he said, his lips curving in a smile. "I think we're on to something. Try again."

She took a deep breath. "My heart. My heart is safe. With you."

"Aye, it is. Try again."

It was easier this time. "My heart is safe with you."

"Your heart is safe to open. Repeat it."

"My heart is safe to open." Her eyes widened. It suddenly felt as if she could take a deep breath, deeper even than she'd ever done before. "My heart is safe to love."

"It is, love." He arched his brows. "Now do you feel it? Maybe a little?"

She was about to say, no, she felt nothing different. But she did feel something. There was desire, of course. His naked body was next to hers, and he was glorious. But there was a sweetness mixed with a kind of pain right at her breastbone.

There couldn't possibly be a physical sensation, could there? To opening one's heart?

"Say it again," he urged.

"My heart is safe to love." She looked into his eyes. "My heart is safe to love you."

"As my heart is safe to love you."

How was it possible? It was like her breastbone was fragmenting, but in a good way. It ached, and yet the warmth that flowed through the cracks stunned her. And while she was shocked by these feelings, he stroked her cheek.

"I love you, Clara. I'll never take away your books. I'll never hurt your body. And I'll always have the time to listen to you."

A sob racked her body. When had she started crying?

"You heart is safe with me, Clara. Just as I know my heart is safe with you."

"It is," she said through tears that smeared her vision. "I'd never hurt you."

"Because my heart is safe with you." He wiped away her tears with his thumb. "Now tell me what you feel?"

"So much," she whispered. Hot. Cold. Excited. Afraid. Wild rushes of elation followed by dizzying whirls of confusion.

"Aye," he agreed. "That's love."

She blinked away her tears. "I love you?" she asked.

"I think so." He dropped his forehead to hers. "What do you think?"

That this had to be love. It was so wild, so uncontained. She felt buffeted by it, and yet she had never felt safer because she was in his arms. "Oh my God," she breathed. "I love you." She looked up into his eyes. "*I love you!*"

"At last," he said, then he kissed her.

She wasn't ready for it. She'd already experienced a thousand different types of kisses from him, from sweetly tender to darkly passionate. She was expecting something like what they'd shared so many times before. What she got instead was a rush of feeling from inside her. Sweet, dark, tender, and demanding all in a wild ride of need and surprise.

So, while he was kissing her, she was loving him. She pressed her mouth to his. She plunged her tongue into his mouth. She angled her body until they were heart to heart. She squirmed as she adjusted her legs to straddle him. And then she ripped herself back from him and gasped out her words over the beat of her thundering heart.

"I love you," she said.

"I love you," he returned.

"Marry me, Liam. Let me be safe with you forever. Let me love you always."

"Always, Clara. Yes."

His hands slid to her hips. He was ever careful with her, but she was in no mood to stop. She gripped his shoulders and arched her back.

"I love you, Liam," she said, now feeling it through every part of her body.

"I love you, Clara."

He thrust.

He filled her body with a sharpness that made her cry out. It was like the last restraint on her heart was torn free. He wanted her, he loved her, and she…she could feel everything for him in return.

He held himself still while she adjusted. And when she opened her eyes, he was studying her face.

"Good?"

She nodded. "Verra good," she said in a bad echo of his brogue.

"It'll get better," he said. Then he lifted her slightly higher on his cock before sliding her back down.

"Oh! That was nice," she said.

"Verra nice," he agreed.

She laughed because she could. Because the feelings were so wonderful even as his tempo increased. She matched him then. Not just in body—rising and lowering as he willed—but in their eyes as their thoughts seemed to intertwine. And in their hearts as they flowed together, one into the other and back.

It made no sense. She had no idea this was possible. And yet it was. He was. They were.

They loved.

Climax roared through her, brighter than ever before.

He cried out as he released within her.

Then he held her safe while they floated. A long, glorious stretch of time when they held one another in love.

She exhaled and settled onto his shoulder.

He pressed a kiss to her forehead.

"I've been so stupid," she whispered.

"You've been you. And you're perfect," he returned.

She loved him. She knew that now. But as wonderful as that thought was, as all-consuming and glorious as it was, her mind would never stay on one track for long. In time, she pressed a kiss to his jaw and started talking about something else.

"And I'm really glad we finished the bathhouse."

"Aye," he said as caressed her sides. "I predict that we'll be using it lots in the coming months—"

"Years," she corrected.

"Years," he agreed.

"Forever."

"Aye, wife. Forever."

She stayed silent then, allowing the word "wife" to sink into her bones. It fit well, she realized. It settled deep inside her and sat right next to the word "love."

In time, she straightened up enough to look him into his eyes. "Husband?"

He grinned. She could see the term pleased him. "Yes?" he asked.

"Can we talk about my plans for next spring? A stillroom is a good start, but we really should make decisions based on how the clan will grow in the coming decades."

He groaned at that, but he nodded. And then he listened to her every word.

About the Author

A *USA Today* Bestseller, JADE LEE has been scripting love stories since she first picked up a set of paper dolls. Ball gowns and rakish lords caught her attention early (thank you Georgette Heyer), and her fascination with historical romance began. Author of more than 30 regency romances, Jade has a gift for creating a lively world, witty dialogue, and hot, sexy humor. Jade also writes contemporary and paranormal romance as Kathy Lyons. Together, they've won several industry awards, including the *Prism—Best of the Best, Romantic Times Reviewer's Choice,* and *Fresh Fiction's* Steamiest Read. Even though Kathy (and Jade) have written over 60 romance novels, she's just getting started. Check out her latest news at www.KathyLyons.com, Facebook: JadeLeeAuthor, and Twitter: JadeLeeAuthor. Instagram: KathyLyonsAuthor.